continued . . .

MONA LISA CRAVING

"Suspenseful twists promise more heart-throbbing surprises in the next installment of this haunting erotic fantasy series."
—*Publishers Weekly*

"Unique, captivating, and sexy . . . Everything you've come to expect from Sunny and more . . . Another remarkable addition to Mona Lisa's saga." —*Romance Reader at Heart*

"The latest chapter in the Monère series is a pulse-pounding erotic adventure . . . narrated in first person by the heroine in a strong yet emotional voice. Sunny creates a fascinating world that's violent and sexual." —*Romantic Times*

"Fans of this erotic fantasy saga will appreciate this powerful entry . . . Once again it is the secondary characters that provide strong support to the plot which makes this an endearing tale . . . Another winner." —*Midwest Book Review*

MONA LISA BLOSSOMING

"For those of you who have been following Sunny's Monère series, run to your bookstore and buy *Mona Lisa Blossoming*!"
—*Romance Reader at Heart*

"Tantalizingly erotic, Sunny's *Mona Lisa Blossoming* seduces readers into the powerfully imaginative world of the Monère."
—L.A. Banks, *New York Times* bestselling author of the Vampire Huntress Legend series

"Sunny is blossoming into a star well worth reading."
—*Midwest Book Review*

"Sunny's fascinating story has interesting characters and a rather unusual origin. There are shape-shifters, blood drinkers, a heroine who's an unexpected unique queen, some bloody violence, and a fair amount of sex." —*Romantic Times*

MONA LISA AWAKENING

"Darkly erotic, wickedly clever, and very original!"
—Bertrice Small, *New York Times* bestselling author

"A terrific debut sure to appeal to fans of Anne Bishop or Laurell K. Hamilton . . . Sunny's characters stayed with me long after I finished the book."
—Patricia Briggs, #1 *New York Times* bestselling author

"A spellbinding tale full of erotic sensuality and deliciously fascinating characters." —Lori Foster, *New York Times* bestselling author

"A refreshing, contemporary urban erotic horror thriller that grips the audience." —*The Best Reviews*

"A lively writer . . . Erotica fantasy that is fresh, engaging, and a damn fun read . . . Sizzling sex scenes." —*Sensual Romance Reviews*

LUCINDA, DARKLY

Book One of the Demon Princess Chronicles

"An awesome story populated with endearing and sexy characters. This unabashedly sensual gothic story will feed your need for something new and fresh. Readers will be loath to put the book down until the final page is read . . . The ending will leave you hungry for more." —*Romantic Times*

"An emotionally intense, sexually charged, gothic romance . . . If you're in the mood for a different kind of paranormal read that is superbly written, marvelously told, and extremely sensuous, look no further." —*Romance Reader at Heart*

"[A] superb fast-paced urban fantasy in the tradition of Laurell K. Hamilton." —*Midwest Book Review*

"Full of paranormal passion, Sunny's fast-paced first in a new erotic fantasy series, the Demon Princess Chronicles, introduces Lucinda, a six-hundred-year-old demon princess who's getting bored with her long unlife." —*Publishers Weekly*

MONA LISA ECLIPSING

A NOVEL OF THE MONÈRE

SUNNY

BERKLEY SENSATION, NEW YORK

THE BERKLEY PUBLISHING GROUP
Published by the Penguin Group
Penguin Group (USA) Inc.
375 Hudson Street, New York, New York 10014, USA
Penguin Group (Canada), 90 Eglinton Avenue East, Suite 700, Toronto, Ontario M4P 2Y3, Canada
(a division of Pearson Penguin Canada Inc.)
Penguin Books Ltd., 80 Strand, London WC2R 0RL, England
Penguin Group Ireland, 25 St. Stephen's Green, Dublin 2, Ireland (a division of Penguin Books Ltd.)
Penguin Group (Australia), 250 Camberwell Road, Camberwell, Victoria 3124, Australia
(a division of Pearson Australia Group Pty. Ltd.)
Penguin Books India Pvt. Ltd., 11 Community Centre, Panchsheel Park, New Delhi—110 017, India
Penguin Group (NZ), 67 Apollo Drive, Rosedale, Auckland 0632, New Zealand
(a division of Pearson New Zealand Ltd.)
Penguin Books (South Africa) (Pty.) Ltd., 24 Sturdee Avenue, Rosebank, Johannesburg 2196,
South Africa

Penguin Books Ltd., Registered Offices: 80 Strand, London WC2R 0RL, England

This book is an original publication of The Berkley Publishing Group.

This is a work of fiction. Names, characters, places, and incidents either are the product of the author's imagination or are used fictitiously, and any resemblance to actual persons, living or dead, business establishments, events, or locales is entirely coincidental. The publisher does not have any control over and does not assume any responsibility for author or third-party websites or their content.

PRINTING HISTORY
Berkley Sensation trade paperback edition / April 2011

Library of Congress Cataloging-in-Publication Data

Sunny, 1965–
    Mona Lisa eclipsing / Sunny.—Berkley Sensation trade paperback ed.
      p. cm.—(Monère, children of the moon ; 7)
    ISBN 978-0-425-23894-3
  1. Supernatural—Fiction. 2. Shapeshifting—Fiction. 3. Louisiana—Fiction. I. Title.
    PS3619.U564M75 2011
    813'.6—dc22

                                                                                        2010051648

PRINTED IN THE UNITED STATES OF AMERICA

10 9 8 7 6 5 4 3 2 1

To two wonderful fans Janon Swink and
Candace Clemons, and my fellow author Mima—
the three angels who convinced me to hurry up and write
this next part of Mona Lisa's story.

ONE

THE SWORD WHISTLED toward me in sharp descent, almost too fast for a human to see. But not for a part human, part Monère, and whatever else part thing I was, which was, oh yeah, that's right—demon dead.

I parried, feinted to the left, then thrust to the right. "Gotcha!" I crowed as I tapped Edmond smartly on the ribs.

My young partner lowered his sword, rubbed his side, and grinned as I did a small victory dance. With protective padding and dulled weapons, he could afford to grin. Practice was much more civilized and far less bloody than real life would have been.

"You didn't let me score on purpose, did you?" I asked suspiciously.

"No, milady," Edmond said. "You've gotten better than me, sure and true."

"You hear that?" I said smugly to the big guy watching us, Nolan Morell, our sword master instructor. "I'm better than Edmond now."

"Progress, indeed, milady," Nolan agreed blandly. "You can defeat an eighteen-year-old boy."

"An eighteen-year-old Monère warrior-in-training who has been practicing with the sword since he was ten, whereas I have been swinging a practice blade for only three months," I corrected.

"And no longer just swinging but thrusting and parrying, attacking and counterattacking," my stern teacher relented with a brief smile that faded all too quickly. "But your footwork is still sloppy, your crossover too slow—"

"Yeah, yeah, yeah." I dismissed the oncoming lecture with a careless finger wave. "Indulge me for a moment. Let me enjoy my brief glow."

Both of them waited a couple of seconds as I rested, sucking in deep breaths.

"Enough glow, milady?" The dryness in Nolan's voice could have rivaled the finest aged wine.

I straightened. "Sarcasm doesn't become you, Nolan."

His tone, if anything, became even drier. "I will be sure to take note of that, milady. Now let us continue. En garde!"

We practiced for another twenty minutes concentrating on footwork, then finished up the session with more challenging blade work. Whatever Edmond lacked in skill, he made up for in exuberance as the multiple sore spots where he had tapped me attested. Of course, I'd delivered quite a few whacks myself, I thought with satisfaction.

I saw my progress in swordsmanship much as I did the ruling of my new territory and its many people—much improved. It had been half a year since I had become a Monère Queen, the Queen of Louisiana specifically. It was a mantle that had been awkward at first but now fit more comfortably. I had over four hundred people under me, Monère men, women, and children. I knew almost all their names now and their varied relationships within our insular community.

"I'm going to miss you, Edmond," I said as we wiped down our equipment and hauled it inside.

"You have only to say the word, milady, and I will be happy to stay with you."

And here was where the easy camaraderie that we had shared over the past few months became strained. Because what he was really asking was that I take him into my bed. That was what Monère Queens did to fresh and dewy eighteen-year-old virgin Monère boys: take them into their beds and enjoy their harmless, lusty vitality for a handful of years before they tired of them or they grew too strong, too powerful, and were kicked out of their Queen's bed. Because then it was not mere copulation anymore, an exchange of pleasure that took place, but an exchange of power and sometimes of talents and abilities.

Awkwardness fell as the *ticktock* of life intruded on us. The summer solstice was coming up, and in several months Edmond would leave his home, all that he had ever known, to seek service in another territory with another Queen, one who *was* willing to make him her lover—our Monère version of going out into the big, bad world. It made worry flutter in my stomach like any mother sending a kid off to college would feel, but to keep him here safe with me would be even crueler because I had no intentions of taking him into my bed. It was much too crowded already.

"Ah, Edmond," I said, sighing. "I would be doing you a grave disservice if I asked you to stay. Find another Queen who will appreciate the gift of your Virgin Claiming. Me? I've got too many lovers as it is."

"Not enough, milady, and half of those are not even with you regularly."

He was referring to Amber, the Warrior Lord who ruled the adjacent slice of Mississippi territory, a portion of my own domain that I had induced the High Queen's Court to officially split off and deed to him. I'd upgraded Amber's status and downgraded his time with me. Gryphon, my other Warrior Lord, my first love, had died and become demon dead. He resided in Hell now, but that wasn't a barrier for me. I could visit him, was the only Monère who could, actually, thanks to that quarter human part of me: my blood was warmer than a Full Blood Monère, allowing me to survive Hell's scorching heat. Of course, the fact that I was out of sorts with Halcyon, the High Prince and ruler of Hell, who not only happened to be my demon mate but also the sponsor of my newly dead first love . . . well, that made visiting Gryphon a bit awkward. My other lover, Dante, was missing. Of course, I'd sort of kicked him out, but I'd had a change of mind and heart. Only problem was he didn't know that. He hadn't come back.

"Only Dontaine is here with you now," Edmond noted.

Dontaine—my breathlessly handsome master at arms. He had stuck despite my best efforts to push him away. I seemed to be my own worst enemy.

"The others might be absent but they still count," I said firmly.

"Still, that is only five men."

"Only." I rolled my eyes, my humor returning. How could it not at such an outlook. "Only five men. If I had it in me, I would blush, but my human upbringing seems to be fading more and more each day I spend with you guys."

"And they are all old," Edmond complained. "You should try someone younger and more tender."

"Yuck," I grimaced. "You make yourself sound like a piece of steak."

A smile widened his lips. "Juicy and succulent, prime and untouched—"

"Stop, just stop. You're turning me off steak, and if you do, I'll never forgive you."

The two of us shared a laugh, then in a more serious vein because I had become fond of my young practice partner, I told him with honest regret, "I cannot give you what you need and deserve, Edmond. I'm weird that way. I happen to like older guys, especially the ones I've chosen. And I know I may be fucked up, because I was the one to push them away, but I'm waiting for them to come back to me."

Edmond gave me a gentle smile. "Then they surely will, milady, for I cannot see any resisting you."

"How about forgiving me?" I asked wryly.

"That, too," he said with an earnest kindness that allowed a glimpse of the strong and wonderful warrior he had the potential of maturing into . . . if the Queens whose beds he passed through in the next few decades of his life weren't totally fucked-up bitches—which, unfortunately, most of them were.

"After you've enjoyed your time with as many Queens as you can glut yourself on, Edmond, when it becomes too dangerous for you . . . you know that you can always come back here, right?" Young and dewy fresh though Edmond was now, he had only fifty years or less to play paramour to a Queen, a century at most after that to serve as guard. Then would come the grim fate of death or desertion. Because most Queens ended up killing their oldest and most powerful warriors, who became not only threats to the Queen's authority but also potential competitors for a territory of their own should they gain enough power to attain Warrior Lord status. Either they were killed or they fled and went rogue. They were never invited back to the territory of their birth, offered a promise of safety and shelter, as I was now offering Edmond.

My words clearly stunned him.

"That is very generous, milady," Edmond said, greatly moved. Kneeling, he kissed my hand.

"Please don't forget," I said, fondly tugging his hair. "You have a place to come back to, okay?"

"Yes, milady." Bowing, he took his leave, tossing over his shoulder as he walked away, "And I'll be older then. Just the way you like!"

Impudent boy. I was still grinning when I left the locker room. Nolan was still at his desk, jotting down notes in the lesson book he kept on my progress.

"Did you mean it?" Nolan asked, looking up to meet my gaze.

"About Edmond being able to come back here?"

"No. About waiting for your lovers to come back to you. About *wanting* them to."

Our relationship abruptly shifted from student and teacher to the more complicated relationship of a woman facing the father of one of the men she loved. "Do you mean Dante?" I asked softly.

Nolan nodded.

"Yes . . . if he can forgive me."

"Goddess bless us. I believe it's the other way around, as does he, likely: whether *you* could forgive *him*."

"I would hope that we could forgive each other." There was quite a lot to forgive, on both our parts. "I keep expecting him to return, but he hasn't. It's been three months since he left." Truth—since I kicked him out. "Have you heard anything from him?"

"No, he hasn't contacted us." A flicker of worry, quickly concealed. "But he will soon, eventually."

"Do you think . . . he wouldn't try to end his life, would

he?" That was my greatest fear. That he would die and this time not come back—be reborn. That was his curse, you see, laid down upon him by none other than yours truly, or who I had been anyway, this fierce Warrior Queen from long, long ago: a curse of dying and being reborn into an ever-diminishing bloodline until his family line finally ended. The number of his descendents was down to a trickle now, just him, his twin brother, Quentin, and his father and mother. But that wasn't really the part of the curse I worried about—Quentin was even now enthusiastically sowing his seed, and Nolan and his wife, Hannah, might still yet bear more children. What worried me most was the possibility that the curse I had laid upon Dante so long ago might have been broken by the life we had created, the child that had lived so briefly within me before I lost it in a traumatic miscarriage.

It had almost destroyed Dante when I'd lost the baby. He'd taken out his grief by slaughtering all of Mona Teresa's warriors, the Monère Queen who had injured me and deliberately caused the loss of our child. Last I'd heard, Mona Teresa still hadn't recovered yet; few warriors had been brave or desperate enough to swear themselves into her service. If Dante had not been legendary enough before, slaying the first great Warrior Queen . . . well, he was certainly infamous now after he had single-handedly sliced and diced, and viciously torn apart Mona Teresa's thirty warriors with exceptionally cold and bloodthirsty proficiency.

Dante and I had a real complicated history, you might say. We had been enemies long ago, then lovers in my second cycle of life in a most ironic twist of fate. The wonder was not that I had pushed him away: it was why I wanted him back.

The answer to that lay in his eyes—what I had seen in them as I had cramped and bled and lost our child, his hope for ending the curse. The way he had touched me and held me with a tenderness and concern that had fractured and broken my heart even more.

I had saved him, started to love him until my memory of him, of my first life, of being *killed* by him, returned. Then I had feared him and pushed him away, ordered him gone. And I was afraid now that he might be gone forever.

I know. I was one really messed-up gal. I pushed the men I loved away from me, and then when they left, I wanted them back. But I was aware of my issues and I was trying to change. Fate had given me a second chance with Dante, and though I had managed to screw up the first part of it, this second opportunity was not yet over. *Please, Goddess*, I prayed. *If you give me another chance, I promise I'll do my best to make it right this time.*

The door opened and Hannah Morell rushed into the room. She glanced quickly at me, then fixed her gaze intently on her husband. "Dante has been seen on the island of Cozumel."

And I discovered, to my surprise, that sometimes prayers really do work.

Two

"Cozumel?" I don't know why, but when I'd imagined Dante alone and suffering somewhere, I hadn't pictured him in a tropical island paradise. "Are you sure?"

"It makes sense," Nolan said, "if he took a boat from New Orleans."

Leaving on a boat, and not just any boat but a cruise ship? I hadn't imagined that either. After killing Mona Teresa's warriors, had he traveled back to my territory, watched us and made sure we were doing well before going off into exile?

"Who saw him?" I asked.

"A group of tourists on horseback came upon him in the jungle," Hannah said.

"Tourists?" I felt my eyebrows climb up my forehead. "Not a Monère Queen or one of her men?"

"No, milady."

"Then how do you know it was Dante they saw?"

"They saw a saber-toothed tiger; that is his other form. It's creating quite a stir since more than one witness saw him."

"A saber-toothed tiger? For real? Aren't they supposed to be extinct?"

"They became extinct over eleven thousand years ago," Nolan answered quietly. "When they died out, so did the animal form in Monère shifters."

Which meant that Dante had lived and died and been reborn for at least that long. Over eleven thousand years . . . Sweet Goddess! I'd laid one whammy of a curse of him. One whose painful depths I hadn't fully comprehended until now. The wonder was that Dante hadn't torn me apart, murdered me painfully and slowly the moment he had seen my Goddess's Tears, the pearly trademark moles embedded in my palms, and realized who I was: that I was Mona Lyra reincarnated. It was a wonder he was capable of having feelings other than sheer loathing hatred for me after what I had done to him.

When I'd asked him once if he remembered his previous lives, his answer had been, *My memories are most clear of my last incarnation and of my first life. That, I never forget. I get random flashes of other lives, occasionally. I think it's my mind's natural defense, that selective memory. Remembering everything would probably be too much for one single mind to handle.*

The last sentence had been a vast understatement.

"I'm going after him," Nolan said.

"Good," I said, nodding. "I'm coming with you." But leaving wasn't quite as easy as that.

My men threw a hissy fit. It might not be the best words to apply to a collection of fierce Monère warriors and former rogues, but that's essentially what they did. They didn't want me to go, too dangerous. Not just where I was going but who I was going after. When that didn't dissuade me, then they all wanted to come along to guard me. I had no problem with that.

"Whoever can be ready to leave in an hour can come with us," I said agreeably. "Be sure to bring your passports. We're catching a six forty a.m. commercial flight that leaves in"—I glanced at my watch—"four hours."

The relief on my men's faces turned back into fierce scowls.

"I do not have a passport," said Tomas, one of my guards, his usual smooth-as-butter Southern drawl completely absent from his voice.

"Neither do the rest of us," said Chami. All of my inner-circle guards were old, but Chami was probably the oldest among them. His full name was Chameleo, for his chameleon's gift of blending in with his surroundings. He could virtually disappear in front of your eyes. "But that won't be a problem for me," he said, smiling.

"And I can fly," Aquila said, stroking his neat Vandyke beard. "It'll just take me a little bit longer to get there." A former rogue, he now served as my steward, handling all of my territory's vast business concerns. He was the only one among my guards with wings; the other form he shifted into was that of an eagle.

"Wait." I held up a hand. "None of you have passports?"

"I do," Nolan said. "But that is because my family and I lived so long among humans." They had had to flee from an evil Queen.

Hearing Nolan had a passport didn't surprise me. I had expected him to have one since he was the one who had suggested taking a commercial flight in the first place, and had called and booked our reservations using his credit card; I had promised to pay him back. It was just easier to let Nolan handle things. Good thing, because Aquila, who handled all my financial matters, likely wouldn't have done it so quickly or easily, not without a great deal of argument and compromise first. Among my people, Nolan and his family were the only ones financially independent. The rest lived the traditional, old-fashioned—and backward, in my eyes—Monère way. They relied on their Queen to supply everything for them, which was a great way for Queens to control their people: keep them needy and dependent on you and make it hard for them to venture out and survive on their own.

I'd grown up thinking myself human and had only recently discovered that I was part Monère, part of a race of supernatural beings descended from the moon. I thought I was making great progress in learning about my new territory and people—then I was smacked in the face with something like this and realized how very little I still knew.

"None of you have a passport?" I repeated, unable to get over that fact.

"Few of us have any form of human identification," Dontaine said, entering the room. Someone must have called him, in the hopes of talking some reason into me, being my lover and all. "A false human identity is very hard and expensive to come by," he said, seating himself near me. "I'm one of the few here who have a driver's license, and that is because I was trusted by my former Queen to oversee her New Orleans businesses."

Well, that answered why so few Monères here knew how to drive. Wow, I had far more work cut out for me than I knew, but that was for another time.

"What is this I hear about you flying out of the country?" Dontaine asked. He had the most beautiful eyes, a riveting pure shade of green, as if his maker had decided he had not graced the physical form enough and had to give him this added touch of splendor.

I had to deliberately shake myself loose from his gaze and focus on his words. "What? Oh, um, Dante's been seen down in Mexico, on the island of Cozumel. Nolan and I are catching a flight leaving in four hours. When everyone raised a hue and cry about me going off alone, I invited others to come along. No one, however, seems to have a passport. Do you?"

"No," said Dontaine. His frown didn't detract at all from his stunning good looks, which I found quite unfair. "I have never had to leave the country before. Why not take the private jet?"

Being Queen of my own territory had some nice perks. One of them was access to a private jet authorized for my use by the High Queen's Council.

I shook my head. "High Court doesn't know anything about this, nor does anyone else, and his family and I want to keep it that way. The plan is to go in quietly, find Dante, and bring him back home."

"With only Nolan, one guard, accompanying you, a valuable and vulnerable Monère Queen?" Dontaine inquired with false calm. His emerald eyes had darkened to jade, a sure sign to those who knew him that he was upset.

"I shall also accompany them," said Chami, my chameleon guard. "Getting on the plane unseen won't be a problem for me."

"But my brother—" I started to protest. Chami's main duty was to watch over my brother Thaddeus.

"Tomas will watch over him while I'm gone," Chami said, looking over at the other guard.

Tomas nodded his silent agreement.

"And I can fly there in my eagle form," said Aquila.

"Across the ocean?" I asked.

Aquila nodded and said, "That is the shortest route, milady."

"No, not that way," I said. "There's nothing but water, no place to land if a storm comes up or you need to rest. How many miles is that anyway? Never mind—no way can you fly all that distance in one stretch."

"But—"

"Absolutely not," I said, cutting off his protest. "I'll have Nolan and Chami with me. There's no need to risk yourself like that."

"Actually," Dontaine said, inserting a calm voice of reason, "if you insist on going, it would be safer if Aquila went as well." He turned to Aquila. "How long would it take to reach Cozumel if you flew along the Gulf Coast, skirting along land?"

"I would need to see a map," Aquila said.

We all trooped into the study that Aquila had officially turned into his office, and looked at the world map he rolled out over the top of the desk.

"I estimate it would take a little over twenty-four hours, flying that route," he said after doing some calculations.

"By then, we might be on a flight back home with Dante already," I grumbled.

"Or you might not yet have found Dante and would be quite happy to have Aquila's eagle eyes and wings to help you search," countered Dontaine. As my master at arms, he was responsible for my safety. He continued with quiet authority, "I would prefer that you take as many men with you as possible. Two guards, no matter how strong or skilled, are not enough to guard a Queen. Three is barely acceptable and only so because of how powerful these warriors are. The most ideal would be if you allowed Nolan to go alone to fetch his son."

"Are you speaking as my lover or as my captain?" I asked. Dontaine was my newest lover and the least secure in my affections. Was he saying this out of jealousy of another rival?

"I speak as your captain, purely in terms of your safety," he said, returning my gaze calmly. "Cozumel, as an island, should be neutral ground, but Mexico is quite different—it has very few Queens or established territories, and most of the country is roamed freely by rogues."

"I can't," I said, biting my lip. "I have to go look for him, speak to him myself. Dante might not come back otherwise, no matter what his father tells him."

Dontaine nodded and said, "Then I would ask that you allow Aquila to fly out to join you in this safer, more round-about route."

"All right." I nodded agreement.

"Thank you," he said, gratified by my willingness to compromise, his manner growing warmer, more relaxed. Making him even more irresistible.

"You're welcome." Giving in to temptation, I lifted a hand to that altogether too-attractive face, shifting our interaction to a more intimate level. We had a lot of hats to juggle in our relationship, but so far, things seemed to be working.

THREE

THE FLIGHT WAS smooth and uneventful. Sitting in the window seat next to Nolan, I kept the shade pulled down the entire flight for Nolan's sake rather than mine. Being a Mixed Blood, I did not suffer the effects of the sun to the extent other Monère did. If you wanted to punish a Monère warrior, all you had to do was expose him to sunlight. It burned their skin, not quickly but surely and steadily. One hour under the sun and their white skin turned lobster red. Four hours of direct sunlight and they had sun poisoning the likes of which those who had ever witnessed such a thing would never be unable to forget—oozing blisters, putrid boils, and sloughing-off skin.

Nolan had built up more immunity to sunlight than most Monères, having raised his children among humans. He was one of the few warriors, in fact, who had a light tan. But still, no need to tempt fate; I kept the shade firmly drawn. We'd be getting plenty of hot sun on the Island of the Swallows—what Cozumel translated to in the Mayan language. I wondered for a moment how Chami was faring and where in the hell he was keeping himself. There was little free space in the main cabin; just because he was invisible didn't mean people couldn't bump into him. But no incident occurred, making me wonder if he had stowed away in the baggage compartment. No danger from the sun there. The chilling temperature might even be refreshing to a Monère; if the lack of oxygen was uncomfortable to a Full Blood, it certainly wasn't fatal. Only sun or silver poisoning, cutting off the head, or ripping out the heart killed a Monère. That hardiness, of course, didn't apply to me, being a mongrel Mixed Blood. But hey, I had some great compensation. Silver didn't weaken or poison me, and I could walk in the sun without being toasted into a gooey, overdone, dying mess.

After a stopover and change of plane, we landed and stepped out onto Cozumel's runway at four thirty in the afternoon. The sunlight was bright and fierce. I hadn't thought of that when I had okayed Aquila's coastline-hugging flight. Had Aquila taken sunlight into consideration when he had quoted that "a-little-over-twenty-four-hours" time estimate? Was he still flying during the day? Did his feathers protect him to some degree?

Crap, I wish I had thought to ask him all this before. I turned to Nolan and asked him instead, "How are you doing? Is the sun bothering you?"

"Nothing intolerable," was his answer. But I noticed he walked quickly off the hot tarmac into the more welcoming shade of the island-style terminal.

I felt Chami's presence as soon as our luggage came into sight on the conveyor belt. Most Monère had a definitive presence you could feel when in close enough range. Chami, however, had the rare ability to mute his energy so that you didn't feel or sense him, allowing him to get within deadly striking distance of another Monère before they were aware of the danger. The perfect assassin. That Chami hadn't bothered to mask his presence meant he either felt no reason to or was too weak to waste energy doing so. I squelched the alarm that flared at that thought, reminding myself that all my guys were big boys. Powerful ones, too. They could take care of themselves.

Only when our luggage was safely claimed and we had passed through customs, which was no more than a quick stamp in our passports, did I speak to air beside me. "I was wondering where you were, Chami. Have a nice flight with our luggage?"

"Nothing that I would recommend," Chami said, dropping his camouflage to become just another guy walking out of a nearby men's restroom. He joined us with a boyish smirk, looking all of twenty-five, tall and wiry thin with adorable curly brown hair. "Lousy seating and no service, but it got the job done. You wouldn't believe how roughly they handle our luggage, though. Not that we have anything useful in them." Flying commercial meant no weapons, nothing that would draw attention to us. I felt almost naked going without a blade.

After picking up a rental car, we drove downtown and stopped at a dive shop to buy some knives—a weapon of sorts, albeit of a fishy kind. Still, a sharp blade was a sharp blade, even though it wasn't silver. I immediately felt better with it strapped to my waist. Nolan and Chami picked up sun-blocking T-shirts and wide-brimmed sun hats, the type that draped down in back, protecting the neck as well as shading the face. With sunglasses in place, smeared with SPF 100-plus sunscreen, they were good to go. Or as good to go as they could be in this hot weather.

We checked into a hotel, unloaded our stuff, and I called the local tour company.

"Adventures Naturale," a girl answered with a musical island accent.

"I was interested in booking your jungle horseback-riding tour," I told her.

"For when, please?"

"Today."

"Sorry, ma'am, too late. We're completely booked. How 'bout two days from now?"

"We're not staying that long," I said, frowning. "What about tomorrow?"

"Nothing. We've been real busy since all the news coverage. You another reporter?" She sounded hopeful.

The *no* I was about to say impulsively changed to, "Yes, I'm with the"—I cast wildly around for a name and said the first one that popped into my mind—"*National Enquirer.* Can I ask you some questions, Miss . . . ?"

"Francisca Montalbo," she supplied eagerly, and spelled out her name for me. Getting detailed information from her was very easy after that.

Armed with a detailed map of the island and the rough location of where Dante had been spotted, we drove six miles south to El Cedral, touted as the oldest town in Cozumel. It turned out to be a little village with lots of stuff to sell to tourists. The Mayan ruins it was famed for was an old, disappointing rock and concrete building the size of an outhouse that we couldn't go into, but since we weren't really tourists, that didn't bum us out.

Ours wasn't the only car parked along the road. I counted three jeeps and four other rental cars, but only saw two tourists browsing the little street-side shops. The other occupants of the vehicles seemed to have disappeared into the jungle down the horseback path, intent perhaps on finding a saber-toothed tiger.

With the sun glaring down on us, we set out on foot. Once out of sight, we stretched our legs and senses, loping quickly down the trail. It was a jungle but the foliage was only just above our heads; it did nothing to shelter us from the direct rays of the brilliant sun. Less than a mile out we came to an abrupt halt, or rather Nolan did. Since he was in the lead, Chami and I stopped as well. "Do you sense that?" Nolan said, gazing ahead.

"Sense what?" I asked, wiping my brow. I was hot and sweaty, but the other two were panting already, their body's mechanism for expelling heat. Their skin beneath the white paste of their sunscreen, I noticed, had deepened to a bright pink.

"There's another Monère here, several miles north ahead of us. And it's not Dante."

"He has humans with him," Chami added, sniffing the air. "Armed with guns."

"We have to go back," Nolan said, turning around.

"No," I said, blocking his path.

"It's not safe for you," Chami murmured behind me.

Typical males, ganging up. So close . . . no way was I turning back.

"You said you sensed only one Monère."

"With other men who are armed with guns," Nolan answered. "We only have knives."

"Then we'll avoid him. Do you think he's sensed us?"

"Likely not," Nolan replied after a brief moment, confirming what I'd suspected, that Nolan's and Chami's senses were keener than most, likely something that increased with age and power. Theirs were certainly much better than my own ability. I couldn't sense the other Monère yet, which meant that he probably hadn't sensed us either. Goody.

"Plus, it's only an hour until sunset. They'll probably head back soon, before it gets dark." I pulled out the map to study. "Instead of turning back, it makes better sense for us to cut east for several miles, then continue north, parallel to them, just out of their range."

Doing so, however, turned out to be much harder than I'd expected. With no trail, we had to pick our way slowly and carefully through the thick brush so as not to make too big a racket and give ourselves away. Nor was hacking out a path acceptable for the same reason: too much noise.

We'd managed to head out only about two miles east when the sky began to darken. Sunset had finally come.

"How are you guys holding up?" I asked in a low, muted voice.

"Better now," returned Chami, just as quietly. Taking out a handkerchief, he began wiping the sunblock off his face.

Noise alerted us. Excited raised voices.

"They must have picked up our scent," Chami hissed. "They're coming after us."

"Split up," Nolan said tersely. "I'll go north. Chami, you go south. We'll act as decoys and make plenty of noise; that plus the obvious smell of our sunscreen should draw them after us. Milady, you keep heading straight. You'll come out of the jungle in a mile or so onto the coastline highway. Stay on the road; there'll be hotels and resorts. Go to the nearest one and wait for us there."

Chami and Nolan turned and started crashing through the foliage in opposite directions. Heart racing, I made my way forward as quickly and quietly as I could.

Rapid commands were issued in Spanish, and twigs and branches snapped and cracked as our pursuers split up. But it wasn't into two parties, it was three, and the one coming after me was moving silently and swiftly with a tangible, distinct presence that brushed up against mine. It was the Monère and he was after me.

No need for silence or stealth now. I leaped and sprang in inhumanly long bounds, crashing through the underbrush at a speed that would have left a human far behind. But my pursuer wasn't human. He proved that by keeping pace with me, and even more worrisome, narrowing the distance between us. The rubbing of awareness between us was like an invisible marker getting closer and closer. Whoever he was, he was superbly fit.

I broke out of the jungle onto the edge of the highway and took in my situation in a brief, panicked glance. The human heartbeats that I had heard and used as guidance were those of men my wily hunter had posted along the road, not of tourists or staff from a nearby hotel as I had been expecting, though one such resort was visible several miles down the road. I knew they weren't innocent tourists because they were carrying small automatic pistols that looked like mini machine guns.

That smart son-of-a-bitch Monère had set a trap and flushed me out into the open.

The gun-toting men posted along the empty, narrow highway seemed as surprised to see me as I was to see them. What to do? Normally I would have tried to bluff my way out: *Nothing but a lost tourist. Thank God there's a hotel down the road! Could you let me pass?* But the hypercharged presence behind me closing in fast negated that option, so I simply turned and ran north up the road, and didn't even try to pass for human. I ran full out, which meant I was just a blurring streak to the other men.

Gunshots *rat-a-tatted* behind me, whizzing by, spraying the ground around me.

"No disparar!" roared my pursuer. I hoped like hell he was telling his men not to shoot me, which it seemed he had because no more gunshots sounded. But my hopes of getting away died when I heard a soft *swoosh* and felt something painful thud into my back. Reaching between my shoulder blades, I yanked out a blood-tipped dart.

Well, fuck, I thought, as I felt the strength leech out of my body at alarming speed. *The bastard shot me with a tranquilizer dart.* I might have preferred being shot with a real bullet instead. This was just too damn embarrassing.

My unchecked momentum took me a few more strides before my legs stopped working. One minute I was running full out; the next moment I slammed to the ground as my legs suddenly collapsed beneath me.

There was a bright flash of splintering pain as the right side of my head hit something hard on the ground. Then, lights out.

FOUR

ONE MOTHER OF a killer headache had me in its merciless grip as I sluggishly rose back to consciousness. I groaned, raised a hand to touch the side of my head, and whimpered when my fingers touched the egg-sized lump over my right temple.

"Easy, *lucerito*," murmured a voice that was velvet soft, an alluring sound that made me want to open my eyes.

I cracked my lids open a cautious sliver. When my head didn't explode, just kept to that constant pounding headache, I opened my eyes fully.

"Ow!" I said for lack of anything else better to say as I stared up at a dark, masculine face. A stranger I didn't recognize, sitting next to me as I lay in bed. Gingerly I sat up and took in my surroundings. A strange man, a strange, luxuriously furnished bedroom . . . and we were not alone. Two other Latino men were in the room with nasty-looking guns in their hands. Bodyguards. Their weapons weren't pointed at me yet, but I had the feeling that they would be if I so much as blinked wrong, which was a complete puzzle. This whole thing was, actually.

"Where am I? And who are you?" I asked woozily, fighting back a groan as my shift in position added in nausea to the mix. I had to swallow and close my eyes for a brief second before the headache lessened back down to not-wanting-to-puke-your-guts-out bearable.

My eyes reopened and focused on the unfamiliar face in front of me. He was a very attractive devil, I observed distantly like someone viewing a lovely work of art. He had glossy black hair and dark eyes, but whereas my skin was fair, his was tanned, though not as swarthy as his two armed bodyguards.

For the moment, my discomfort preempted feelings of anything else like alarm, but it hovered close, within touchable reach.

"You are in my home in Cancun," said Mr. Dark and Lovely. His English was perfect, accented lightly with a sexy Latin cadence and fluidity. "My name is Roberto Carderas. What is your name?"

"Lisa. Lisa Hamilton." I blinked again, as if that would help clear up his words better. "Cancun? You mean, like in Mexico?"

Roberto nodded, his dark, intelligent eyes observing my reaction.

"Why the hell am I in Mexico? I live in Manhattan. My job . . ." Worry spiked, intensifying the blistering headache.

"What do you do?" asked Roberto.

"I'm a nurse." God, there was nothing but confusion in my head. Confusion and pain. "What day is today?"

"Wednesday."

"Crap, I should be at work! It's nighttime. Is Mexico in the same time zone as New York? What the hell am I doing in

Mexico?" I muttered. "I have to call the hospital and let them know I won't be able to come in tonight." Carefully, I turned my head, searching for a phone.

"Easy, *lucerito*."

I didn't know what the heck *lucerito* meant, only that it sounded almost like an endearment. "Do I know you?" I asked.

"You don't remember?"

"Remember what?"

"Meeting me on the island. On Cozumel," he clarified.

"No. Where's Cozumel?" I'd heard of the popular vacation destination but didn't know its exact location on the map.

"It's an island not too far from here," he said. "You fell and hit your head, and I brought you to the mainland. The hospitals are much better here than the small clinic they have on the island. They x-rayed your head and determined that you had no fracture, just a bad concussion, so I brought you back to my home to rest. Did you come with anyone else? A boyfriend or perhaps a husband?"

"No, no one. Just me."

"No family?" he persisted.

"No."

"What about friends?"

I shook my head, immediately regretting the action as another severe wave of pain pounded my skull, enough to make me cry out. When the sharp pain eased back to a bearable throb, I focused on . . . what was his name again? . . . Roberto.

"Why did you help me?" I asked. "We obviously don't know each other that well, do we?"

"No, I saw you on the island. I was vacationing there myself. As to helping you—it was the decent thing to do."

"Thank you," I murmured, touched by how much trouble

and expense he seemed to have gone to help me. "I'll pay you back," I assured him.

"*De nada,*" Roberto said, dismissing my pledge with the easy, telling grace of someone accustomed to wealth. "No need to pay me back. Medical care is much less expensive here in Mexico than in the United States. It pleases me to be of service to you."

"No, I insist." Then wondered if I could make good on my words. I didn't know how much money I had with me, much less why the hell I'd traveled here in the first place. "Where is my purse?"

"You did not have one. Just your passport, credit card, and some cash you were carrying in your pocket—" Roberto gestured to the bedside table where the items he had mentioned were laid out. "—and a knife."

"A knife?" That was a surprise. The knife, I noticed, wasn't with my other things. "Are you sure it was mine? I don't carry a knife."

"You had it strapped in a sheath around your waist."

"I did? How odd. I wonder why."

My reply had him studying me more closely and no wonder. He was probably wondering if the strange woman he had played Good Samaritan to was crazy or violent. I was wondering that, too. For the life of me I couldn't remember what had happened to me, or make any sense of where I was or what the hell I was doing in Mexico.

I eased my way carefully over to the bedside table to look over my stuff. The passport was familiar, but I didn't recognize the credit card. My uneasiness grew. It had my name printed on it, but it was as unknown to me as the knife they claimed to have been strapped to my waist, and was issued by a bank I didn't recognize.

I counted out a little over two hundred dollars in cash,

American money, nothing converted to local currency yet. I held out two hundred dollars to Roberto. "I know it's probably not enough—"

"Keep it," he said in that smoothly accented voice. "I insist."

It felt oddly vulnerable to be here, among all these strange people.

"Are they your bodyguards?" I asked, glancing nervously at the men standing by the door.

"*Sí.*"

"Why do you have bodyguards?"

"I am a wealthy businessman, and as such am a target," Roberto said. "Kidnapping and ransom, unfortunately, is common here in my country."

"Oh, for a moment I thought they were here to protect you against me," I said with a weak grin, inviting him to share in the humor of the ridiculous thought. But Roberto didn't smile. Just gazed at me with careful, probing intentness.

"Why would you think that, *querida*?"

"I don't know. Maybe because they're staring at me so suspiciously." That and the fact that their guns were drawn, if not pointed.

The reassuring smile he gave me made him even more attractive. "Forgive their diligence. They are paid to be suspicious, and you are, after all, a strange woman that I have brought into my house." He murmured something in Spanish and his men holstered their weapons. And some tension I hadn't known I felt eased within me.

"Can I use your telephone to call my work?"

"Of course," Roberto said graciously. He stood up, and I noted that he wasn't just handsome but tall as well, an inch, perhaps, shy of six feet. "I have a phone in the other room. I will get it for you."

It was only when he left the room that I noticed something I hadn't noticed earlier, in those first confused moments after waking up with that dreadful headache. I *felt* him. Was aware of him in a way I wasn't aware of the other two men in the room. When Roberto returned a few seconds later with a cordless telephone in hand, that sparking awareness shimmered between us again, growing stronger with each step he took closer to me, something I'd never felt before. A connection, for lack of a better word.

My heart kicked up its rhythm with a few hard beats and my hand trembled, faint but visible, as I held it out for the phone.

"Allow me," Roberto said. "It's a bit complicated to call out of the country. If you will be kind enough to give me the numbers, I can place the call for you."

He punched in a set of numbers then entered in the area code and phone number of the hospital I gave him. I heard the call go through, and he handed the phone to me. Four rings later I got an automatic recording that said, "This number has been disconnected or is no longer in service . . ."

I hung up. "I'm sorry, I got an out-of-service recording," I said, thinking that he must have dialed it wrong. "Can we try again?"

I waited until he had entered in the country code. "Can I try dialing the rest of it, please?"

"Of course." He handed me the phone.

"Do I need to dial 1?"

"No, just the area code and phone number."

I entered the numbers and got the same recording. "That's odd." I frowned. "I know for sure that's the correct number. We must be doing something wrong."

"I have placed many calls to the United States and have

had no trouble before," Roberto said. "Is there someone else you can call?"

Only one other number came to mind, a nearby restaurant where I frequently ordered takeout. Roberto entered the first string of numbers and allowed me to input the rest.

"White Elephant," answered a familiar voice. "How can I help you?"

"Hi, Joey. It's me, Lisa."

"Hey, Lisa. Long time no hear," Joey said cheerfully. His strong Brooklyn accent made me feel almost homesick, though his words puzzled me. I didn't think a day or two constituted a long time, even though I practically ate there every day. "Listen, Joey, I tried calling St. Vincent's Hospital and got this no-longer-in-service recording. Did they change their number or something?"

"What number did you call?" Joey asked. I could hear sounds of the small, busy restaurant in the background.

I repeated the telephone number.

"That's the old number, honey."

"The old number?"

"Yeah, before they moved to the new location on Twelfth and Seventh."

"The hospital moved?" I said, feeling as if the whole world instead of just the hospital had shifted.

"Yeah, but they might as well not have. They went bankrupt shortly after you left and shut down, a couple of weeks ago, actually."

"I left?"

"Yup, you quit and left New York."

I unconsciously gripped the phone tightly enough to make the plastic casing protest. Lightening my hold, I asked, "Do you know where I went?"

Joey laughed. "What is this? You pulling my leg?"

"No, I, um . . . I hit my head and have a concussion. I honestly don't remember. I thought I still worked at St. Vincent's."

There was silence at the other end for ten long seconds with nothing but the distant sound of customers and cooking drifting faintly over the line. When I heard Joey's voice again, it sounded gruff and concerned. "Lisa, honey. You quit your job here almost six months ago. I haven't seen or heard from you since then. Sorry, honey, I don't know anything more than that."

After saying thanks, I numbly hung up, feeling dazed by more than just the blow to my head. "I think I asked the wrong question," I said, looking up at Roberto. "What date is it?"

When he told me, I felt a slight roaring in my head—a silent rush of feeling, of panic.

I had lost more than *half a year* of memory!

I had made a new life somewhere . . . and couldn't remember a single moment of it!

There are movies about people who lose their memory—total amnesia. It makes for a great story, with lots of drama and stuff. Having it happen to you, however, was not as much fun as watching it being enacted by talented actors. Granted, I only had partial amnesia. I knew who I was, knew my name—Lisa Hamilton—and where I used to live. I hadn't lost myself completely. Just a significant chunk of time.

I spent the next half hour trying to hunt up more clues of where I had moved to and what sort of new life I had built for myself. St. Vincent's was completely shut down, as Joey had said, with no one in administration to talk to at all. What the landlord of my old apartment had to tell me was more helpful, and highly disturbing.

There had been four men with me when I had moved out of my apartment and turned in my key.

"Four men? Did they seem like friends?" I asked after my initial surprise.

"Yeah, sure. Or why else would they help you move out of your apartment?"

"Can you describe them?"

"Why?" he asked, suspicious.

"Because I hit my head and"—a weak laugh at having to say the next part—"I can't remember them or where I moved to."

"No shit!" My old landlord sounded impressed. "One was a real big guy—tall, six and a half feet at least, heavily muscled like one of those pro-wrestler types. Another was movie-star handsome. The third guy had this old-fashioned beard and mustache like those people in the Victorian age, and the last one was just average looking, you know."

None of this struck a familiar chord in me. One huge wrestler type, another looking like a movie star, another sounding like an Englishman? It didn't describe any of the doctors, orderlies, or tech guys I knew from work. The average-looking fourth fellow might have been one the few guys I had dated, but none of those brief relationships had ended well, certainly not well enough for them to help me move out of my apartment. "Were they young, old?" I asked.

"A little older than you. Late twenties, early thirties, maybe."

"Did I leave any forwarding address?"

"Nah, you best check with the post office. Maybe they can help you."

"Thanks, Mr. Samuels." I hung up with even more questions whirling in my damaged brain.

"Do I have competition," Roberto asked lightly, "these

four men I heard you mention?" He had been sitting so quietly I had almost forgotten that he and the two bodyguards
were still in the room. I blushed when I saw his smile and
the intent look in his eyes. My headache and wooziness had
lessened in the half hour of time I had spent hunting up
more information. And the can of soda and analgesic he had
brought in helped as well.

What had Roberto asked? Oh, yeah. If he had any competition. He was teasing me, of course. Latin gallantry. As if
the idea of a man as dashing and wealthy as he obviously was
being attracted to me wasn't ludicrous.

"I have no idea who those men he described to me were.
They don't sound like anyone I know. Maybe my landlord
mixed me up with someone else who moved out recently. I
didn't have any friends, just acquaintances from work."

"No old boyfriends?"

"None that parted on good enough terms to help me move
out of my apartment."

"They did not end well?" Roberto asked with warm
sympathy.

"Or last long. Only a couple of dates." Just enough to hit
the sheets once, after which it became clear that a physical
relationship was not going to work out between us.

"What about your patients? Did you befriend or get
romantically involved with any of them?"

For a moment, something tickled the edge of my mind,
then was gone like a phantom breeze. "No," I said slowly, "I
never got involved with any of my patients."

"Was it, what you say, professional ethics?"

"More like no interest, on their parts," I said with rueful
honesty.

"A lovely woman like yourself?"

"What is it, Latin genes or something, flattering any

woman you come across? I know I'm a very average-looking woman. And, no," I said, holding up my hand when he opened his mouth, "I'm not trying to fish for more compliments or flattery. I'm simply stating the truth. You are very gallant, and I am deeply in your debt for your help and letting me rack up a huge phone bill with all these telephone calls. I'll pay you back, I promise . . ."

Words died in my throat as he reached out and grasped my hand. That awareness, that strange humming energy between us intensified into sudden blazing brightness at physical contact, and all I knew and felt was him. Like he was my moon, my stars, my entire freaking orbit . . .

"You are far from plain or average, Lisa. You are like me." Cradling my fingers between his own bigger, broader hands, he clasped my hand as if he was savoring our contact, our connection. "Just like me."

FIVE

Touching Roberto was overwhelming. I felt like I wanted to tear off his clothes and jump his bones . . . and that was just so not like me. I'd never felt physically attracted to anyone ever before. Never felt this overpowering urge to mate, like some irresistible force pulling him and me together. It scared me enough to tear my hand away from his, to stand up and back away from him. Distance, I found, helped. Whatever it was I was feeling, it lessened the farther I distanced myself from him.

His bodyguards drew their guns at the sudden movement. And the fact that I had two deadly firearms pointed straight at me was less alarming than the way I reacted to Roberto: like he was a flame I wanted to bask myself in . . . to be consumed by.

Lust.

Holy crap! What I was feeling was lust. Me, the coldest fish in the world.

My heart pounded like a giant drum gone crazy, and my breath sawed in and out of me as Roberto spat out harsh orders in Spanish. I smelled my sweat and some other unfamiliar odor emanating from my body as his men put their guns away, leaving the room.

That, unfortunately, didn't make me feel any better.

"Easy," Roberto murmured.

"No," I said, gritting my teeth, knowing my eyes were wide and wild. "I won't let it control me." With those words, that willful determination, I felt that maddening pull start to ease up between us.

Silence followed, broken only by the sound of heavy breathing. Silence like what a bomb squad must hear after they've successfully prevented an explosion. Roberto eased closer to me, and I did nothing to stop him since his nearness no longer made me want to tear off my clothes and offer myself to him.

His breath came as heavy and fast as mine. Farther down, his pants tented out stiffly with unmistakable prominence. My face flamed, and my unfortunate headache chose that embarrassing moment to reassert itself.

"Argh!" I said, gripping my poor head. God, I ached, not just the bump on my head but the entire right side of me—shoulder, arm, leg, and hip. When the merciless pounding eased, Roberto was standing before me.

"What the hell was that?" I asked, breathless.

"That, *querida*, was a miracle—it was attraction."

I would have snorted if it wouldn't have split my head open. I made a faint, disbelieving noise instead. "I think it was much stronger than attraction. More like this unthinking raw urge to mate."

"It was attraction—lust," he said, echoing my own earlier thoughts. He looked curiously appalled and eager, wary and amazed at the same time. "I have never felt anything like that before."

"Then you were lucky."

"No, I thought I was cursed. I have never been attracted to any woman before, until you." Carefully, delicately, he touched a fingertip to my face.

There was that sensation, that odd zap of energy and awareness again, but muted now. I had somehow reined it in, smothered down the raw intensity of the primitive urge. It still hovered, however, like dry tinder ready to take spark again, but I was in control now: the reason, maybe, why I didn't freak out when his other hand joined the first and his fingers explored my face with something almost like reverence.

"Your skin feels so soft," he murmured in wonderment. His eyes dipped down to my lips, and slowly his head lowered down to mine as hesitation and curiosity held me still. Strong attraction zinged between us again.

I drew back, more than startled by my response. "Oh!" I exclaimed, my hand flying up to cover my mouth.

It had always left me feeling nothing before, men's kisses, their touch. Left me feeling empty, dispassionate. But not now. Whatever chemistry had been missing before was present in full, blazing glory with Roberto.

"*Oh* as in *I did not like it?*" asked Roberto in a low, throaty murmur. "Or *oh* as in *That was unexpectedly good . . . wonderful . . . something we should do again?*"

"The latter," I whispered, holding up a hand when he started to press forward, "but not now. I'm . . ." Overwhelmed, confused. Like a tiny, drifting boat caught up suddenly in powerful, swelling waves that drew me further and further away from all that I had ever known or thought about myself.

"Forgive me, you are injured and in pain." He visibly reined himself in and stepped back. "But tell me," he said, passion vibrating his voice, "tell me that it is the same for you, what I am feeling."

Words I could easily give him. "It's the same," I assured him. "I have never felt attracted to another man before. Until you."

Strong emotion—fierce satisfaction—tightened his face, making the bones stand out strong and masculine. "Rest now and recover," he said in a husky murmur. "We will speak more of this later." Stepping away from me, he left the room.

I took the opportunity to shower and wasn't surprised to discover colorful bruises and red chafed skin on my body, both sides, though more on the right. The hot water eased some of the soreness, and being clean made me feel even better. The only pain I could not account for was in my upper back.

My first glimpse of myself in the mirror was a bit of a shock. My dark hair, so naturally dark it had almost been black, had been skillfully lightened to a color ranging from dark blonde to ash brown, and the cut was more sophisticated than the blunt, straight style I'd always worn my hair before. I lifted a hand to touch the lightened strands of my hair and felt a small twinge of pain between my shoulder blades. When I twisted around to check out the sore spot in the mirror, there were no bruises or signs of falling, just a tiny, barely visible red mark.

Others' pain, their sickness and injury, had always held a special pull for me—what had drawn me into becoming a nurse in the first place. I could take that pain, draw it away from those sick and unwell, and take it into myself. But I could not take away my own pain. Taking away the pain was not my intention, however. Finding out why it hurt, was.

I stretched back and lay my hand over the tiny red mark. With contact, I felt that special ability I had spiral out of the round, pearly mole centered in the heart of my palm and wind itself down, exploring the half-inch depth of the healing injury. It was a puncture wound, though what could have caused it, I had no idea. It was too clean and precise to have been a branch or stick poking into my back when I had fallen. Only a needle could have caused this.

Had they have given me an injection in the hospital? A tetanus shot, maybe? That would make sense, but not the location there in my back; the shot was normally given in the arm. And it was too high up to have been a spinal tap.

A knock interrupted my thoughts and a woman's voice came through the closed bathroom door. "Miss? I am Maria. Senor Carderas asked me help you. I come in, please?"

Wrapping the towel around me, I opened the door. A short, middle-aged Latino woman attired in a maid's uniform smiled pleasantly up at me.

"There's no need for your help, Maria, I've got it."

Maria's pleasant smile slipped away as I began to close the door. Something almost like panic sprang into her eyes. "No, please, senorita. Senor Carderas. He very upset if I no help you." Fear coated Maria's voice and quickened her pulse, filling the air with sharp scent. It was enough for me to open the door and allow her in.

Why had she been so afraid? Was she so terrified of losing her job?

"*Gracias, gracias.* Here, I help you dry hair." Eagerly she blotted the wet strands with another towel and gently combed out the tangles. After blowing it dry, she parted it down the side and gathered my hair back into a simple, elegant chignon. The hairstyle exposed the delicate features of my face, which she then proceeded to enhance with makeup: mascara to thicken my lashes, smoky dark eye shadow, light blush, and red lip gloss—all items she had brought along with her in a small makeup bag. When she was done, the overall effect was quite pleasing.

"How lovely I look. Thank you, Maria. You possess a much more skillful hand with hair and makeup than I do."

Maria beamed with pleasure as she ushered me back into the bedroom where clothing had been laid out on the bed: a sky blue dress, clean underwear, and sandals that looked to be my shoe size. All new.

"These aren't my clothes," I said, looking at the items.

"Senor Carderas asked me buy you something clean and pretty to wear. You try, yes? You wish I wash and fix old things or throw away?" She nudged the shirt and pants I had left on the bathroom floor, torn and covered with dirt and blood.

A good question, considering the condition my old clothes were in. Yet they were the only things linking me to that half year missing out of my life.

No, I wasn't ready to toss them just yet, I decided. "If you could wash and do your best to mend them, please."

Maria wanted to help me dress, but there I stood firm. I would dress myself. With heavy assurances that she had been of great assistance, I ushered her out and closed the door.

The dress fit me almost perfectly; it flattered my tall, slender form, and the color looked good against the creamy white of my skin, my light brown hair, and red lips. I looked quite unlike myself, so smoothly polished and feminine. Not my usual jeans and T-shirt and sneakered self. It was almost startling to realize that with a little effort, I could look attractive. Not something that had interested me much before, but now with Roberto and that potent, shimmering attraction between us, looking nice for him was an appealing idea. The few times I had tried men and sex before had been unpleasant. Painful, even. But things seemed to be different between Roberto and me. Dare I try one more time?

A knock drew me away from my thoughts as Roberto's voice came through the bedroom door. "May I come in?"

"Yes, please do," I answered.

Roberto and another older Latino gentleman entered. "You

look lovely, Lisa." Approval and appreciation lit Roberto's eyes, causing a strange fluttering sensation in my stomach.

"Maria is wonderful," I responded, blushing. My words reminded me once again of her strange behavior. "I tried to send her away, but she seemed almost, I don't know . . . afraid of displeasing you."

The muscles in his face tightened subtly before easing back into relaxed blandness. "I pay my staff very well," Roberto informed me. "She must have feared losing her position. I told her how very important a guest you are to me and how I wished you treated well and with all courtesy."

"You hardly know me," I said, flustered.

"Enough to know that you are very important to me," Roberto responded warmly.

I found myself blushing, remembering our brief kiss.

"Dr. Torres here has come to examine you," Roberto said, introducing the other man.

The doctor took my blood pressure, pulse, and respiratory rate, listened to heart and lungs, palpated my abdomen, and did a full neurological exam. Roberto stayed the entire time. It should have been embarrassing, but it wasn't. Medical stuff I was familiar with, and his presence in the room was reassuring more than uncomfortable. It proved the truth of his words, that I was indeed important to him.

I passed with flying colors: both pupils equal and reactive to light, all reflexes normal. My lack of memory, however, specifically the long months of loss, seemed to stump the good doctor.

"What you have is posttraumatic amnesia," Dr. Torres said in surprisingly good English. "Retrograde amnesia, to be precise, loss of memories formed shortly before the injury."

"Usually it is only a day or two of lost memory, not half a year of it," I said.

"You seem familiar with the diagnosis."

"I'm a nurse. I've seen it in the ER, usually high school or college football players knocked out during a game."

"Then you know as much as I," Dr. Torres announced, closing his bag. "Medicine and the human body is not an exact science unfortunately. I called the hospital and spoke to the doctor who examined you. You suffered a traumatic brain injury, enough that they initially feared a skull fracture and hemorrhaging inside the brain."

"A fracture? Bleeding? Just from tripping and hitting my head on the ground?"

"You hit your head on a rock very hard, according to Senor Carderas. The doctor swore you had a positive Babinski when he first examined you." He gazed at me as if that should have some meaning, and it did. A positive Babinski reflex, fanning of the big toe upon stimulation of the sole of the foot, indicated a significant problem in the central nervous system . . . like cerebral hemorrhaging.

"But your CAT scan was negative, and you proved only to have a concussion," he concluded.

"And amnesia," I added. "Mustn't forget that. Will I regain my memory?"

"What would you tell your own patients?" Dr. Torres asked.

"That I may or may not. That no one really knows. Only time will tell."

"Precisely. I am a general practitioner, not a specialist, however. I will be happy to refer you to a neurologist."

"No need," I said. "He'll probably run a bunch of tests, charge a lot of money, and then tell me the same thing you just did."

Dr. Torres gave me a sympathetic smile. "Look at it this way, Miss Hamilton. You lost only a small part of your memory, and have kept the most important parts: you still know who you are. Your injury could have been much worse."

The doctor's words stayed with me after Roberto saw the doctor out.

Your injury could have been much worse.

I wondered for a moment if it had been.

A positive Babinski . . . Could my skull really have been fractured? Could I have been bleeding into my brain and my body's unusually rapid healing ability repaired the damage in the few hours it had taken to travel here and have the CAT scan done? Most likely I just had a simple concussion, but the long length of time I must have been unconscious—several hours—bothered me.

"Darn it," I said when Roberto returned. "I forgot to ask him about this." Turning around, I unzipped the back of the dress enough to reveal the tiny red mark between my shoulder blades, wondering why the more severe injuries had been healed while the lesser injuries still remained. "I noticed this while showering. It looks like a puncture wound."

"A puncture wound?" Roberto said. "Where . . . here?"

I shivered as I felt his finger lightly brush over the spot. Awareness flared up bright and hot between us but controllable, or more accurate to say, controlled.

"Do you know what it is, what caused it?"

"Perhaps you fell on something sharp when you hit the ground," he said.

"Like a sharp stick that happened to be shaped exactly like a needle?" I asked a little dryly.

"Why do you say that?" He gently turned me around to face him. "Do you remember anything?"

"No, it was just that it was my first thought also, that I had fallen against something sharp on the ground. Only it looks more like a needle mark to me. Did the doctors give me a shot or something?"

"In your back? Not that I know of."

"Maybe they did, and you just don't know about it."

He took my hands in his, making me shiver slightly with awareness. "I was with you the entire time, *querida*. It does not look like a needle mark to me." He looked a bit concerned over why I was pressing the matter.

I couldn't explain my certainty to him without revealing my ability, and despite the sense of intimacy that was quickly flaring up between us, I wasn't ready yet to do that. Hiding my differences from other people was a lifelong habit, deeply ingrained.

"I'm sorry. You're probably right. It was likely from just a sharp twig on the ground."

He smiled, releasing my hands. "I shall have Maria bring you up a salve."

"No, no. I'm fine, really. I feel much better after taking a shower and getting cleaned up. Dr. Torres mentioned a CAT scan. That's much more expensive than an X-ray."

"Please, no more mention of money," he said, laying a kiss on my hand. The sizzling sensation of his lips brushing my skin and the bright flare-up of that tightly contained attraction between us snatched my breath, and any further words, away from me. "Just rest and recover for now. We shall talk more later."

Wow. Talking later wasn't what came to my mind. More like seeing if his lips running over other parts of my body would be as staggering as that light brush against my hand. His touch left me in a mute sensual daze; it was almost a relief when he closed the door behind him.

Lying down on the clean bed, which had been freshly changed, and remembering the extremely dirty state of my clothing when I had first awakened, I mentally added a new bedspread as well as the CAT scan to the growing tally of what I owed my gracious host.

SIX

I RESTED, NOT for the brief fifteen or twenty minutes that I had expected, but for several long hours during which time I slept deeply. When I awoke, I found my hand reaching for something that was not there.

I sat up and thought, *Where is my necklace?*

A panicked rush out of the bedroom brought me my first glimpse of the main house. It shouted of a degree of wealth that was far beyond anything I'd ever seen before. Roberto's home was styled like a grand palazzo, with marble floors, fluted columns, massive windows, and ceilings that were impressively high—classical elegance blended with modern sophistication. The dress Maria had provided me, that had felt too formal and overdressed before, now seemed perfectly fitting in the graceful splendor of the residence. I ventured down the wide staircase feeling a bit like Alice dropped down the rabbit hole.

Heartbeats sounded toward the back of the house. I was about to head over there when Maria came through a door bearing a tray. On it was a plate of some sliced exotic fruit and a glass of orange juice, freshly squeezed, if the juicy pulp was anything to go by.

"Miss Lisa, you up. Good, I tell Senor Carderas. Come." Leading me to another room, she set the tray down on a small table overlooking the gardens outside, and gestured for me to sit. "This for you. You eat and drink now. You want *medicina* for head?"

"Medicine? No, thanks. My headache's gone now." And not only was my headache gone, but the lump on the side of my head had disappeared. The purple bruises on my arm, openly displayed by the short-sleeve dress, were also yellow now. Five days of healing accomplished in several hours of rest. If Maria thought it odd in any way, she didn't comment on it.

I was savoring the last bite of the delicious fruit when Roberto appeared. I hadn't thought much of his clothing before, only that he favored white and cream-colored clothes that set off his dark skin tone rather nicely, but on closer inspection I saw that it was very much in keeping with his home, a casual lord-of-the-manor style of dress.

"You look much better," Roberto said, sitting down beside me and taking my hand so that a sharp frisson of awareness flared up between us again with the contact.

"I feel much better. This is the most delicious fruit I've ever tasted. What is it?" I gestured to my plate where only the thick outer green peel and black discarded seeds of the fruit remained. I had spooned out and eaten every single bite of the inner, custardlike white flesh.

"Cherimoya," Roberto answered, looking divinely handsome sitting there. "Mark Twain once declared it the most delicious fruit known to man."

"I would have to agree. Do they have this in the United States?"

"Why?" asked Roberto.

"Because it would be criminal if I never tasted this again."

"Stay here with me and you can have all the cherimoya you can eat."

Our conversation had been the easy kind that casual acquaintances had with one another. His last comment, though, had been uttered with what sounded very much like sincerity. As if he had truly meant it.

Stay here with me . . .

I did what any woman who wasn't sure if the man she was speaking to was joking or not would do. I laughed and withdrew my hand from his light grasp. "Wow, if you're an example of that famous Latin charm, no wonder it's, well . . . famous."

He held my gaze. "Will you consider it?"

"What?" I needed him to say it, in case I was mistaken.

"Staying here with me."

I blew out a breath. "You're kidding."

"I do not kid," Roberto said with grave sincerity. "I ask that you think about it."

The idea that he was serious—that he meant it—was overwhelming. "Why? You hardly know me. I hardly know you."

"I know that you are like me, and that I have been alone all my life until now, as have you. I know that our chemistry is alike, a small miracle to me." He grazed his thumb lightly over the back of my hand, sparking that strange surge of energy between us again. "It does not sound as if you have much to return to: no job, no family, no close lovers or friends. You have been alone all your life, like me, and I have never felt anything like this before with another woman. It would be criminal, as you say, not to taste this, explore it . . . savor it."

Oh my. For someone who had never been attracted to a woman before, he was very, very good—smooth and suave and tantalizingly seductive.

My hand crept up automatically in a nervous gesture to touch the necklace I had always worn. "My necklace," I said, reminded of its loss. "What happened to my necklace? I know I was wearing it when I fell. I always wear it."

"Do you?" he asked curiously.

"Yes, it was the only thing I had when they found me abandoned as an infant on the doorsteps of an orphanage."

"So you have had it ever since you were a child?"

"Yes, it's the only thing I have from my mother. Please tell me you have it."

He nodded, and I felt a surge of relief well up within me. "Oh, thank God. I would have been devastated if I had lost it."

"It looked valuable, so I put it in my safe for safekeeping and forgot about it until you reminded me. I shall go get it. No, stay here. Allow me to bring it to you."

My joy, when he returned, turned to puzzlement. The item he laid carefully down on the table was a necklace all right, but one I had never seen before. "What's this?" I asked.

"Your necklace. The one that you were wearing when you fell and hit your head."

"But the necklace I've always worn is just a simple cross. This . . . I don't recognize it." I looked down at an exquisite cameo, the likeness of a man carved upon its ivory surface with scroll-like writing framing the rim. The bottom was engraved with the fierce image of a stylized dragon. As I ran my finger over the engraving, the present world hazed over and the man whose likeness was carved onto the cameo was looking at me. His eyes were a deep, rich chocolate brown.

"The dragon denotes my lineage and is the crest of our family line. Will you wear this?" he asked.

With an abrupt wrench, I returned back to present reality.

"What's the matter?" Roberto asked, grasping both my hands.

I was shaking, trembling.

"I don't know. I think . . . I remembered something—some*one*. The man who gave me this necklace. He said the dragon denoted his lineage, his family line."

"Who was he?" Roberto demanded.

I shook my head. "I don't know."

Roberto stared at the cameo image as if by sheer will he could make it impart its secrets to him.

Picking up the bright silver chain, I examined the scrolled writing more closely to see if it might jar loose some more memory.

"That does not hurt you?" Roberto asked, sounding odd.

"What?"

"The silver chain you are holding."

"No? Why should it?" I asked.

He gazed at my fingers holding the delicate chain. When I continued to simply hold it with no sign of discomfort, he pushed his chair back and stood. "How interesting," he murmured. "Do you remember anything else?"

"No. Nothing else," I said, disappointed and highly perturbed. Who was that strange man with the dark chocolate eyes? And why was I wearing the necklace he had given me instead of the silver cross that meant so much to me? Could he have been the fourth man my landlord had mentioned? The one he described as average looking?

"Lisa," Roberto said, drawing my attention back to him,

"we have mentioned that we are alike, you and I, but have tiptoed around the matter. I think it time to lay our cards on the table. I shall go first. I heal unusually fast like you do," he said, gesturing to the fading bruises on my arm. "I am also faster and stronger than anyone else I know. I can hear things other people cannot hear, and see things from a great distance away that other people cannot see."

I felt as if my heart stilled for a moment as he said aloud the secrets I had kept from others all my life.

"What about you?" he asked softly.

As my heart regained its rhythm and thumped loudly in the silence, I realized something else I had not noticed till now. Roberto's heartbeat was beating as slow as mine, at around fifty beats per minute. Most heartbeats ranged from sixty to a hundred beats per minute. Another shared oddity between us.

"Me, too," I whispered, intimidated even now by speaking of these things aloud. "Ever since puberty I've been faster and stronger than other people, my senses—hearing, seeing, smell—all sharper, more acute."

"But this." He gestured to the silver chain I still held in my hand. "This does not hurt you or weaken you in any way?"

"No. Why should it?"

He searched my eyes as if he would glimpse all their secrets. "No reason," he said, sitting back down.

I blew out a breath, feeling a curious relief from unburdening myself. "Oh my God, I can't believe it. You're just like me." Hesitantly, shyly, I laid my left hand over his chest to feel his unusually slower heartbeat. "Your heart even beats slower, like mine."

He held himself very still beneath my touch.

"What?" I asked. "Why are you grinning and looking at me like that?"

"Because it is the first time you have voluntarily touched me."

I drew back my hand, flustered. "I'm sorry, I—"

"No, do not apologize. I like it very much when you touch me. Why are *you* staring at *me* like that?"

The words left my mouth before I had a chance to think. "Because when you smile you go from being remarkably handsome to almost irresistible." I felt my cheeks grow warm. "Did I just say that out loud?"

Roberto laughed, and the sound of his laughter was as compelling and tantalizing as the rest of him. "Yes, to my great enjoyment. I shall endeavor to smile more for you, my sweet Lisa," he said, reaching for my hand.

I drew back, my gaze dropping to the necklace that lay between us. "No . . . I'm sorry. You make flirting so easy, so fun, and I admit to a powerfully strong attraction to you . . . but I don't remember the last few months of my life. I don't know if there might be someone else I'm committed to, unlikely though that may be."

"You do not wear a wedding or engagement ring," Roberto observed carefully.

"No." I looked down at my bare fingers. "I don't."

Gently he lifted my chin until our eyes met again. "Then count me in the running."

"Of what?"

"A suitor, like this other man you remember may be."

"More likely he was just a new friend I had made, or perhaps a neighbor or a coworker."

"There you go again, denigrating yourself."

"With good reason. I know I'm not beautiful. I'm just a very plain-looking woman."

"You do not know what I see. But, *gracias Dios*, I know that you feel what I feel." That ever-present heat flared up between us like an invisible muscle flexing, testing. "You are special to me, as I know I am to you."

Roberto started his campaign that very night.

The coastal city of Cancun, I found, had a high-gloss charm. Sprawled like a languid queen amidst the natural splendid beauty of white-sand beaches and indigo sea, it abounded with four-star hotels, glittery nightclubs, and international tourists roaming the night looking for fun.

"It's just dinner," he said when I protested the expensive-looking restaurant his driver pulled up in front of. "You are doing me a favor by keeping me company while I eat, truly."

We dined in discreet luxury, ushered immediately to a corner table, bypassing the line, the maitre d' and waiter treating us like royalty.

"They seem to know you," I said, grateful for the lace shawl that hid the yellow bruises on my arms.

"I dine here often," Roberto said.

Digging immediately into the food, I found myself unexpectedly ravenous. "Everyone's looking at us," I whispered.

"That's because they are all wondering who my lovely companion is."

It proved to be an accurate surmise. Not that I was lovely, but that people here were curious as to who I was. Other diners, acquaintances that Roberto knew, stopped by our table—a dapper gentleman who proved to be the mayor of the city, a local real estate mogul, even the owner of the hotel we were dining in. It appeared the crème de la crème of society was here, all peering at me with avid interest in their eyes.

Roberto introduced me simply by my name. The proprietary hand he laid casually around my shoulder, however, defined our relationship more clearly than any words he could have uttered.

"What are you doing?" I asked in a low voice.

"I am staking my claim to everyone." With a smile, he laid a gallant kiss on the back of my hand, sending a chorus of whispered speculation buzzing anew throughout the dining room.

"I told you before," Roberto murmured, stroking my hand, sending tingling warmth coursing through me, "other women have never interested me the way you do."

"So I'm the first woman you've dined with in public?" I said skeptically.

"No, I have had other dining companions. But you are the only one I have ever touched or kissed like this."

Roberto, when he turned on the charm, was mesmerizing, and despite myself, I found myself relaxing beneath his warm, intoxicating attention. Two glasses of fine wine also no doubt helped.

"Are you enjoying yourself?" he asked as our waiter discreetly cleared the plates from our table. Not only had I eaten a main entrée and dessert, but I had guzzled down soup and salad and an appetizer as well—much more than I usually ate.

"The food was divine, the company wonderful, and the setting exquisite," I said, sitting back happily replete.

"I am only wonderful, while the food was divine and setting exquisite?" he said sadly. The twinkle in his eyes told me he was teasing.

"You're good," I drawled back, "but not as good as the food. Especially the dessert."

"Oh, you wound me." Mockingly he clasped his chest.

When I giggled, he smiled happily. "You know, I have never had a more wonderful time. Dance with me."

"Where?" Live music was playing, but there was no space to dance.

"Outside on the patio." He drew me to my feet and pulled me out the terrace doors.

"It feels unreal," I said as he enfolded me into his arms outside. "*You* feel unreal."

"I'm very much real," Roberto murmured as he brought me close against the hardness of his body. We swayed in time to the music as a cool sea breeze blew across our skin.

"Kiss me," I said, lifting up my face, feeling more relaxed than I'd ever felt in my entire life. Feeling almost beautiful.

"I've been wanting to all night." His head dipped down and claimed my lips, and with sweet magic that ever-present chemistry flared up between us.

His kiss, his touch, sent pleasure thrumming through me. With a small sound, I parted my lips, inviting his tongue in to tangle with mine. I ran a hand through the thick silk of his hair, touched the close-shaven side of his face, and felt desire—wonderful, miraculous desire—course through me like a shaft of brilliant sunlight, as if the sun was shining brightly beyond my closed eyelids.

Roberto's abrupt withdrawal opened my eyes, and I found that the light I had thought I'd imagined was real. Only it wasn't sunlight, it was our skin: my skin blazing brightly with white luminescence, Roberto's skin a dimmer glow.

I gasped. "My God. We're glowing! What did you do?"

"Nothing," Roberto said, as startled as I. "I thought you might know what this was."

To our vast relief, the glowing of our skin dimmed and disappeared after we broke apart.

"No one saw us," Roberto said. "What just happened?"

"We lit up like two freaking lightbulbs. That's what happened!"

"Yes." He gave a brief, shaky laugh. "But what caused it?"

Reality shifted suddenly again.

The moon full and round, pregnant with light and energy. Rays, shafts of light, coming down from it. No, that wasn't quite right— pulled down from it. *By me. Hitting me, filling me with buzzing power like a battery getting a sudden blast of charge. Light filling me, pouring out of my skin, setting me aglow . . .*

I crashed back to the present. To Roberto's voice.

". . . it was almost as if sunlight emanated from us—"

"No," I whispered hoarsely. "Moonlight . . . moonlight spilling from our skin. What in God's creation *are* we?"

Sudden awareness rippled across my skin, that feeling of like to like, as energy brushed faintly across me.

"What's that?" I asked as my skin prickled. Turning in a circle, I tried to pinpoint where that feeling was coming from.

"What is what?" asked Roberto.

"That. Don't you feel it? It's like what I feel with you, only it's more distant. It's coming from . . . the sky. There!" I pointed to a bird on the distant horizon and wondered if I was crazy. No airplane, no crazy tourist hang gliding or parasailing. Just the bird—my vision zoomed in. An eagle.

Roberto suddenly urged me inside.

"What is it?" I asked. "What's wrong?"

"It's another like us," he said, sounding grim.

"Where?"

"Where you pointed."

"I pointed to a bird."

"Exactamente."

"You can't be serious." I stopped. Turned to look at him. "You are! You think that eagle is someone like us?" I said with disbelief.

He nodded. "If I can take on the form of an animal, so can someone else."

My voice squeaked up an octave. "You're telling me that you can shift into an *animal*?"

"Into a jaguar. Can you not shift into animal form?"

"Uh . . . no."

That seemed to surprise him. He shook his head as urgency regained its hold. "Inside the restaurant, quickly."

"Why? If it's someone like us, don't you want to meet him?" I asked, bewildered.

"It's a male," Roberto said. Opening the door, he ushered me inside the restaurant. "I have found other males to be quite dangerous."

"You've met others?" Aware of our environment, I lowered my voice. "Like us?"

"Met them and killed them."

"You killed them?" I said in a shocked whisper, swinging around to face him. We were drawing attention again, but our voices were lowered beyond what normal humans could hear.

"It was kill or be killed," he said, gripping my shoulders. "Other males come here occasionally to challenge me, to try and take my territory." Planting a quick kiss on my mouth, he spun me around and led us back to our table. With a gesture from Roberto, our attentive waiter rushed over. A quick spatter of Spanish later, Roberto was leading us out the front door. His two bodyguards, waiting near the entrance, fell into place, one in front of us, one behind.

"I didn't see you pay," I continued to whisper, even though there was no longer a need to.

"I had the waiter charge the bill to my account."

No credit cards, just charging things to your account. It struck me as hilariously funny for some reason. I started laughing as I almost ran to keep up with Roberto's brisk pace, his hand tightly clasped around mine.

"What's so funny?" he asked, glancing back.

"You are. This whole situation—bodyguards, just signing instead of paying a bill, running from a bird." And unsaid, our skin glowing with moonlight, and learning that there were other people like us who Roberto had killed and who had tried to kill him. And discovering that people like us could shift into animal form!

Our car quickly pulled out in front, and we slid inside into the dark, tinted interior. The two guards squeezed in front with the driver, and off we went, blending swiftly into traffic. There were fifteen minutes of alert tension but nothing happened, and I began to think that we had lost whoever, *whatever*, had been flying toward us. A bird. *A freaking bird*, I thought with disbelief. Had I not felt that frisson of awareness, I would have wondered whether Roberto was paranoid or deluded.

Shifting into an animal . . . Roberto had claimed he could as well. Never in my wildest dream had I imagined being able to do something like that. But as we pulled off the main highway and threaded our way onto less crowded residential roads, I felt it again, that sharp frisson of awareness.

"He's here," I said a second before something big struck the roof. The car jolted with the impact, and taloned claws—alarmingly big, almost the size of a man's hand—punched through the metal above us with a screeching, tearing sound. Gravity tilted as the car was jerked abruptly onto its side, my scream lost among the blistering sound of metal scraping along asphalt and the loud, explosive din of guns being fired at close range.

The taloned claws disappeared, and the car careened to a stop. We were amazingly uninjured, I saw, as I climbed out of the upended car. I looked wildly around for a large eagle and felt him close by but had only a fraction of a second to glimpse a naked, bleeding man sprawled on the road before my senses were awash with another onslaught. *Not just one but many*, I had time to think, and then three men were suddenly attacking us.

Our two bodyguards had crawled out of the car and were shooting in a wild burst of fire but seemed unable to hit any of our attackers. Roberto came closer to hitting his target with the gun he had pulled out and was firing. Close but no cigar. His bullets struck and deflected off the thick, metal bracelets his attacker wore on his forearms, using them like an ancient warrior of old to block the shots—a wild-looking man with long, dark hair and a thick, unruly beard. It was a scary and impressive skill he had. Even more impressive were the three-inch-long claws curving out of his fingertips!

I blinked my eyes to make sure what I was seeing was real. Holy crap, it was.

He was a seasoned fighter, much better than Roberto, it became quickly obvious as the two neared each other. Blood scented the air, pungent and coppery thick, as he sliced across Roberto's chest and, spinning nimbly, cut deep bleeding furrows down his back. Before I had time to think, I was in motion, as with cold, eerie calmness he executed another neat rotation, raising his right hand—his right claw—for a beheading stroke.

"No!" I threw myself in front of Roberto, coming face-to-face with eyes so pale a blue that they looked like ice. I saw my death in those eyes and had no time to brace myself for the oncoming blow that would end my life.

Emotion flashed in those arctic eyes, something like confusion, maybe even surprise, as he twisted himself violently away. I felt his claws whistle pass my neck, felt the brush of passing wind whip across my skin, and braced for pain, but none came. No blood, no wet splatter. He'd missed . . . he'd deliberately missed.

"Mona Lisa," he rasped hoarsely, words that jolted me. As I stared into those odd, pale eyes, his body jerked as a gun fired behind him, blasting my eardrums with the close shock of the loud noise. My eyes dropped down to those deadly claws, so long and lethal and inhuman, and watched with awful fascination as they shrank down in a fluid wave of transformation to become normal nails on normal hands.

"Silver bullets," the pale-eyed attacker said, looking down at his unblemished chest. No exit wound. The bullet was still inside him, buried in his flesh.

As he dropped to his knees, Roberto came into view, his dark eyes shining with satisfaction as he shot the man a second time. The bandit jerked again and collapsed on the ground.

One moment I was alone with the fallen attacker, shielded behind Roberto and the two bodyguards; the next instant a hand grabbed me out of nowhere, an invisible hand I could not see, matched by an invisible voice that said, "Let's go, milady, quickly."

"No!" Frightened and bewildered, I instinctively resisted the invisible hand gripping me. "Let me go!"

Roberto aimed to my left and fired. More bullets whined. I heard, even felt, some of them passing by. Heard two of them hit their invisible target as I twisted and fought against my unseen captor. My wrist was abruptly released, and I sensed whoever had been holding me move away. He made it only a few yards away before the first drops of red blood spilled out at stomach height, as if from the very air itself. Then abruptly, as if a veil had been yanked away, a man suddenly appeared, tall, wiry thin, with short, curly brown hair. He looked like a young graduate student instead of a road bandit; certainly not someone capable of playing the invisible man and inspiring the choking amount of terror he had in me.

All guns trained at him and fired. If I had wondered before if we were capable of moving faster than a speeding bullet, the answer is yes, sort of.

Roberto and I were the only ones who saw the other attacker move, the biggest one, tall and strongly muscled, with a beard like the other man but shorter and more neatly clipped—the only one left uninjured among our group of attackers. He moved as I moved when I ran free, out of sight of prying eyes: inhumanly fast. He snatched up Mr. Invisible (who had now turned visible) and darted out of the way of fire before the bullets reached where the other man had been standing.

Roberto was the only one fast enough to fire a second round. The big guy deflected two of the bullets with metal wrist guards similar to what the arctic-eyed bandit wore. Even as he ran, fast, so fast that it was nothing but a blurring streak to human eyes, I saw him turn back and look at us . . . no, not us. At the other man who had fought like him and been shot down, fallen near me, blocked from rescue behind Roberto and the bodyguards.

"Go! Leave me," I heard the injured man say as he tried to crawl away from us, making pitiful progress. The words should have been lost beneath the gunfire but I heard him and so did the big man.

The large bandit raced to the naked eagle guy and swung him over his shoulder. Unhindered by their weight . . . indeed, acting as if they weighed nothing more than a feather each, he sprang into the air, one impressive bounding leap that took him to the end of the block where he veered around the corner, disappearing from sight.

I was still reeling from what I had seen, not the world-record-breaking leap—that I could do myself, though maybe not with two other men hanging over my shoulders—but rather from what I had glimpsed when he had swung the naked man onto his shoulder: the neat Vandyke beard and mustache adorning the bird-man's face.

Looking just like a character out of England's Victorian age.

SEVEN

T HE DRIVE BACK home was made in tense silence, with the prisoner gagged and bound in handcuffs—silver, I noted, not the stainless steel they appeared to be. My nose smelled the difference. The cuffs had the same sharp metallic scent as the fired bullets, and seemed to physically pain the prisoner upon contact—no sound, just a subtle clenching of his face and arm muscles. They had dumped him in the trunk of our car, and though he was out of sight, it was impossible to forget him.

For some reason, I didn't like knowing that we sat comfortably in the car while a shot and injured man lay locked in the dark and cramped trunk space behind us. Could he breathe? Did he have enough air? He must have or Roberto would not have put him there, I didn't think, but I couldn't even ask Roberto. He had been on the cell phone speaking in rapid Spanish ever since the car started moving.

I had a number of questions I wished I could ask the captive. Number one was how he knew my name, my secret name that no one else knew. Mona Lisa. The second was about his companions—the big wrestler-type, the guy with an old-fashioned Vandyke beard and mustache, and Mr. Invisible. Together, with him, they made four men, half of whom clearly matched the description my landlord had given me. The other two descriptions were off, however. The poor schmuck bound and gagged in the trunk was neither movie-star hand-some nor average looking, though the latter might apply to Mr. Invisible—a startling trick, by the way, turning invis-ible; almost as good as turning into a bird and being able to flip big cars onto their side. I felt an edge of hysteria grip me for a frantic instant and didn't know if I was going to laugh or start crying. Thankfully I did neither, just sat there feeling my world, my reality, distorting.

Okay, deep breath. Clear thinking.

No telling what the guy in the trunk looked like with all that mountain-man hair and beard covering his face. He didn't look movie-star handsome, but maybe he'd dressed better and hadn't had all that facial hair when my landlord had seen him. Maybe he'd been smiling instead of tearing his way through flesh with horrific clawed hands. First impres-sions really did matter, you know.

Another surge of demented giggling threatened for a thin, precarious moment, then subsided.

Jesus. Maybe I was going crazy because now that I'd had time to think about that chaotic fight, a couple of things bothered me. For one, they didn't seem to be trying to rob us as I had first assumed. My second thought had been kidnap-ping; Roberto was wealthy, after all. But the guy had clearly been about to kill Roberto, not hold him for ransom. I wasn't too familiar with the profession, but I believed kidnappers generally kept the person they wanted to demand money for alive, not cut their head off, which I was pretty sure Mr. Pale Eyes had been about to do before I stopped him. He had been willing to hurt everyone but me. And what had the Invisible Man called me? My lady. *Let's go, my lady, quickly.* As though he'd known me and had expected me to come with him.

I hadn't been able to see his eyes but I wondered if Mr. Invisible might have had the same confused and surprised expression on his face as the man in the back of the trunk had when I'd thrown myself in front of Roberto and stopped his killing blow.

I had assumed Roberto had been their target, if not to kidnap him then to kill him. That seemed to be what Pale Eyes had intended, his death. But if that was their goal, then why try to take me away?

I was confused—confused and feeling something almost like dread rising within me.

Roberto ended his phone call.

"Why did they attack us?" I asked him.

Did Roberto hesitate a moment or was I just imagining it? And if not imagining it, then reading something more into it than I should?

"I told you before, *querida*. Sometimes others come here to try to take what is mine."

Reasonable answer. But I wasn't satisfied. "They were trying to kill you but not me. They did their best, in fact, not to harm me. No one shot at me, not once. And the guy in the trunk pulled his blow, the one he had intended to take off your head with, or it would be my head rolling on the ground right now. Why didn't they try to hurt me?"

He must have heard the rising note of agitation in my voice because he put his arm around me and soothed me with a soft shushing sound, gently urging my head to rest against his chest. But I resisted, the first time I'd done that. I pulled away so I could see his face. It was important that I do that, see Roberto's face when he answered me.

"You are a woman. I have seen other men like myself but never a woman before," Roberto said, choosing his words carefully, making me wonder how much English his two bodyguards spoke and understood. "Of course they would wish to kill me and take you for themselves."

It all sounded true, reasonable, consistent with everything he'd told me. I would have been satisfied if two of our attackers didn't match the description my landlord had given me of my four "friends" who had helped me move out of my Manhattan apartment.

Had they—bizarre thought here—had they been trying to rescue me? If so, that would imply that they thought Roberto was the bad guy. It would also imply that I was a captive, which I wasn't. Was I?

"We'll drop you off at the house first," Roberto said, interrupting my train of thought.

"No, the police will need my statement. I was a witness. For that matter, why didn't we wait for the police? Aren't we supposed to stay at the scene of a crime?"

"Normally we would, but it was too dangerous to remain there. The men who escaped might have returned."

Roberto and his two bodyguards had tipped the car back onto all four wheels, roughly stowed their captive in the trunk, and taken off like a bat out of hell. Roberto could have straightened the car himself, single-handedly, but he'd asked his bodyguards' help, likely in case anyone in one of the homes along the street were watching. As if a giant eagle turning into a naked man, and people moving at faster than human speed, able to leap an entire block in a single bound, were not strange enough.

"I will take you to the house first. No need for you to be involved," Roberto said in a soothing tone. "If the *Federales* wish to take your statement, they can come to the house to do so." He dropped me off, leaving the taller bodyguard with me, following me inside like a looming shadow as Maria opened the door.

I escaped upstairs to my room, very aware of the guard's presence outside my door as I wrestled with my sudden, odd suspicions. Roberto had been nothing but kind to me so far, more so than he needed to be. And they had attacked us, not the other way around. But still, so many things didn't add up, and my questions would not be answered unless I asked them.

I made my decision and opened the door. "Excuse me," I said to the guard standing outside my room. "Do you speak English?"

"*Sí.* A little."

"Good." I looked up into his eyes and captured his will. Mesmerism, compulsion—whatever name you wanted to call it. I considered this my most dangerous power; as a nurse, I'd only used it to help people, to provide a momentary balm to soothe sick and injured patients.

"What is your name?" I asked.

"Carlos Hernandez."

"Come inside, Carlos."

He entered and I shut the door behind him. He waited for my next command, his face slack, eyes fixed on mine.

"What type of businessman is your boss, Roberto Carderas?"

"A ruthless one," Carlos said, answering the question, but not in the way I had hoped.

I rephrased it. "What type of business is Roberto in?"

"He is a drug lord."

My sluggish heart started to pound. "What type of drugs?"

"Crystal meth, cocaine."

Okay, definitely the illegal stuff. Even though I didn't feel the strain yet, I knew I couldn't keep up the compulsion for much longer and asked the next question quickly. "How did I come to be here in Roberto Carderas's house?"

"He shot you with a tranquilizer dart and brought you here."

My hand flew to where that red spot on my back had been, an injury caused not by a needle but a dart!

"When he shot me with the dart, was I alone?"

"*Sí.*"

"So the men we just fought, I do not know them?"

"The big man and the invisible one tried to help you, but Senor Carderas put a knife to your throat. Threatened to kill you if they did not leave."

"They *are* my friends!" It was a stunning, devastating realization. "The man they captured . . . I have to rescue him! They're bringing him to the police."

"Senor Carderas did not take him to the *Federales*. He is taking him somewhere to be questioned."

"And after he questions him?" I asked.

"He will kill him."

EIGHT

I WAS OPERATING blindly in so many ways, I should have been terrified. And if not terrified, then exhausted and drained, as I usually felt after expending so much energy to compel another's will. But I was none of those things. I was flying on fear and adrenaline instead of crashed out on the floor in a weak and helpless puddle, not at all tired, even though I'd held the compulsion for more than five minutes— by far the longest I'd ever done so. A lot of things, it seemed, had changed in those six months of lost memory.

I changed back into my own clothes, which Maria had neatly mended and washed. Grabbing my passport and money, I left with Carlos before the additional guards Roberto had called in to protect the house arrived. Moments later, I was in the car, being driven by Carlos to wherever Roberto had taken the prisoner—a friend whose name I didn't even know yet—to be questioned. Or, in franker terms, to be tortured and then killed.

I looked nervously over at the swarthy bodyguard behind the wheel.

With a final flexing of will, I had implanted in Carlos the false impression that we were fleeing an attack on the house. Things seemed to be going well so far—no suspicious glances at me yet. I didn't know how long the compulsion would last. In the hospital in New York, I'd used my ability only in short spurts, to provide quick comfort. Not for anything as elaborate as what I was doing now.

"How much farther?" I asked.

"Just ahead." He seemed to mean it literally as he turned into a driveway and pulled in front of an old house that would have looked quite ordinary were it not for the two men posted outside armed with small machine pistols. A rapid flurry of Spanish was exchanged between Carlos and one of the guards, the other bodyguard who had been in the shoot-out, and I wondered for the umpteenth time if what I planned to do wasn't just crazy but maybe sheer suicide. Then I was inside, with Roberto walking toward me, frowning fiercely. Two other armed men, new guys, followed behind him wielding more of those nasty-looking weapons.

"Thank God!" I cried, throwing myself into Roberto's very surprised arms. "The big bandit attacked the house and may have followed us here."

At Roberto's sharp command, the two guards rushed outside.

"This is not acceptable," I said, words that at my implanted suggestion caused Carlos to slump to the ground sound asleep. In a flash of speed and strength, I slammed the silver bullet I was holding into Roberto's back, embedding it deep in his flesh, somewhere he would have a hard time reaching.

The silver rendered Roberto weak and slow, just as it had done to his captive. I stuffed a handkerchief in his mouth and secured it with Roberto's own silk tie, all done in the blink of an eye. In the next ticking second, both of his arms were cuffed behind his back, the handcuffs borrowed from the sleeping Carlos.

"That should do it for you," I said, satisfied. Not bothering to secure him further, I pulled Roberto's gun from its holster and dashed outside. It was almost unfair how easy it was to knock out the two guards with careful, restrained blows to the backs of their heads. A quick hunt for the other two men, who were checking the perimeter, and it was over by the time Roberto stumbled outside, enraged sounds coming from his gagged mouth. I threw the automatic pistols, one after the other, into the surrounding forest.

"Join me," I said, pulling Roberto back inside. He struggled but in his weakened state was no match against greater strength. I followed the smell of blood and the sound of a slow heartbeat, even slower than mine, to the basement.

I ended up carrying Roberto down the stairs with me—easier to do that than get him to voluntarily walk down them—and set him back on his feet at the bottom of the steps. Tugging him behind me, I threw open the door to the room where that single slow heartbeat thudded.

NINE

THE PHYSICAL PAIN was agony, the silver bullets burning like fiery brands lodged within Dante's flesh. But the mental agony was greater. She had betrayed him. In what explicit words, Dante could not say or express coherently in his current haze of rage and pain, only that she had betrayed him and caused injury to all but his father.

It had been many lifetimes since Dante had been a captive, bound, gagged, and helpless. Yet in this current cycle of life, this was his second time in such a state, in as many months. The first time, Mona Lisa had saved him. Now she was the reason he had been captured, his body writhing in silver-ridden pain . . . because she cared more for a handsome stranger than she did him or her own people.

Dante's thoughts and emotions were in chaotic turmoil. He loved her, hated her, wanted her like no other . . . and despised her with almost blinding, seething fury for kindling that want, that helpless need within him.

As if Dante's very thoughts had procured her, he heard her

voice above. Heard the treacherous news fall from her own lips that she had yet again fled a rescue attempt by his father. The Warrior Queen had indeed served vengeance upon him cruelly well.

You made me love you! Made me think you might love me, too. Betrayed, betrayed . . .

It seeped within him and rose like a poisonous well until livid fury drowned all thoughts in a deafening roar for blood and vengeance. The sight of her, as she came through the door, was like a blow bludgeoning his chest. Love and hate, yearning and betrayal, mixed together in tumultuous disorder.

He twisted against his silver bonds, shouted muffled words of wrath. Then fell silent as she pulled Roberto in behind her, bound and gagged, with his arms handcuffed behind his back.

Mona Lisa hesitated at the sight of the wild captive chained to the wall. She had thought him frightening before in his eerie fighting calm. Now the calmness was gone and something akin to madness gleamed in his pale silver-blue eyes. The sight, the shock of it, jarred loose another broken memory.

The same young man in a near-naked savage state straining against silver chains, padded oddly with fleece, his hair unkempt and wild, eyeing her like a famished beast.

It overlay the current reality like a ghostly afterimage for a heartbeat, and then disappeared. The momentary shift in reality unsettled and confused her enough to make her ignore the dangerously enraged state of the bandit.

She ripped off his gag, asked him desperately, "I . . . I know you, don't I?"

Her question punched through Dante's rage and shocked him still. "Mona Lisa. What game are you playing at?"

"Do I know you?" she persisted.

"Hell, yes, you know me!"

His shout galvanized her into action. "Where are the damn keys?" she asked. Turning to Roberto, she searched his pockets.

"You don't need keys," Dante snarled. "You're strong enough to break the chains yourself."

"I can?" She seemed surprised.

"Yes, silver doesn't weaken you."

"No, you're right. Silver doesn't bother me." Still, she seemed astonished that, with one simple tug, she was able to wrench open the shackles that had contained him.

The chains fell away with a clank, and he was free, looking wildly dangerous and threatening, those pale blue eyes burning so hot and fierce as he stepped toward her.

"What's your name?"

Her question stopped him cold in his tracks again. "You know my name," Dante said, jaw clenched.

"Maybe once but not now. I don't remember. I hit my head. I don't remember any of you."

He stared at her intently then said, "I'm Dante." When she showed no reaction to his name, he nodded toward Roberto. "What about him?"

"He's the bad guy, right?"

A cold, deadly smile lit Dante's face. "Yeah, he's the bad guy." He moved toward Roberto, who fell back, mumbling frantically, trying to force words out past his gag.

"Wait." She gripped his forearm. "What are you going to do?"

"I'm going to kill him." He had fallen back into that eerie calmness. Said it as if it were a foregone conclusion. As if it was normal practice for him—and her—to kill the bad guy. But whatever Mona Lisa didn't remember, she couldn't have changed that much. The thought of killing Roberto made her instinctively recoil.

"No, leave him! We have to go. There were other guards coming to the house. I took off before they arrived. They may be on their way here."

The sound of a car pulling up and people getting out, weapons being readied, filtered down from outside.

"Too late, they're here," Dante said and ran up the stairs as fast as his wounds allowed, cursing the silver still lodged within him limiting him to only human speed.

He grabbed a knife from a fallen guard and one of those automated pistols—.22 caliber, Dante noted, why the bullets hadn't blown through him like a more powerful 9 mm weapon would have. Mona Lisa followed behind with Roberto. Stuffing the pistol in his waistband, Dante grabbed Roberto, bringing the naked blade to his throat. "Knife, I think. A more visual threat. You're going to tell your men to throw down their weapons, understand?"

Roberto nodded frantically as Dante ripped off the mouth tie, allowing him to spit out the gag.

Dante glanced around for Mona Lisa, but she was gone. He felt his heart give a frantic thud at the discovery. "My lady doesn't want you dead," Dante snarled in fluent Spanish as he jerked Roberto outside, using him as a human shield. "But give me a reason and you will be. Tell them to drop their weapons now!"

Roberto yelled out the order. There were four men, all armed with automatic pistols. Two of them started to drop their weapons, but the two others farther away still held their guns trained at Dante. In a fast, blurry motion, Mona Lisa came up behind them, knocked the two armed men unconscious, and followed suit with the two surrendering guards.

"I did what you said!" Roberto babbled in English as his men thudded to the ground.

"Pity," Dante said, removing the sharp knife from his neck. He shoved Roberto down onto his knees. "Stay here. You move, you die." He strode to Mona Lisa, stopping two feet away from her. Any closer and he would be tempted to grab her and shake her. "What the hell did you think you were doing?" he gritted out as fear and adrenaline pounded madly through him.

"Disarming them." She started gathering up the weapons, handling them with dainty distastefulness.

"You should have stayed safely inside instead of risking yourself," he growled.

"I didn't want any more bloodshed, yours or theirs," she replied softly. Only a discerning ear would pick up the faint, trembling edge in her words. She was not as calm as she appeared. That sign of nerves oddly calmed his own fear and rage.

Dante watched as she went to the car parked farthest out in the driveway. Popping the trunk, she hastily dumped the weapons she had collected in there.

"You should kill them," he said with calm practicality.

"No." Just one soft word.

"They'll follow us."

Slowly, carefully, she took the knife from Dante's hand. "Not if I can help it." Going to the other cars, she slashed their tires with quick efficiency. "Let's go," she said, sliding behind the wheel of the last car, the only functioning vehicle left.

"What about him?" Dante asked, casting a hard glance back at Roberto.

"Just leave him, please."

She scrambled out of the car in alarm as Dante went back

to the other man. "I'm just getting his wallet and leaving him a warning," he said. Crouching down, Dante whispered low into Roberto's ear, "Be grateful for your miserable life. Come near her, or any one of us again, and I will kill you slowly and very painfully. *Comprende?*"

Roberto nodded frantically.

Dante returned to the car and they drove off.

TEN

GOD, WHAT AM I doing, leaving with someone even more dan-gerous than Roberto, the asshole drug lord?

My eyes couldn't help glancing down at Dante's hands. At where those long and lethal claws had sprouted out from his fingertips. He'd used them like knives. Fought with them calmly, as if he'd done it many times before. It was hard to tell how old he was under all that hair, beard and mustache covering his face.

"How old are you?" I finally asked.

"Twenty."

Twenty to my twenty-one. Jesus Christ, I'd thought him ten years older. He was one year younger than I was but only in physical years. His eyes were those of a much older soul. That of a hardened soldier's.

I eyed him warily as he slumped back against the seat. "You're injured," I said, feeling silly stating the obvious, but in the midst of all the fighting he'd acted with such competence and menacing purpose I had completely forgotten the fact that he had been shot twice.

"Yeah, the bullets are still in me," he said, eyes closed. "You have to get them out."

"I'll take you to the hospital."

"No, too long. You'll have to take them out."

"With what? My fingernails? Unfortunately, they don't grow out long like yours do."

He grinned, actually grinned. A slight, brief upward tug at the corners of his mouth. "You can dig them out with the knife." The knife he had held to Roberto's neck.

I didn't know whether to believe him or consider it a joke. It didn't sound like the latter despite that brief grin. I drove blindly, wondering if my companion was a madman.

I made random choices whenever the road forked or intersected, but some deity must have been watching over us because after several minutes of blind driving, we somehow found our way back onto the highway. Ten miles later, smelling the ocean, I exited onto a smaller road, following the briny scent.

"What are you doing?" Dante asked, opening his eyes.

"Getting rid of the guns." Nodding to the blue ocean looming up before us, I parked and popped open the trunk.

Dante silently watched as I grabbed the guns and tossed them one after the other into the crystal blue seawater.

"Keep one for yourself," Dante instructed.

"I'm not too familiar with guns," I said, watching as he pulled out his own automatic pistol and competently popped the clip to check the ammo.

"My father trained you. You can shoot a gun."

"I can? Well, that's certainly news to me." Gingerly, I took the gun he handed to me.

"How much memory did you lose?" he asked.

"Six months. The last thing I remember is being a nurse working in Manhattan."

"You were a nurse? I didn't know that." The gun was shoved back into his waistband.

I stopped fiddling with my gun and glanced at him. "So you weren't in Manhattan? You didn't help me move out of my apartment."

"No, I met you in Texas near the border of your Louisiana territory."

"Louisiana? What, I own property there?"

"Yes. Quite substantial property."

"I do?" This was getting more and more bizarre. "Where did I get the money to buy property? First you tell me I know how to shoot a gun. Now you tell me that I'm apparently quite wealthy, too. Are you sure you haven't mistaken me for someone else?"

Or maybe the answer was even simpler than that. Maybe he was crazy. Out of his mind.

"You're a Queen. A Monère Queen."

I was getting an awful feeling in the pit of my stomach.

"Monère?" I tested the word carefully. "Is that one of those small countries somewhere in Europe?"

"Nope." He looked at me as if I were the unhinged one. "It's not a country. It's a race of people descended from the moon."

With blurring speed, I snatched his automatic weapon away from him. Pointing the gun at him, the gun he had assured me I knew how to handle, I backed carefully away. "I'm sorry but I don't know you, and the only memory I have of you is chained up in this wild, crazed state."

"You think I'm crazy."

"In a word—yes."

"You saved me from that. From going crazy."

"How?"

"By sharing the moon's light with me."

His words halted my retreat as I recalled that other memory fragment I'd had. Of moonlight filling me up with indescribable energy, and, more recently, of my skin glowing, illuminated, along with Roberto's.

"How much do you remember of me like that, in that wild state?" he asked.

"Just that you were shackled . . ."

". . . with fleece-lined cuffs around the wrists and ankles."

"Yes," I whispered. Licking my lips, I asked, "How did I share the moon's light with you?"

"By having sex with me," he said plainly, pale eyes locked with mine. "Your skin filled with light and you shared it with me."

The gun dropped limply to my side.

A part of my brain still screamed denial of everything he told me. Another part of my brain told me he was telling the god-awful, appalling truth. "So we're . . ."

"Lovers."

It was hard looking at a complete stranger who'd just announced that he had been intimate with me.

"My skin didn't glow before when I had sex," I said, grabbing onto something concrete, something that I knew for certain.

"Did you feel pleasure?"

"No."

"Then your partners were human."

"Yes," I said hesitantly. "I'm still trying to wrap my mind around the idea that I'm not human."

"But you are. You're a Mixed Blood—one-fourth human,

three-quarters Monère. The first Mixed Blood Queen in Monère history."

There he went throwing that queen stuff at me, but I stayed on track, sticking to one thing at a time. "My skin glowed just from kissing Roberto, even though we didn't have sex."

Dante's hands, I couldn't help noticing, curled into fists. "We glow only with pleasure, and only at the touch of another with Monère blood."

"I didn't know Roberto was a bad guy when he kissed me," I offered lamely, driven, for some reason, to explain that to him.

"Do you believe me now?"

"Yeah I guess . . . though I still have a lot of questions."

"They'll have to wait. Can you get the knife from the car? It's on the front dash."

"Why?"

"To dig the bullets out of my back."

"I thought you were kidding."

"I wasn't."

"I'm a nurse, not a doctor," I felt compelled to point out.

"I know. Don't shoot me," he warned, going to the passenger seat. I watched carefully as he retrieved the knife. Gesturing me over, he handed the blade to me, hilt first, then, unbuttoning and removing his shirt, he presented me with his bare back, hands braced against the side of the car.

I cast an appalled glance at him, which he didn't see. "I don't have anything to sterilize the knife with."

"I'm a Full Blood Monère. We don't get infections. If you don't cut it out now, the wound will heal over and make it even harder to get the bullets out."

It had been less than an hour since he had been shot, but the wounds were already starting to knit together at the edges.

"Mona Lisa, you have to do it now. We don't have much time."

"Why? You think Roberto will still come after us after the way you threatened him?"

"He's a wealthy and powerful, arrogant drug lord who grew up faster and stronger than anybody else. This is probably the first time he's ever been humbled, so, yes, I think he'll come after us. You should have let me kill him."

"You know, you're pretty bloodthirsty for a twenty-year-old." More than a little ticked off at him and the situation, I stomped around the car and rummaged inside. Nothing but a box of tissues, but at least we had that.

"Okay, brace yourself." I felt him tense as I laid my hand over the first bullet hole and let my senses sink down into the wound. When I had ascertained the depth of injury, I moved to the second hole. "The bullets are in pretty deep," I muttered. "Here goes."

I prodded gently with the sharp tip of the knife and cursed when the wider part of the blade started cutting into his flesh as I inserted it deeper. "Goddammit, the knife is too wide."

"Don't stop," he said through clenched jaw as the knife clinked up against the bullet.

"It's hurting you and you're bleeding. A lot!" Enough to completely soak the wad of tissues I had pressed to his back.

"It doesn't hurt as much as the silver stuck inside me— burns and acts like poison. Weakens me. Just get the damn things out. I'll heal up."

I was unable to get any leverage and finally had to remove the knife and make a new incision along the outer edge of the wound, cutting deep down into muscle before I came to the end of the bullet. Deep enough that I started worrying about puncturing his lung. Deliberately cutting into him was one of the most horrible things I'd ever had to do. Then came the awkward maneuvering with the blade.

He endured the torture in silence while my hands shook. Tears ran in a silent stream down my face. *Stupid tears*, I thought, wiping my face against my shoulder. He was the one hurting, not me. "It's out," I said hoarsely after what seemed like eternity.

"Get the other one out."

"You're fucking kidding me!"

He turned impatiently. Stilled at the sight of my tears. "Don't cry," he said, looking unexpectedly bewildered. "It feels much better with the silver out."

"Oh yeah? You didn't see the mess I made of your back," I said, damning the tears. A sob jerked out of me and then I was crying, really crying, no longer silent.

How oddly natural it felt for him to draw me against him, press my tear-drenched face against his bare chest.

"This is so screwed up," I muttered against his hard shoulder. "You should be the one crying, after what I just put you through."

"I know this must be confusing . . . overwhelming to you. You've been so brave." He stroked my hair with a tenderness that made the tears flow even more. "I just need that last bullet out, and then I can start healing and be strong for you."

"God! You don't ask for much, do you?" I snorted and pushed away from him. Scrubbing my face dry, I took a deep, cleansing breath. "Please tell me there's something else we can try to get that last bullet out of you."

He hesitated.

"There is, isn't there?" I said, pouncing. "Tell me."

"You have an affinity for metal," he finally said.

"I do?"

"You can draw metal objects to you with these." Taking my hands, he stroked the moles embedded in my palms.

I blinked down at my hands. "How?"

His lips twisted wryly. "I don't know. That's why I hesitated to bring it up, but I've seen you do it. Watched you pull two swords out of their sheaths from a distance of over ten meters away and fly them into your hands."

It seemed fantastical, what he was saying, almost unbelievable were it not for the fact that I had seen other fantastical, unbelievable things happen tonight.

Okay. I took another deep, steadying breath. He could make claws sprout out of his hands, and I could apparently draw metal things into mine. "All right," I said, deciding there was nothing to lose by the effort. "Let's give it a try."

With odd reluctance, he turned around, presenting his back once more. As I laid my palm over the second bullet wound, the muscles in his back and arms bunched and tightened. "Think of pulling it out," he said in a voice that sounded terse and strained. "Call it into your hand."

"Relax," I muttered. "You seem even more nervous about this than I am." Focusing on that part of myself, I felt my palm begin to thrum, felt it stroke his surface skin and start to reach deeper into his injured flesh. I stopped it there, holding the power, keeping it leashed close to its origin.

Not in, I told myself. *Don't go in to it. Make it come out to you.*

I concentrated and fought against the pulling need of the power to seep down and in, mapping out the injury as it had before. Visualizing the hole made through his flesh, I fixed the image of the silver bullet in my mind, and the mole in my palm heated, grew physically hot against his skin.

Without warning, Dante yanked away and swung around to face me, his pale eyes glittering, his face damp with perspiration, chest moving in deep breaths.

"Did I hurt you?" I asked, worried.

"No," he said, but he looked totally spooked. "I felt your palm grow hot." Snatching up the knife, he slapped it into my hand. "Here, use this. It'll be faster."

"And much more painful. Not to mention gory and bloody. I think I almost had it. Let me try again—"

"No!"

The loudness of his voice startled me.

"No," he repeated in a more restrained tone. "Please, just do it this way. Cut it out. Do it fast."

Too late. The sound of a car turning off the highway. "There's a car coming."

"Get in the car," Dante said, grabbing his shirt. "Drive!"

The car peeled out, spewing dirt and gravel behind us. "Is it Roberto?"

"You tell me. My senses are crap with that silver slug still inside me."

I quieted my pounding heart and listened. Words spoken in Spanish. A voice that sounded like Roberto's. A heartbeat that was slower than the others, like mine.

"Yeah, it's Roberto with some of his men."

"Shit, they're closing in on us," Dante said, glancing behind. "Speed up."

"I'm already going past the speed limit."

"Doesn't matter. Floor it."

Twisting awkwardly, he positioned the knife behind him, blindly probing his back with the other hand.

"What are you doing?" I asked as I zipped around slower-moving cars. Settling onto an open stretch of road, I pushed the gas down until it hit the floor. Until we were going over a hundred miles per hour.

"I'm getting the bullet out of my back. Keep it nice and steady for a minute."

A minute, at this speed, was a very long time. With a quick, horrified glance, I saw him stab the knife deep into his back. When he pulled the blade out, fresh blood gushed out.

"What did you just do?"

He scooted over and presented his bleeding back to me. "Stick your finger in and fish out the bullet."

"You're crazy, absolutely crazy! You could have killed yourself!"

"I can't die, Mona Lisa. I'm Monère. We only die in certain ways: if you cut off the head or rip out the heart, poison us with silver, or expose us to the sun for several hours. But you and Roberto are part human—you're probably easier to kill."

"Good to know," I said tightly. "I still say you're crazy!"

"Dig the bullet out before they catch up to us."

"It's unbelievable what you're asking me to do! Completely unbelievable."

"Do it—please. Trust me."

With a curse, I eased up on the gas pedal.

"You're slowing down."

"Yes, I know," I snapped back. "If you want me to grope around in your back for a bullet, I'm not doing it while going a hundred and ten miles per hour. I'm not Wonder Woman, you know."

Amazingly, he turned his head and grinned. "You're better than her," he said, humor lightening the grim lines for a moment. "But don't tell Linda Carter I said that."

I laughed and shook my head. "I can't believe you just made me laugh. We're being chased by bad guys with guns, and you make a joke."

"Do it quickly," Dante urged, growing sober. "If I didn't cut deep enough, just push through with your fingers— you're strong enough. Doesn't matter if you tear up my flesh. Just get the damn slug out of me."

Without thinking about it, because if I did, I would scream, I stuck two fingers into his wound and pushed my way slowly down. Blood squished out, sliming my fingers and hand.

Shots sounded, thudding into the rear window. Bullet-proof glass apparently. My hand on the wheel jerked in surprise, causing the car to swerve. I had to put both hands back on the steering wheel to regain control as I sped up.

Lowering his window, Dante leaned out and fired back. After several seconds of return fire, our car suddenly dropped a few inches on the passenger's side, pulling the steering violently to the right. I knew in an instant our back rear tire had been shot out. Our smooth ride turned bumpy as we rode the metal rim of the hub.

"Good news and bad news," Dante said, sticking his head back inside. "I shot out his front tires, but he blew out our rear wheel."

"I can tell," I grunted, fighting to keep our car straight without overcompensating so much that I accidentally ripped out the steering wheel. Despite the lost tire, the car was still drivable, though at a much slower speed. But with two of their tires out, our pursuers weren't going any faster.

"Pull over," Dante said.

"What?"

"Pull over and get out!"

I started to ask why but then glimpsed the reason in the rearview mirror. Roberto and his men had abandoned their car and were coming after us on foot. And Roberto was running with superfast speed, faster than our car was going, apparently no longer hindered by the silver bullet I'd jammed in his back, though Dante did his best to remedy that by shooting at him. But he missed. Didn't even come close to hitting Roberto, moving as fast as he was, and with Dante slowed down to sluggish human reflexes and speed.

I jerked the car to a halt and sprang out, gun in hand. Roberto's men were firing at Dante—not me, just Dante. Some of the hail of bullets struck our car, others Dante managed to deflect with his wrist bracelets—a pretty miraculous feat considering how much the silver slowed him. He slid back into the protection of the car, but Roberto had come close enough that he now had a clear shot at him. They drew on each other, but it was an unfair match. Roberto was much faster.

I fired before I gave myself a chance to think and watched blood blossom on Roberto's right shoulder. He cried out, dropping his weapon.

I turned and emptied my gun, laying out a round of fire that hit the asphalt in front of the four bodyguards, making them scramble back to their car for cover. Before Dante had time to lift his gun and fire at Roberto, I yanked him out through the driver's seat door and took off, carrying him. A quick sprint and we reached the cover of trees. I heard Roberto yelling orders at his men. No gunshots followed us, but I didn't bother slowing down, just kept moving deeper into the forest.

"You missed his heart," Dante said after ten minutes of running through the woods.

"Surprisingly, I hit exactly what I was aiming for—his shoulder. I guess you're right: I do know how to shoot a gun."

He closed his eyes, shook his head. "You can put me down now. Are they following us?"

I listened and heard only the quiet life-sounds of the jungle, no sound of pursuit. "Not at the moment."

"Roberto will want to get that silver bullet out of his shoulder before coming after us again. He'll go to a hospital," I said, setting Dante on his feet, dropping down to the ground to rest for a few moments. "Several hours at least."

He eased down to sit beside me. "You're amazing, you know."

"No, you are. You must be hurting terribly—you were shot twice, stabbed once by me, a second time by yourself!—and yet you can still smile." More softly, "You should do that more, you know. Smile."

"As you wish, milady." He took my hand, kissed it unexpectedly. "One more thing I must ask of you."

"Your back," I groaned. "God, you have a one-track mind."

"Hard not to. The silver burns my flesh unpleasantly."

I sighed. "Do you have the knife?"

"Sorry, left it on the floor. I was fortunate to hang on to the gun, not that it will do us much good," he said as he popped the magazine out and counted. "Only three bullets left. One of them was aimed quite nicely at Roberto's heart before you jerked me out of the car."

"Would it have killed him?"

"Maybe. He's a three-quarters Mixed Blood like you."

"You're too bloodthirsty, Dante."

"And, surprisingly . . . you are not."

"Why is that surprising? Was I different before?"

He gave me another one of those small, fleeting smiles and turned, presenting his bloody back to me.

"All right, all right! You want the damn bullet out, I'll get it out." I pushed and squeezed my fingers down to the end of the cut he had made. "You were off by an inch," I muttered, feeling viciously angry, at him, at myself.

"Hard to aim when you can't see a bloody thing," he returned through a tightly clenched jaw.

"Goddammit, I hate this. I really, really hate this." No

help for it. As he said, I was strong enough to tear through his flesh with my fingers, and almost puked as I did so.

I finally came to the bullet, curved my fingers around it, and pushed the troublesome thing back out the hole. Then I proceeded to throw up.

ELEVEN

I SHOULDN'T BE *so happy*, Dante thought with remorse. *Not when the lady I love is heaving up her stomach contents.* But the truth of the matter was, it was more than he had expected, to be with her again like this—the ease and trust between them.

"Gee, that was fun," Mona Lisa muttered when her stomach finished its violent heaving. "You really know how to show a girl a good time."

His lips quirked. "My pleasure, to be alive and here with you."

"Even with me torturing you and getting you caught and injured? Why the hell are you smiling?"

He smoothed her hair back in a gentle gesture. "You."

"But I'm not the *you* that you knew. I'm different, aren't I? Because I can't remember."

"You're still the same person at your core. And I like seeing the core you—someone who's upset enough after inflicting deliberate, unwanted pain on someone she cares about to become physically ill."

"Cares about?" She aimed a mean, narrow-eyed glance at him. "Honey, I don't even *know* you."

His small smile grew broader. "You will."

Funny, she thought. *He doesn't look so fierce or frightening when he smiles.*

The smile evaporated as resonant energy swept across them. Monère—more than a half dozen.

"Your friends?" she asked.

"No." One word, icily sure.

"Roberto's men?"

"They're coming from the opposite direction." Grabbing her hand, Dante sprung them forward in large, bounding leaps that took them sailing over the eight-foot-tall brush in graceful arcs, the fastest way of traveling through the jungle-like forest, heading back where they'd come from.

He jerked to a halt that had Mona Lisa stumbling into him as they both felt another wave of men closing in on them from that direction. Not Roberto and his thugs, unfortunately. These were all entirely Monère.

"Organized group," Mona Lisa noted in a soft whisper.

"This way," Dante said, heading north.

"What if they're deliberately herding us this way?" Mona Lisa asked as they went sailing over the thick brush again like human kangaroos.

"No choice."

Behind them they felt the hot energy signatures of their Monère pursuers and heard the sound of swift movement, many of them. They weren't even trying to muffle the sounds of pursuit. Indeed, a primitive, undulating hunting cry sliced the air like a sharp blade, quickly taken up by others. The excitement in the raised cries raised the hair on the back of Mona Lisa's neck. "What the hell is that?" she asked.

"The sounding of the hunt."

Something whizzed by them during one of their leaps.

Dante cursed. "Stay on the ground." Holding her hand in a tight grip, he began bulling his way through the dense foliage.

"Was that bullets?" she asked. "I didn't hear any gunshots."

"Silver darts."

No one was trying to be quiet, at this point. The loud, undulating cries reminded her of baying dogs. Whatever was hunting them seemed more animal than human.

"Let go of my hand," Mona Lisa said. "I'll keep up."

He released his grip. "Stay with me."

"No problem."

Each time Dante tried to veer east or west, they were herded back, more of those silver darts flying their way. Then suddenly the end of their path loomed up: a cliff. A sheer drop-off that was so steep and high that looking down into the deep gorge below made her feel sick and dizzy.

Their pursuers emerged from the thick brush and they saw their hunters clearly for the first time: savage, half-naked men whose faces, arms, and bare chests had been painted in primitive patterns of black and brown swirls. They were barefoot, their long, dark hair braided down their backs.

They were the darkest-skinned Monères Mona Lisa had seen, all lean and hungry looking, like starved wild beasts, every ounce of their flesh strappy muscle.

An image shimmered and condensed in her mind.

A young boy with the same starved musculature, tangled hair matted into an Afro, his chest and feet bare and the only thing he wore, pants, torn and ragged. A boy snarling like a wild animal as he strained against his chains, the heavy smell of urine mixing with the scent of dirty, unwashed skin.

The image broke and dissolved back into current reality,

and faced against that sudden, sharp memory, the men closing in on them didn't look so bad anymore; at least they were
clean. But they still looked pretty darn scary.

Their leader had the figure of a red eye painted on his
forehead, the only one among them with a splash of color.
He looked at Dante and bared his teeth, not in a smile but
in a look of menace. *"Smäileden,"* he said with fierce satisfaction. The look in his eyes when he turned them to Mona Lisa
wasn't any kinder.

"What do we do now?" Mona Lisa asked in a small voice.

Dante gave her no warning. Grabbing her, he turned and
leaped off the cliff, and then they were hurtling through the
air. For a moment, she thought he would transform into a
bird, like the eagle-man she had seen, but they began to fall
rapidly.

"You can fly," Dante shouted. "Transform now!"

"Into what?" she yelped.

"A vulture!"

As soon as Dante said the word, a picture formed in her
mind and she felt energy start to surge and prickle along her
skin.

"Good girl," Dante whispered, releasing her. Just letting
her go.

In a slow and painful outburst of power, she transformed
in a puff of feathers, clothes tearing, shredding. A human
scream turned into a vulture's snarling shriek. And still she
continued to plummet.

"Open your wings," Dante cried below her, in freefall.
"Dammit, open your wings!"

Her wings snapped open, and Mona Lisa's hurtling descent
slowed into a veering, teetering spiral. You'd think she'd
know how to fly, being a bird and all, but nope, wasn't something that came naturally to her. If she'd ever flown before,

she couldn't remember it. After a few awkward, experimental shifts of her wings, she got herself angled down after Dante, but the gap between them had grown substantial. Why wasn't he shifting?

Mona Lisa opened her mouth to yell at him and found a hissing sound emerging from her beak instead of words. A hissing sound that grew louder and more distressed as the bottom of the rugged gorge loomed alarmingly closer, and still he just fell, making no effort to change, his pale blue eyes glittering, lifted up to her.

She tucked in her long span of wings and dived, but it was too late; there was too much distance between them. He hit the ground feetfirst with bone-crunching impact and slammed into the dirt, landing on his side. Blood sprayed the air with metallic scent.

She hissed and snarled, misjudged the landing distance, and hit the ground harder than she had intended. Dante was still conscious, a broken, bleeding mess. His eyes, only his eyes shifted to her, his head and neck unmoving. Blood, mixed with clear sanguineous fluid, seeped out like in a tiered halo around his head, reddening the ground.

"Take us away," he croaked in a barely understandable rasp.

She wanted to yell and scream at him, tell him he was too injured to move, but a vulture had no vocal cords, no way of speaking. Only her eyes flashed her ire and sick worry as she hopped agitatedly around him.

He smiled, goddamn him, seeming to understand her distress. "Won't kill me . . . but they will." He shifted his eyes to look up. Turning, Mona Lisa saw them in the far distance, scaling their way rapidly down the cliff like giant spiders.

Mentally cursing, she hopped onto his chest, surprised a little at how big she was. Grabbing each arm with a claw, she spread out her long-spanned wings and flapped hard. Taking off with deadweight wasn't easy. She ended up dragging his body more than ten feet on the ground before she finally gained air. Flying with him was more strenuous than she had expected, and to think that eagle had flipped a car onto its side with four heavy people inside it. What did the guy eat? Wheaties? Well, if he could do that, she could do this, but it sure wasn't pretty or easy. Her flight had absolutely no grace or finesse. It was jerky and erratic and rough, real rough. And all the while she worried about dropping Dante and seeing him falling . . . falling like before, that endless plummet, the brutal landing, the crack of bones and spray of blood, the pooling of it around his head in a growing splash of red.

She flew for what felt like forever, with the heavy, dragging weight of Dante clutched in her talons, and still she flew on, until her wings ached so badly she was sure they'd crack and fall off—was surprised they hadn't done so already.

During all this time, he didn't make a single sound—not one grunt or moan of pain during the jerky flight. Just the harsh noise of his breathing.

Following the sound of water, Mona Lisa eventually came to a river and landed, laying him as gently as she could on the bank, which was not gentle at all; it was as rough and clumsy as her first landing, maybe even worse. It took two tries before her tightly clenched talons—could talons cramp?— finally got the message and released him. A slight lift and hop away from him and she staggered, let herself fall over, wings folded.

Human, she thought, and pictured it in her mind: her normal self.

A faint, weak shimmer of energy, a swirling and morphing of reality, and she found herself gazing at her bare arm, followed it down to see the skin of her chest, stomach, and legs. "I'm naked," she slurred, pushing up onto her elbow.

"Tore your clothes . . . during transformation," Dante said with painful effort.

He was conscious.

Oddly, ridiculously shy, she crept over to where he lay. "You okay?" she asked, wishing for longer hair—something, anything to cover herself with.

"Could be better," he rasped. "You can use my shirt . . . quickly. Don't have much time."

"You think they're following us?"

"Yes . . . hunting me."

"You?" Carefully she unbuttoned his shirt and eased it down his left arm. "I'm going to have to lift you a little."

"Do it."

The entire left side of his face was grotesquely swollen and matted with blood. She couldn't tell if his temple and the back of his skull were fractured. His cheekbone was definitely broken, as were both his legs, she noted as she slipped the shirt off his other arm. Blood soaked the left collar and almost the entire back, but it was still a relief to slip it on over herself and button it up. She had lost everything, not just her money, credit card, and passport, which had been in her pocket, but her socks and shoes as well. All but the necklace she still wore around her neck. Only that hadn't slipped or torn off when she had transformed into a bird . . . a vulture, of all things!

"Build a raft," he told her. "We'll float down the river."

TWELVE

"BUILD A RAFT," I muttered as I pushed over my fifth tree and ripped off the branches. I felt better now with a little rest. Enough to feel resentment building up at the situation—lost in the mountainous wilds of Mexico with a demented pack of native Monère savages still hunting us . . . hunting *him*.

"Why the hell are you so sure they're still hunting us?" I asked as I dragged the trunk over to where he lay. I'd never realized how pampered and tender my feet were until now, walking around barefoot in a jungle.

"What he called me. *Smãileden.*"

"What's that?"

"That's me—what I turn into."

"Which is?"

"A saber-toothed tiger."

I stopped what I was doing. "You're kidding."

"Nope."

Brushing off my hands, I crouched down beside him. "You know how I said that you should smile more?"

"Yes."

"Well, I changed my mind. It's starting to irritate me."

His smile deepened enough to form crinkle lines around his eyes. "You're cute when you're irritated." During the half hour of his rest and my labor, his voice and breathing had evened out. Broken ribs healed perhaps.

I rolled my eyes. "And you're obviously feeling a little better—as much as someone with a cracked face and broken legs can feel better. Oh, and I forgot, you've been shot twice. In all the new trauma, I almost forgot that minor detail." I shook my head at him, at the situation. "Really? A saber-toothed tiger?"

"Yes, it's a rare form, and why you're in this mess. Some tourists saw me and it was reported in the news. My father said that's why you came here looking for me."

"Why was I looking for you?" I asked.

"I don't know." He sounded honestly puzzled.

"I mean, why were we apart? You said we were lovers."

His gaze fell away. "Things happened. I left."

I looked thoughtfully down at him. "You said the first time, I shared light with you. Light that you needed. Was it just that once?"

"No, two more times."

"Were those two other times a therapeutic necessity?"

He shook his head

"Did we break up?"

"Yes." The affirmation clearly hurt him.

"So why was I looking for you?"

His gaze lifted back up, his odd pale eyes somehow managing to look both tender and tormented. "There are things I have to tell you. But later, not now. They're hunting us."

I cast my senses out. "I don't feel or hear anything."

"Neither do I, but I know they're coming."

"You've encountered them before?"

"Yes, a long time ago." He turned his eyes to the tree trunks I had laid out on the ground. "Gather some vine and use it as rope."

His sense of urgency communicated itself to me, and I had the trunks crudely rafted and knotted together a few minutes later.

"Let's see if this thing works," I muttered. Dragging it into the river, I hopped onto the makeshift structure. It wasn't the most stable thing, but it floated. Pulling it onto the bank, I returned to Dante.

"Bring some tree branches," he instructed.

"Why?"

"For cover when the sun comes out. One of the ways to kill us, remember? Me, at least. You, it doesn't seem to bother."

I went back and gathered an armload of the most heavily leafed branches. "Enough?"

He nodded and I piled it onto the raft, then went to fetch him. "This is going to hurt," I warned.

His mouth remained a tight, thin line as I carried him over to the raft and set him gently down.

"Push me into the water. Then I want you to go."

"Go where?" I asked.

"Shift into a vulture and fly back to where we came from, back to Cancun."

"No. I refuse to leave you."

"Fly back and find the others, and return with them for me."

"That's a ridiculous idea."

"No, it's not. It's the quickest and most efficient rescue."

"I won't leave you stranded on a raft, floating in the water, completely helpless." My mouth firmed. "You'll snag on something, get stranded, or capsize."

"That won't kill me," he said with exasperation.

"Oh yeah?" My voice rose. "Well, what about being eaten by a damn crocodile?"

"It's me they want, not you."

"So I should just leave you?" My eyebrows lifted in disbelief.

"For a little while, until you get help."

"I'm not that stupid," I said, shaking my head. "You're trying to protect me. You believe that Roberto and his thugs are less dangerous to me than these other men."

"These hunters will kill you. It's what they do." His silver-blue eyes flashed with disquieting emotion. "Roberto, if he manages to get his hands on you, wants you alive at least."

"No."

"Chances are you'll be able to find my father and the others without tangling with Roberto again."

"Your father?"

"Yes, the big guy with the beard who scooped the others onto his shoulders. Mona Lisa—"

"Shut up, Dante," I said, not unkindly. Setting the raft in the water, I pushed off and hopped on board.

We floated down the river without speaking. For the most part, the raft drifted without guidance. It was actually soothing, the gentle bobbing of the water, enough that Dante gradually fell asleep.

I looked down at the mess of him. Blood matted his hair and beard, making his appearance gruesome even though the swelling had gone down significantly on the side of his face. *My wild man*, I thought. *So dangerous before. So broken and helpless now.*

When the sun came up, I twisted the branches into a makeshift construct that sheltered him from the brightening light. "What about you?" he murmured, awakened by my movements, watching me quietly.

"I'm fine," I said, shrugging. "I could do with a tan."

He shifted himself, grunting. "Good, I seem to have the use of my arms back."

"You didn't before?"

"No, I think I broke my back. That part, at least, seems to have healed."

It was amazing how he seemed to take it all for granted, healing paralysis in a handful of hours. His body had to have expended a great deal of energy to accomplish such healing in so short a time. Remembering how ravenous I'd been after waking up from my own accident, I asked, "You hungry?"

He nodded.

I slipped into the water and scissors-kicking, guided our raft closer to shore.

"What are you doing?" he asked, propping himself up on one arm.

"I'm bringing us to shore. Maybe I can find some berries."

"No need. Come back up."

"No need as in, I'm not hungry. Or no need as in, I can get food another way."

His eyes crinkled down at me. "The latter."

"Okay." I heaved myself lightly back on board, dipping the raft down.

"Help me closer to the side," he said.

I did so and watched Dante dip a finger down into the water. "What are you doing?" I asked.

"Fishing."

He continued staring intently at the water. A swirl of energy slapped my senses, and for a moment I thought his eyes glowed silver. I didn't know what I expected, but it certainly wasn't the leaping fish that suddenly came out of the water onto the raft.

"Catch it, quick," he said as I scrambled after the flopping fish. It was a good arm-length size.

Grabbing it up by the tail, I clubbed the fish against the rough wood of our raft and it stopped moving. "Is it stunned or dead?" I asked.

"Probably just stunned. Here, let me." Dragging himself over to me, he extended his hand. I watched his nails extend into two-inch-long claws. With a quick, neat slice, he cut off the fish's head.

"Neat trick," I observed. "Wish I could do that. It would have been much easier to fish the bullet out of you that way."

"You probably will be able to in time." With neat, efficient strokes he sliced off the skin and tail, filleting the white flesh into one-inch strips. "Here, try a piece."

"No, thanks."

"Think of it as sushi," he said, eyes crinkling, "which it essentially is."

"I never ate sushi."

"Your first time then."

"No. I don't think so."

The smile disappeared. "You need to eat and replenish your energy. Just a small piece," he urged.

He refused to eat until after I had done so—the only thing that made me swallow a slice of the slippery, raw fish. "It doesn't taste that bad," I said with surprise. A belated thought popped into my mind. "What about worms or parasites?"

"It didn't have any," he assured me. "Even if it did, your body would easily rid itself of them."

"How do you know? I'm part human, remember?"

"Have you ever been sick?"

I squinted in thought. "No, never. No colds or ear infections as a child. I've never been sick or ill before at all, come to think of it." Pushing up my left sleeve, I glanced at the clear skin of my arm. The yellow bruising had disappeared. "This is the worst I've ever been injured. I can't believe it's healed so quickly, even though it took longer than my head."

"Our body heals our worst injuries first."

"Is that why your legs are still busted up?"

Dante nodded. "Yes. Back, ribs, and head first—the cheekbone was a simple, clean break and easy to fix. Legs next—a lot of bones were shattered. At least I can wriggle my toes now."

He made me eat one more slice, and then he finished off the rest of the fish himself. He tossed the skin and bones into the river, and I splashed some water over the side to clean away the blood-tinged residue.

"How did you make the fish jump up like that?" I asked.

"I lured it close with my finger and then compelled it to jump out of the water. A trick I learned over the years."

"Hmm. Never thought to apply that trick to a fish before."

We had another aquatic meal for lunch, and a third one for supper. By that time, I was thoroughly sick of raw fish. "I think I've had enough sushi to last me a lifetime," I said. "Berries tomorrow."

"We'll see," he murmured, drowsing under the shaded canopy of the woven branches. It seemed adequate cover for him. I was glad when the sun finally set and the cooler darkness of night set in.

His legs, by that time, had healed enough for him to stand up and stretch.

"The wounds on your back"—from his knife and my fingers— "still haven't healed."

"They'll go last—the least serious. Still finishing up the legs," he said, glancing down the river. "Do you hear that?"

"What?"

"Listen."

I did. After a moment's concentration, I heard what he had: the sound of water was louder ahead of us. It grew louder still as we journeyed forward, until, finally, we saw with our eyes what we had first heard with our ears. Ahead of us, the river abruptly ended, plummeting down into a waterfall. From the sound of it, it was a long drop.

"I guess we go to shore," Dante said, gazing out over the distance. I felt him cast his senses outward, and in response, loosened my own senses as well.

"No sign of our pursuers," I murmured. "I think they stopped following us a long time ago." If they had even bothered to.

Dante didn't say anything as I slipped into the water and guided the raft with strong kicks toward shore.

"Just let me do it," I said in protest when he eased himself into the water. "You're still healing up."

He ignored me. "Don't pull the raft ashore. Let it float down and go over the drop. We'll follow along the bank."

"I don't think it'll survive intact. It sounds like a pretty big drop, and I spent a lot of time and effort making this raft," I said, frowning. "Maybe I can carry it down."

"No, I'd rather you had your hands free. I'll help you gather up the logs again if they separate."

It turned out he didn't need to. The moment we were onshore, a net came flying over us. Silver, I realized, at Dante's sharp hiss of pain, but it had no effect on me—no pain, no lessening of strength. I tore it apart easily and flung it off us.

Familiar undulating war cries shrilled the air, two close by that we somehow hadn't sensed. The eerie chant was taken up more distantly by the rest of our pursuers.

Before we could spring away, another silvery net came down over us, entangling our limbs. I started to rip that away also and felt a stinging prick on my arm.

I yanked a dart out. Silver. But with something else as well. Drugged or poisoned, I had a moment to realize as my limbs grew unbearably heavy. Then darkness muffled me and swept me under.

THIRTEEN

WHEN I CAME to, it was not with a simple and easy drift-to-wake consciousness. No, it was much cruder than that. Pain first, a rough shaking of shoulder, then even rougher slaps across my face. Two voices yelling, angry. One of them was familiar—someone I knew, if only I could wake up. Then a cold, wet splash of water—a bowlful dumped across my face, I saw as I blinked the heavy lids of my eyes open. A dark, frightening face, painted black and brown, with a red eye drawn crudely on the forehead, looked down on me.

Ah, yes. It was all coming back to me: silver nets, a drugging dart, capture by these heathenish Monère. My impression of the race so far wasn't that great. First a drug lord. Then what I had thought were bandits. Now this half-naked primitive bunch.

I turned my head and saw a familiar face belonging to the familiar voice. Dante. My poor comrade-in-arms. Me, I just hit my head and spilled out some memories, and, oh

yeah, turned into a vulture. He was, however, by far getting
the worst of things. Atop of his old injuries, now his right
eye was swollen shut, with new bruises adorning his chest
and arms in garish disarray. Couldn't tell if his poor legs had
been rebroken or not because he was lashed to a pole, arms
and legs tied. His single unswollen eye glittered like a hard,
pale diamond.

For all that he was bound, he looked more scary than
scared.

At a woman's command, I was pulled to my feet and
secured to a similar pole, my wrists bound together with
silver ties similar to the material used in the nets that had
captured us. My arms were lifted up, tied, and my legs bound
in likewise manner below. I was helpless to stop them—my
limbs felt leaden and my wits just as heavy and slow. What
the hell had they drugged me with?

A woman sauntered into view. The woman who had given
the command, no doubt. She had black lustrous hair. True
black, not the shade mine had been before, a brown so dark
that some had mistakenly called it black before a talented
stylist had skillfully lightened the color.

She had threads of gray streaking through the black
strands—odd to see against an unlined face. Without those
betraying gray hairs marking her age, she could otherwise
have passed for thirty. How old was she now, midforties
maybe?

She was lighter skinned than her men. Would have been
the fairest one here but for myself. Even with my newly
acquired tan, my skin was almost white compared to the
brown pigment clearly marking her Latino ancestry. There
was a curved roundness to the pretty features of her face and
a softness to her small and shapely build, all but the eyes.
Her eyes, the color of dark soot, fringed with long, fanning

lashes, were hard and frightening, with not a smudge of soft-ness in them.

"You have caused my men much trouble," she said in lightly accented English. Her voice, like her eyes, was hard and authoritative. It was a bit disorienting. Like hearing a sol-dier's voice coming out of a pretty doll's mouth. Did she com-mand all these hundred-odd poorly clad people surrounding us? Most of them were men, less than a handful were women, and even fewer, children. She seemed way overdressed stand-ing next to her people in the long black gown she wore.

"Sorry," I replied. "Wasn't my intention. We weren't try-ing to bother them. Quite the opposite."

She assessed me coolly. "They said you broke our silver nets as easily as ripping through paper."

"I'll be happy to repay you their cost," I offered.

She sneered. Not the answer she was looking for appar-ently. "And yet you are held by them now."

Because you drugged me! I wanted to say, but kept my mouth shut. No need to give the enemy any more knowledge or advantage than they already held. But it seemed they had already figured out the reason for my weakness.

"Our venom affects you oddly," she said in chill observa-tion.

"Venom?"

"Viper venom." She gave me a most unpleasant smile. "It kills humans but acts only as a brief sedative to those of our kind. It affected you more than him." By *him*, I assume she meant Dante. Had he been knocked out by it also?

"You have the faint smell of human in your blood, and yet you feel as powerful as a Full Blood Monère."

I didn't respond. She hadn't asked a question, after all.

Her voice suddenly dropped down into an ugly snarl. "What are you doing here, another Queen in my territory?"

Her territory? Had that leisurely drift down the river brought us closer to danger instead of taking us farther away from it? And here was that Queen stuff again. If it was confusing to me before, it was even more so now with a thick head and dulled wits. I bypassed it and stuck with what I knew. "We were running away from your men. They were the ones who drove us here; it was not our intent to trespass. We will be happy to depart as soon as you release us."

Her cold smile told me it would not be that easy. "Of even more interest, what are you doing in *his* company, this Queen killer?"

Huh? "What Queen killer?"

"Him!" Her finger speared at Dante.

"Dante? He's not a Queen killer." Was he?

"Dante . . . is that what he calls himself now?" An alarming mixture of hatred and vicious satisfaction glittered her obsidian dark eyes. "He is the most legendary Queen killer in our history. And not just merely for the death of my mother."

I swallowed sickly. *Oh, crap.*

"She deserved killing," Dante said clearly, heard by all. "I spared your life, an innocent child, but that seems to have been a mistake."

A child, I thought in confusion? How old had Dante been when he had killed her mother? Five? Had he lied to me about his age, or was this angry Queen younger than she looked?

She whirled to face him like a rabid badger. Small and mean—something that could tear your limbs off. "So you admit it," she growled.

"Yes. I am who you seek."

Triumph and an almost sick ecstasy filled her face, as though she had just gotten the confession she had expected to take hours to beat out of him. She sucked in a harsh breath in delight. "Queen killer. I have waited a lifetime to meet you again."

"I dispensed justice. Evil deed for evil deed. Your mother was one of the most vicious I have ever met in my long existence," Dante said with a calmness I sure wasn't feeling. "Is what I did any less foul than you do, murdering other Queens?"

"It is not forbidden for a Queen to slay another Queen who challenges her."

"Whereas if a male does the same, it breaks our most sacred law." Dante's lips tautened with cynicism. "You have twisted our law into gross turpitude, Mona Sierra. If I am guilty, you are guilty ten times more so. Even from far away, I have heard of your slaughter of other Queens."

A kind of panic was fast clearing my mind. My body, on the other hand, still felt weak, my muscles unable to obey the urgent command I sent to break free of these bonds.

"This Queen with me is different from the others," Dante said.

"Yes, she tried to help you." Mona Sierra made it sound like the most heinous crime ever committed.

"This Queen is the one who started my legend." He addressed his next words to me. "Show them your palms."

With my hands tied above my head, all it took to do so was uncurling my hands. I opened my palms, wondering all the while what Dante was up to. Nothing to see there but my moles. They were unusual, yes, but not so unsightly as to cause the vastly startled reaction that ran like bolts of lightning among those gathered. More than a few choked out a name. *Mona Lyra*.

Mona Sierra strode over to me, stopping a foot away to stare intently at my hands. "Who are you?" she asked.

"Lisa Hamilton," I answered, wetting my lips.

"She is Mona Lyra reincarnated," Dante said, his voice ringing out.

Mona Sierra whirled like a scalded cat. "Then why was she helping you? If she is Mona Lyra, why would she help the one who killed her?"

It was more than confusing now. It was becoming surreal. And I had absolutely no idea what was going on, or what Dante was trying to accomplish with this fantastic claim of his.

"She does not know or remember," he said.

"That may explain her actions, but not yours. Why would you try to help the one who killed your father and laid this curse upon you? No," she said, shaking her head, "you lie."

"You see with your own eyes the Goddess's Tears embedded in the heart of her palms. The mark of favor from our Mother Moon never seen in any other."

The feeling of unease was palpable now among the crowd. I could even see it subtly affecting Mona Sierra. She shook it off. "Pah! Nothing but lies. She is tainted with human blood."

She made that sound akin to a butt-ugly mongrel dog.

"This Queen is not one you should toy with," Dante said with calm reason. "Let her go. You have me—I'm the one you seek."

Things became clearer then why he was making all these outrageous claims. He was trying to free me. A variation on the old take-me-but-let-her-go ploy.

"You bargain with nothing in your possession," Mona Sierra spat back at him. "Nothing but false claims to try to trick us."

"If you do not believe the mark of favor everyone sees plainly embedded in her palms, then believe this. The woman before you is the High Prince of Hell's chosen mate. Kill her and you will bring down Hell's wrath upon you."

"Another lie. You grow desperate trying to save your little Queen."

"She wears his necklace," Dante stated.

Mona Sierra faced me again, eyes narrowed into slits. "That should be easy enough to disprove," she sneered, reaching down my collar to lift out my necklace.

There was a flash of blinding light and the sharp smell of burning flesh. Mona Sierra's scream shrilled the air. I blinked, momentarily blinded by the light. When I was able to see again, I saw the other Queen fallen in front of me, clutching her hand. Black burn marks were visible on her seared fingertips. Six hunters ran to her, pulling her away from me, eyeing me warily as if I had been the one responsible for hurting their Queen.

Not me. I didn't do that, I wanted to babble but was not stupid enough to do so. If they wanted to account me powers I didn't possess, far be it for me to correct their false assumptions. I wondered, though, how Dante had pulled off that impressive bit of magic. If he could do that, why the hell didn't he free himself?

"What did you do?" Mona Sierra hissed from behind the wall of her men.

I didn't have a clue and didn't know what to tell her. It was Dante who answered. "It was the necklace you touched. It reacts against those who intend harm against her."

She rapped out a command in Spanish, and a hunter with the red mark on his forehead advanced with knife drawn.

"Uh, Dante . . ." I said uneasily.

"Be still," Mona Sierra snapped, pushing her men aside. "We only wish to see your necklace."

I swallowed as the hunter carefully inserted the tip of his knife down my shirtfront and drew out the necklace with his naked blade. "The chain is silver," he murmured in heavily accented English. It was odd hearing words come out of his mouth. Like hearing a wolfhound unexpectedly talk.

Another murmur of unease rippled through the crowd.

"She has many differences—a special Queen," Dante said loudly. "Even if you cannot read the script, you can see the likeness of the Demon Prince clearly on the necklace"—I startled over that pronouncement—"declaring his protection over her. Beware, lest you make yourself an enemy you cannot afford."

Mona Sierra drew near enough to peer at the necklace, as did the other hunters surrounding her. Even I craned my neck down to catch a glimpse. Demon Prince? Was that whose likeness was carved on the cameo? Was there even such a person, or was Dante making it all up?

"Prince Halcyon felt that touch, Mona Sierra," Dante said, "when you grabbed the necklace just now. He will know that someone with ill intent came in contact with his beloved, and may even now be on his way here."

He was spooking them with a bogeyman and it was apparently working. Two young children in the crowd started crying and were quickly shushed by their mothers.

"You are trying too hard to convince me to let her go," Mona Sierra said warily.

"How about this?" Dante offered. "If you release her and allow her to go on her way, you have my word that I will not seek reprisal upon you or your people when I am reborn again. Otherwise you have my promise of vengeance."

More mad claims atop other mad claims, of reincarnation and curses, Hell and Demon Princes, and now rebirth. Rebirth after they killed him, I presumed. And yet, no one was laughing. I didn't know whether just Dante was mad or all of them.

The knife eased away and the necklace dropped down,

clearly visible to everyone. They eyed it with fascinated revulsion, as if it were a viper about to strike them.

"Enough," Mona Sierra proclaimed. "I will not allow you to distract us with your baseless, futile claims. Shave off his beard," she said, gesturing to Dante. "I wish to see his face and remember what it looks like."

Her words broke the still silence, and people moved once again, murmuring among themselves as Mona Sierra and her men left.

A woman came to tend to Dante. First the beard and mustache was trimmed with scissors, then the stubble was shaved off with a disposable razor—odd signs of civilized living dispersed among the, if not quite squalor, then clearly not wealthy, living conditions here. She fussed with his hair, braiding it back in the fashion the men here wore their hair, and then stepped away.

My breath puffed out in surprise at the first clear sight of Dante's face. He was indeed twenty years old, a young man's face atop a grown man's body.

I thought he had looked wild before with all that hair covering him, but now, clean shaven and unadorned, he was even more dangerous looking. He wasn't handsome so much as striking, with a proud nose, a clean, chiseled jawline, and those queer eyes . . . so old and cold. Silver-blue. As distinctive as his saber-toothed tiger form would be. Looking into those eyes, you could almost believe that he had lived many lifetimes, dying and being reborn again and again.

Madness. I was starting to become affected by all the other craziness going on here.

When Mona Sierra returned, sooner than I would have liked, her fingertips were healed. Unblemished, unscarred skin. The people that had been milling around gathered into attention once again.

Pulling a knife from the sheath at her waist, Mona Sierra walked up to Dante and without ceremony sliced him across the abdomen. It seemed like a small cut until the blood started streaming, a crimson tide flowing out in a line that slowly widened into a wash of blood as his tissues opened up. I glimpsed a deeper layer of fat and cut muscle as she made a second slice, chillingly silent. No sound. No cries from Dante, or even me—I was too shocked. It didn't seem real to me until the loops of his bowel spilled out of him. Then it was all too real.

I screamed and twisted against my ties so that they creaked and strained. The silver ropes binding my arms broke. I was dropping forward, my upper body free, when a dart pierced my neck. I yanked it out, tried to aim it at a hunter—there were so goddamn many of them—but already lethargy was assailing me. A tingling numbness spread outward from the tiny wound in a rapid wash of weakness, and I sprawled limp, elbows on the ground. A haze of darkness and sparkly lights filled my vision, but I didn't pass out. I clung to consciousness, barely. After a second or two, my vision cleared and returned.

"The diluted venom seems to work. Good," Mona Sierra said with satisfaction. "I want you to see this."

"Why?" I mumbled—it felt like marbles filled my mouth.

"Because your distress will pain him even more." She nodded to a man who was clothed more than the others, wearing shirt and shoes as well as pants. He stepped before Dante and pulled the edges of his eviscerated abdomen together, with the intestinal loops still trailing out of him. Even in my dulled state, I felt the wash of energy coming from his hands. When he drew his hands away, the gaping wound was sealed back together, all but a central area, an inch-and-a-half-wide hole, where Dante's intestines spilled out of him.

"It will get even tighter as your own body heals," Mona Sierra said, trailing her fingers over the intestinal loops, smearing Dante's blood on them as though she were finger painting. "They tell me it's quite painful, feeling your guts being sucked back into you as you heal, which should take several long hours." She wrapped a small hand around the bunched loops, pulling gently. No sound came from Dante, but his face grew more ashen. "Quite a skill to eviscerate without cutting into the loops themselves. A nasty smell, I've found, when you perforate the bowels. This way is much better, cleaner." She smiled up at him with quiet ecstasy, drinking in his stoic pain. Sticking her finger into the hole, she stroked inside him.

I gagged, watching her, as two hunters bound me again to the pole.

This was one sick chick!

She glanced from me back to Dante. Her scary smile grew even wider as she purred, "Oh, how much fun this will be."

She tortured him like this throughout the night. Watching his entrails squeeze slowly, painfully back in, pulling them back out. When the last small loop finally slithered back inside him, it was almost anticlimactic. I kept expecting the crazy bitch to slice him back open and spill them out again. I think Dante did also, because his face remained as expressionless as mine was wildly expressive, as blank as mine was by turns sickened, angry, then pitiful, and always, always frightened. For both him and me.

So far Mona Sierra had limited her interactions to having Raúl—the guy with the red eye painted on his forehead— shoot me with a dart me every two hours with attenuated venom. It left me in a groggy, limp state. Alert but helpless to do anything. I had a strong feeling that had it not been for the necklace I wore, the necklace that had burned her fingertips black, Mona Sierra would have tortured me as well, just to get a response out of Dante—he had shown far more interest for my well-being than his own. For himself, he had bargained not at all, opened his mouth not once on his own behalf. Just kept his slitted eyes—the swollen eye had finally healed—focused on Mona Sierra with his last words lingering in the air: his promise to seek vengeance if she did not let me go.

I think all of us were waiting to see which way she would go on that, including Mona Sierra herself. Would she let me go or kill me?

Dawn was just beginning to creep over the horizon when they finally untied Dante from his pole. Two men unwound my bindings as well, though they kept our hands tied. No matter, as long as they were through for the night. Couldn't torture us while they were sleeping, right? Which I presumed they would be, since they'd been up all night. Only, it seemed they could.

It didn't occur to me what they were doing until I was standing over the pit. One of the men hefted me over his shoulder and walked a fair distance before setting me back on my feet. I had a moment to see the deep, crater-sized hole before I collapsed in a jellied mass on the ground, unable to stand, not even able to lift up my head. The multiple doses had accumulated within me. I was doped up to my gills at this point.

"Carry her down," Mona Sierra ordered Dante.

It seemed an innocuous thing to ask of him, but Dante reacted as if she had just told him to stab me in the heart. The expression on his face grew frightening and his body seemed to swell larger, even though he didn't move a single muscle. It wasn't my drugged imagination either, because the six men surrounding him stepped back and drew their machetes.

"You will regret this," Dante promised, icy rage flashing from his pale eyes.

"Not as much as you will," Mona Sierra said smugly, "and that is all I care about. Maybe if you had given me a better show, I might have spared her, but you were such poor entertainment."

"Lies," I managed to slur out. "Bitch jus wansa torment you."

Mona Sierra cast a venomous glance at me. "Perhaps. Perhaps not. He'll never know. And that will indeed torment him as you and he boil under the sun. As he watches your skin blister and peel away."

Oh, so that's what she had planned. I blinked and kept my mouth shut. Sunlight didn't bother me. Sunlight, in this case, was my dear, dear friend. It would give me time for the venom to wear off and let me recover my full strength, after which I'd break us out of this creepyville of horror.

"You can carry her down, or I will have her thrown down," Mona Sierra said indifferently. "Your choice."

Dante scooped me up and set me over his shoulder much more gently and carefully than the other man had. I hung over him like a limp rag as he descended the ladder, two men in front of him, another two behind. We went down twenty-eight rungs before hitting the bottom, and it was a tricky bit of work for Dante because his hands were tied together in front and he couldn't hold me as he climbed down. I couldn't even help. Another treacherous mind game Mona Sierra played with Dante—more guilt to heap upon him if I slipped off his shoulder and fell. But we made it down without mishap.

"Over there," Raúl said, pointing.

Dante moved to the indicated spot and set me down on the cool cement floor. Dante's eyes, the brief glimpse I had of them, were wild with anguish, turmoil, and rage. More emotion than he had shown throughout the entire night of tug-of-war Mona Sierra had played with his intestines.

"Step back away from her," Raúl commanded.

I think Raúl and I were both surprised when Dante obeyed without putting up a fight. I watched as he let Raúl's men untie his hands, only to retie them behind his back. They attached a long silver rope to his bound wrists and then secured the other end to a metal rung anchored into the concrete.

They did the same to me, and then the four of them climbed back up, pulled the ladder up and over the side, and drew an enormous silver netting, the ropes twice as thick as what they had used to capture us, over the top of the pit.

"Think of me as you burn," Mona Sierra said in parting. But they didn't leave just yet. Not until two darts, accurately thrown by hand, came sailing through the net to stab me in the thigh. Already I could tell that they had used full-strength venom. It would knock me out for hours. Hours during which Dante might die.

No, I wailed inside as consciousness dimmed. *Noooo . . . Dante!*

FOURTEEN

I woke up to the smell of something burning. For a moment I thought I was back home, and something was burning on the stove. But my home didn't have a concrete floor. And that didn't smell like food cooking. This odor was noxious and distinctive and somehow familiar . . .

I cracked open a heavy eyelid and took note of several things. One, I wasn't home. I was outside, with the hot sun straight overhead, filtering through a silver netting placed there, I remembered, by Mona Sierra's primitive thugs. I was also sore and achy and had my hands tied behind my back. Then I forgot all about myself as I caught sight of the source of that noxious burning smell.

"Dante," I croaked, my lips cracked and dry. The inside of my mouth was gummy, and my skin was pink and flushed. But that was nothing compared to Dante's condition, I saw as he looked up. His face, his chest, were unburned where he had curled. The rest of him, however, was a red, oozing, blistering wreck. His back, arms, even the soles of his feet, were an angry, swollen mess of weeping boils and melting ooze. His flesh was burned, all but where the silver rope bound his wrists just below the bracelet bands he still wore. There the skin was a weeping, crusty black beneath the painful silver binding.

"Oh my God . . . Dante!"

"How are you feeling?" His voice was unbelievably calm and evenly metered.

"How am *I* feeling?" Horror choked my voice and hysteria hovered nearby, but I battled it down.

"Your respirations slowed. Thought you were going to stop breathing." Only then did any emotion leak into his face—the sick worry he had felt for me.

"How long was I out?"

"Six hours, at a rough guess."

Six hours while he had literally broiled.

"I'm sorry I didn't wake up sooner." I tried to roll over onto my knees, but my body didn't seem to want to cooperate. It was as if an anchor was weighing down each of my limbs. The two darts were still stuck in my thigh, their feathered tails sticking up like tiny flags. "I'm awake, but my body still seems to be asleep. I think there's a paralytic component to the venom."

I was awake but useless to him. Fucking great. Wetting my cracked lips, I looked around. With the sun cast high overhead, the only sliver of shade was against the far wall. "Can you reach the shaded area?"

"Already tried. They tethered us out in the center. My rope doesn't reach far enough."

I tested my fingers and toes and found I was able to curl and wriggle them, move my arms and legs a feeble bit. "How much longer can you hold up?"

"Not much longer." His voice held none of the enormous

pain he must have been in, but there were still signs of it—I could hear his distressingly fast heartbeat, his almost panting breaths. "I passed the critical point already. It'll go quickly downhill from here."

"How fast?" I asked, licking my dry lips.

"Maybe another half an hour."

"After so many doses, I'm getting to be a bit of an expert on this venom. I might be able to stand in half an hour"—if I was very, very lucky and determined—"but I'm not going to have my full strength back by then."

Our eyes met, held across the short distance separating us.

"It doesn't matter. It's already too late for me. As least I know you'll survive."

"No, it's not too late," I said, rejecting his words as my mind revved back into gear. I couldn't reach the darts, with my hands tied behind my back, but I could jiggle them loose by awkwardly rubbing my thighs together. Ouch! Not the most pain-free method but . . . yes! There they went, nicely dislodged, falling to the ground. I twisted myself around, fumbled them blindly into my hands, somehow managing not to stab myself, then inchwormed myself sideways toward Dante.

"What are you doing?" he asked, panting.

"I'm crawling over to you. Meet me halfway."

He had to walk on his knees—he couldn't stand, his feet were too blistered—and he was very weak. He moved laboriously slow, like an arthritic old man as I crawled like a slug toward him across the hard and hot concrete. My muscles were quivering by the time I reached the end of my rope to where he was waiting for me at the end of his own tether line. If our hands had been bound in front of us, I could have reached him, but with our hands tied behind our backs . . .

There was just enough length for my forehead to brush up

and rest against his kneecap. One foot more on both our ends and I could have used the sharp ends of the darts to slice away at Dante's bindings . . .

"Fucking bitch," I snarled in anguish. "God, she's sadistic, leaving our ropes just long enough to touch, but not enough to be of any real help. I can't even provide you with any shade."

Dante made a vague sound. We just stayed like that for a while, touching. "You feel so cool," he murmured, closing his eyes. He, on the other hand, felt alarmingly hot.

A minute passed, another precious minute of my weak body resting while my thoughts flew at a hundred miles an hour, thinking, considering options, ideas.

"Probably would have taken too long to free my arms anyway," Dante murmured.

As an alternative, I could use the darts to saw away at my own wrist ties, but for what purpose? I still wouldn't be able to reach him. Not in time.

"There is one thing you can try," Dante said after a moment.

I turned to look up at him.

"Your Goddess's Tears—"

"My what?"

"The moles in your hands. I've seen you do things with them—"

"Take away pain?"

"No, I've seen you . . . project energy, use it like a shield, deflecting daggers and swords."

That sounded astonishing. Even niftier than being able to fly metal objects into my hands. Also completely unhelpful to our present condition.

"I've also seen you use it to burn through a man's chest, take out his heart in a powerful blast of energy."

I felt the blood drain away from my face. "Oh, was that

why you pulled away when my mole started to heat up?" I asked faintly.

"Yeah, knowing you can do something like that, you can see why I preferred you use a knife instead to dig out the bullets."

Definitely safer in comparison.

"Why are you telling me this?" I asked.

"Thought maybe you can try to use them to burn through your ropes."

"I don't know," I said uncertainly. "I'll give it a try."

I couldn't grasp the binding around my wrists, which was just as well for this experiment. Didn't want to accidentally blast off—or through—my opposite wrist. Wriggling back a few inches provided enough slack to grab hold of the long rope with both palms. A moment to calm and center myself. To dive deep into myself and open that door to where that power dwelt within me like a sleeping beast. To try and call it forth, and when that didn't work, to try and pull and yank it out.

Not even a flicker of heat or power.

"Too weak," I said after several fruitless attempts. Was I too drained or simply too drugged? The thought triggered another idea. With more effort than was pretty, I struggled to my knees, putting me face-to-face with Dante. His face was lobster red, but there was no perspiration. His skin was alarmingly dry and as hot as a furnace, giving off palpable heat even from a distance of several inches away.

"Dante, you said I saved you before. How did that work?"

"We had sex. You shared your light with me. But that was different. My body—my mind—craved moonlight after being deprived of it for so many years."

I remembered the vision of the moon's energizing rays pouring into me. Remembered again how my own skin had glowed with Roberto. "It's not just light, is it? We share energy, don't we?"

"It's a lovely thought, a wonderful one," Dante said as he realized where I was heading, "but I don't think sex would be possible. I doubt I could even get my pants off, and even then I don't know if we have enough slack to connect that way—"

"Kiss me," I said, interrupting his flow of words.

"What?"

"We glow with pleasure. We don't have to have sex to share light; all you have to do is kiss me. I could share energy with you that way, maybe enough to help you recover a little, at least give us some more time." My excitement suddenly faltered. "Or maybe I'd just *drain* energy from you—"

He kissed me.

I pulled back. "Wait, maybe this will hurt you more than help."

"Then I shall die happy." He brushed his lips over mine, sweet, simple, soft, the brush of hot, dry lips over my own chapped lips. And then a wet stroke of tongue, smoothing the way to a more slippery friction, and with it a sudden explosion of sensation, more than I had expected from such a dire, battered condition of its participants. It was like a detonation of feeling, a bombardment of things that were the opposite of pain—pleasure, yes, but even more than that. A seeking of life, a last quietly desperate sip of bliss, of enjoyment. A precious, unexpected treasure stolen out of the misery of the moment.

He kissed me with wave upon wave of feeling. All that he had withheld before now came flooding out. A raw surge of seeking, melding, joining with me.

Incomprehensible murmurs came from Dante's throat, from mine. A few husked words . . . *Mona Lisa . . . my lady . . . love you . . . yes . . .*

If we had kissed before, I did not remember it. And it was so much more than the surge of pleasure I'd gotten from kissing Roberto. Like digging into ground looking for a trickle of water and finding a gushing well instead. Dante kissed me as if he would pour his soul into me and pass it into my keeping—a plentitude of giving, not a taking. A benediction of words and sweet sentiment and hotly sprinkled passion over my mouth, my chin, down my neck, touching off zinging sensations, an abundance of it, wherever those firm and tender lips roamed, pulling forth my own gasps and whispers of his name, spurring him more heatedly on.

A seeking nuzzle of those hot lips over the swell of my breast, against my skin. A light, potent brush over my nipple that felt like an unexpected jolt of lightning within me. A sensation so intense it almost frightened me.

"Dante!" I opened my eyes to see my skin and his aglow in luminescent light.

"Sweet, so sweet," Dante murmured as he tugged my open neckline down with his chin so that it exposed one nipple, pert and erect. "Beautiful . . . lovely."

I watched his mouth envelope the hard tip, felt the heat and moisture of his mouth, felt the stroke of his raspy tongue, felt the bolts of amazing sensation that pulled cries from my mouth and more light from my skin until I was glowing like a small nova, overshadowing his own light, as he licked and teased and suckled and pulled at the reddened peak, enjoying himself with utter carnality.

He pulled his mouth free with a tight, pulling sensation that arrowed straight to my womb. "Lie down," he said roughly.

"What?" I was half-blind, dazed from the bombardment of strange and new sensation.

"Lie down on your side. Scoot your legs toward me . . . yes, like that."

That gave us a little more reach, a little more overlap. His mouth, those soft-hard lips, peppered kisses over my quivering abdomen. "Lift your hips a bit. Perfect." He nuzzled the shirt up above my stomach, exposing my triangular thatch of hair to his gaze. "So beautiful," he murmured.

I watched with both curling dread and anticipation as he lowered his mouth to lay a gentle kiss on my inner thigh. "Open your legs for me." His breath wafted over my thatch of curls—a curiously exquisite sensation.

"What are you doing?" I gasped, shocked and appalled as he nuzzled his way between my legs. The sound turned into a moan as he did something even more shocking with his tongue.

"I'm kissing . . ." The pause was punctuated with like action. ". . . licking . . . tasting you. Open your legs wider . . . yes."

He lapped and laved and pleasured me until I was half-crazed and wholly blinded, overwhelmed with searing sensation, beyond thought, beyond embarrassment. And still there was more.

Searching deep in my wet folds, he licked and sucked over an area that arched my back and spasmed my legs, building a tense, spiraling, frightening pleasure that suddenly crested and ruptured, free of skin, body, and fleshly containment. Light blazed forth in a rapture of incandescent brilliance as I cried out and seized in ecstasy.

A blissful moment where time seemed to suspend for an indefinite moment as I felt his tongue thrust deep inside me, as I felt him pull my light into him, illuminating his own skin more brightly. A moment of connection, of shattering, of giving and receiving. Of being flung up in pieces toward heaven and then falling back down reassembled.

He pressed a gentle kiss to my hip. "My lady," he breathed, resting his forehead there.

I opened my eyes and blinked.

Same place but different reality.

Dante's blistered back, buttocks, and weeping arms were healed. No redness. Even the black charring burns over his wrists were gone, leaving healthy, healed flesh in its place. My own scrapes and bruises had vanished as well, and the leaden, drugged weariness was gone. I felt refreshed, at full and normal strength.

A twist—an easy, simple pull and twist—and my arms were free. "What happened?" I asked.

Dante's glittery silver-blue eyes opened. "You can also heal with sex."

I could heal? That was my most heartfelt desire, an instinctual yearning I had felt my entire life—the ability to heal. The manner of doing so, however, was . . . well, let's just say—unexpected.

"That technically wasn't sex, was it?" I said doubtfully. I rose to my feet and rubbed my sore arms to get some painful circulation going.

"Part of my body was in yours," he answered.

Yes, I recalled that quite vividly: his tongue buried in my spasming depths.

I felt my neck and face flush as I freed Dante's wrists.

"How do you feel?" I asked, helping him stand.

His hand lifted, not to rub his sore arms, but to lightly touch my face. "Well and renewed by your light and healing grace. We can correct that technical point later, if you like, when we have more time."

Imp.

I smiled as a new and deeper intimacy stretched between

us. "I would like that," I said, nodding, then smiled. "So that's what all the fuss about sex is about. I never knew."

"Next time," he promised, "will be even better." He brushed an all too fleeting kiss against my lips. "Let's get out of here, shall we?"

It was about thirty feet up to the netted ceiling covering the pit, a bit more distance than what I could jump straight up. I solved that problem by springing off the side of the wall, launching myself farther upward. Grabbing hold of the center of the silver net, I tore it open down the middle. Using the natural swing as it gave, I went backward, then propelled myself forward, flipping myself up and out to land on the edge of the pit. An alarm suddenly screeched, ruining our quiet getaway. A motion detector—a surprisingly sophisticated bit of gadgetry in these primitive backwoods.

Dante sprang up and out in a straight jump through the torn silver netting to land lightly on his feet beside me. Six guards came bursting through the trees, hands reaching for venom-tipped throwing darts sheathed in straps slung across their chest. More voices raised in the distance, slower in coming, as if they were being roused from slumber. When they came, however, they would arrive in overwhelming numbers.

"Shift your form and fly away! I'll hold them off," Dante yelled as he leaped toward the six men. At the highest point of his jump, he transformed himself with a palpable wave of energy and the loud sound of ripping clothes. Bits of cloth sprayed the air in all directions as a one-hundred-and-eighty-pound man transformed suddenly into a five-hundred-pound-plus saber-toothed tiger. He was huge. Massive. Even taller than the men.

He was the most terrifying creature I'd ever laid eyes on. The sheer size of him, not to mention those wickedly long saber teeth, complete with a spine-chilling roar, stunned the attackers. If I was standing in their shoes, I would have shit myself.

Two hunters managed to hurl their darts and roll out of the way. The rest froze in that critical moment as they saw death racing toward them in prehistoric form. The beast swiped with his enormous paws, claws fully extended, several inches long, sailing past two attackers and grabbing up another in his jaws. The two long ivory sabers sank through the hunter's chest like the weapons they were named after. A savage chomp with the powerful jaw, and most of the hunter's chest, including the heart, was bitten off as easily as taking a bite out of a hamburger. Before the body, what remained of it, hit the ground, there was a bright flash of light.

The body *poofed* into ashy dust, empty clothes and weapons falling to the ground.

I thought for a moment the tiger had missed the other two hunters because they stood frozen there like statues. Then in slow, ponderous motion, as they started toppling over, a thin line of blood appeared across their necks like red paint seeping out. As their heads slowly separated from their necks, a bright light leaked from their open bodies. With an immolating *poof*, two more piles of ashes dusted the ground.

With an easy pounce, the creature swatted the three other men into the air like a big cat playing with amusing mice. He broke the spine of one, by the sound of it, partially eviscerated the other, and tore through the ribs of the last, sending them thudding to the ground, an incapacitated bloody mess.

The prehistoric tiger glanced back at me.

I stood there with my mouth opened, stunned by the carnage and odd light-and-*poofing*-dust display—was that how Monères died?

The two darts protruding from the tiger's chest didn't

seem to bother him; too big, perhaps, to be knocked unconscious by them. He chuffed at me, a loud coughing sound,
and tossed his head in a gesturing motion, like he was trying
to tell me something. Oh yeah, to run away. Or more like,
fly away.

I tried. I brought the image of a vulture to mind and tried
to picture myself becoming that image, but nothing happened. I didn't know why—perhaps it was the shock of seeing Dante becoming that tawny, striped, enormous beast. Or
maybe sensing more than fifty hunters running toward us
wasn't enough peril yet to force the change. Maybe I had to
be hurtling down a gorge, in eminent danger of going splat,
before I could shift.

"I can't change," I said to the huge creature, not sure if
Dante even understood me. "I tried but I can't shift, and I
know you want to be heroic and hold them off while I escape,
but hello, here. I need some help. For one thing, if you didn't
notice, I have no shoes, and my feet don't have the inch-thick
calluses these guys seem to have. Are my words even reaching
you? How about this? Here, kitty, kitty," I coaxed.

The big, magnificent cat eyed me balefully.

My heart lifted into my throat as I felt—and saw—the
first wave of reinforcements crest the small ridge above us.
"We have to hotfoot it out of here, Dante, and I can't do it
without you. Please, Dante. I need you."

With a hissing snarl, the saber-toothed tiger delicately
snatched up with his teeth the dark, reddish bracelets from
the ground where they'd fallen in his transformation. Then
he was in front of me, crouching down on his belly.

"What do you want me to do? Climb aboard?"

Dante chuffed and nodded his head, so much bigger than
my own. Jesus, was he big! Big, but not invulnerable. Especially against fifty of those heathenish hunters who were

streaming down the hill in a dark, brown-skinned wave, holding spears, swords, daggers, and those nasty venom-tipped darts, which reminded me . . .

I dashed in front of Dante to pull the two darts out of his chest and throw the nasty things away, then leaped onto his broad back. "Go," I cried, clutching a thick ruff of fur. Powerful muscles bunched and rippled beneath me, and he leaped away. Too late, I saw, looking back—my fault. Dozens of launched darts were coming at us like a dark and feathered malevolent cloud. Dante and I were about to look like a por-cupine. Forget about knocking me out—that many venom-ous darts would be lethal! Me, definitely. Maybe even to him.

With a quick, desperate pull of power from my inner-most core, I threw out my left hand and let energy spill out from my mole, familiar yet different. Broadening the focus, I spread it wide with a grunt of effort. Instead of acting like a shield, which was what I was aiming for, it did even bet-ter. When the oncoming darts collided with my streaming energy, it not only repelled them but also launched them back at the hunters, some of whom had shifted into their animal forms—leopards and hyenas—all of them notably smaller than Dante's prehistoric tiger form. Then my pulse of power hit the wave of attackers themselves like a soundless sonic blast, and sent them flying backward.

I glanced down at my hand, staring at my innocent-looking mole from which that surprising blast of power had come, then hastily gripped fur with both hands to secure myself as Dante stretched out in a loping run.

FIFTEEN

W E RAN FOR several hours. The jungle was denser this far south, and the trees taller, providing more shade. Riding the back of a huge tiger might have been better than running barefoot through the jungle, but it had its disadvantages. Especially when you didn't have any underwear. Going commando was not something I planned to do ever again.

While he ran for our lives, I was being tortured and flayed with erotic stimulation, and had become embarrassingly wet while riding him, not just perspiration of skin but damp between my legs where his thick but surprisingly soft fur brushed up against bare and sensitive parts of me. Dante, polite saber-toothed tiger that he was, didn't say anything when I first became stickily moist, not that he could anyway. But the heavy, musky scent of arousal I began to emit soon made my condition pretty obvious, if the honeyed wetness starting to drip down his sides wasn't a big fat clue already.

If that wasn't bad enough, the stimulation down below stirred things up above. My nipples peaked into hard pebbles and swelled my modest bosom, made worse by the rhythmic surge that rubbed them against the soft, furry pelt. I had more nerve endings than I had ever imagined. Nerve endings that became increasingly sensitive at each brush, each back-and-forth movement atop stimulating fur as Dante ran in long, loping strides.

I alternated my position, trying to ride more up on my knees to alleviate the torturous fur-rubbing friction, but that just made my weight harder to balance; alas, riding on top of a giant prehistoric tiger was not at all like riding a horse. When I almost toppled over, Dante turned his head and growled softly. Plastered tightly against him once more after almost falling off, I felt the deep rumble pass right through his back up into my own chest, and more jarringly, between my thighs. "Oh God," I gasped, swallowing down a moan. "Don't growl. I'm sorry!"

Boy, was I sorry. If he growled again, I was going to light up like a freaking lightbulb and give our position away. Not that I'd heard any signs of pursuit after that surprising power blast I had thrown at Mona Sierra's minions, knocking over their front line like ninepins.

I clung to Dante and endured with gritting teeth and glazed eyes for another hour before we finally stopped at a stream. By that time I was thirsting for something far beyond water.

Sliding off him was almost unbearably, sensually painful. I was never going to look at fur quite the same way ever again. By now, I was so aroused, I wouldn't have cared if a horde of hunters were about to descend on us. I just wanted, needed, something I couldn't name, but that wasn't quite true because in the next second I opened my mouth and did so. "Dante," I whispered, my eyes huge as I panted and trembled with need.

That great jaw opened, dropping the bracelets he had carried, then transforming light sparkled and glimmered as fur formed back into naked skin, silver-blue eyes, and a prominent state of arousal. "Mona Lisa," he growled.

He was magnificent: that arresting face, the riveting body. A gorgeous study of pure masculine form. I touched his chest—smooth skin flowing over hard, rippling muscles, softness over leashed power—trailed my marveling hands down the ridges of his abdomen, finally touching what, two days ago, would have sent me shrinking away in anticipation of pain, not pleasure. My fingertips trailed lightly over his jutting arousal, feeling him, learning him.

"Your skin is even softer here," I murmured in wonder, "like smooth silk over hard iron."

Dante's eyes blazed. He held still, so still, not even breathing as I slowly leaned forward and pressed my nose, my lips, against his throat, inhaling deeply. "I still smell you— tiger . . ." And the animal scent of him was as compellingly attractive, as enticing and intoxicating as the rest of him. "Taste you . . ." My lips trailed down over the graceful slope of his chest. Strength, power, pleasure . . . all inherently combined in him.

Moving farther down, I pressed a kiss over the firm, round head of him, finally eliciting a reaction, a sound. His hands buried themselves in my hair, gripping tight as I licked and delicately tasted the drop of wetness at the tip and found it salty sweet, such contrast, like the rest of him. Discovered that it could be a delight, a pleasure in itself to learn, to taste and touch, the male form, envelope it into your mouth—the smooth, hard slide of him in. To suckle and lap and stroke over that silky, plump smoothness, the vein-rich shaft, testing the firmness beneath.

I moistened him there, as much as I could take of him into

my mouth. Then, pulling away with a gasp—both his and mine—I stood and pressed myself against his strong, smooth chest, his hard, wet shaft rubbing above my own wet feminine folds. His harsh moan twined with my breathless mew of need. "Dante, please . . . I ache."

His hand reached down and pulled my leg up around his hip, opening me fully to him so he could rub against me, once, twice, letting my swollen, sensitive tissues ride along the turgid ridge of his length. The movement, the pressure, made me cry out. An exquisite bombardment to my senses . . . sharp twinges of pleasure and even more throbbing, aching need.

I wrapped my hand around him to guide him in.

With a wrench, he pulled away, whirled me around. "No, this way," he said in a guttural tone and dropped me down to my knees, guiding my hands to the ground. "Yes," he murmured as I felt him kneel behind me, one hand reaching beneath my shirt to knead an aching breast, the other hand splaying over my triangular tuft of hair, tugging it gently, teasingly, before stroking me down farther below.

Sublime bliss. Whimpers, cries, indecipherable words.

More primitive, urgent sounds from my throat as he pushed a finger into me and stroked wetly, one finger, two . . . Oh, God, oh, God! Stretching wetness, more melting honey. The withdrawal of those fingers. My protesting cry of distress. Then those wet fingers touching me behind in a spot that shocked me still.

"Shh, it's all right," he husked as he spread the honeyed wetness over my surprisingly sensitive rear hole.

I whimpered with distress at the unfamiliar touch.

"No condom. Let me love you this way," Dante said hoarsely, and I understood then that even now he was trying to protect me.

My tenseness and uneasiness melted away. "Yes," I breathed. "I need you inside me, any way."

There was the touch of lips to my back, then the press of his shaft pushing into me. Pressure . . . so much pressure. As the tip of him breached me anally with a forceful push, I felt his fingers push into my welcoming wetness in front, a twin forging into me combining stretching pain with sobbing pleasure.

Glimmering light and sweat dewed our skin, glowing brighter and brighter as he pushed his way steadily into me with both cock and fingers, and my body accepted him, if not easily, then hungrily, with wet, thirsting desire.

So good, so good . . . So unbelievably, wonderingly good to feel him inside me, so deep and full. Then the slow drag of him back out with both fingers and shaft, almost to the end but not quite, fingers sliding out completely to search out my hidden pearl.

"Oh!"

A light touch over the swollen nub to send exquisite bursts of spreading sensation within me. Licking, teasing fire that grew hotter and hotter with each burning stroke in, each heavy pull back out with that thick, stretching shaft while those clever, wet fingers played over me, stroking my pleasure higher and higher, winding me desperately tighter as he moved in and out, smoothly, fluidly, in increasing force and rhythm.

His fingers shifted—thumb pressing my swollen pearl, two fingers thrusting back into my tight sheath—his shaft drilling me, filling me behind, and I exploded in screaming climax. He drove into me one last time, his own body convulsing in release.

The light around us, from us, was so blinding that for a moment the moon's light outshone the day's sun, then slowly,

slowly, it began to fade until our skin no longer glowed, no longer shimmered and shone.

He pulled out with a heavy groan and drew me into his arms, both of us lying on the ground, breathless.

"Better than before?" he murmured.

"So much so that I almost fainted."

"Good," Dante murmured. "Wanted to keep my promise."

"You absolutely did."

SIXTEEN

I WAS WALKING, I told Dante. Better my feet than the torture of riding him again.

"You might enjoy riding me later, when we have a condom," he said with gleaming eyes, pulling me to my feet.

An intriguing prospect. "Another promise?" I asked. Pulling off my borrowed shirt, I waded into the stream to scrub it clean.

"At least as good," he said, lips curving in a hint of a smile. "Maybe even better."

"Promises, promises." I splashed him with water and he retaliated. I squealed and he laughed, and we frolicked in the water for a bit. And that was almost as much a marvel to me as sex with Dante had been.

My lover, I thought, running my eyes over him in wonder as we resumed our journey, walking at an easy pace, holding hands. He was unabashedly comfortable with his nudity, with good reason. There was nothing to be embarrassed about with a body like that.

"Eyes forward, you shameless wench," Dante said, amused at my frequent sideways peeks at him, "or you'll get me too stirred up to walk comfortably."

"Would serve you right after teasing me with that comment about riding you."

"I've created a sex fiend," he said in mock dismay.

"That you have," I said, surprised at the truth of it. It was a bit mind-blowing, going from thinking myself frigid to eagerly looking forward to the next time we could make love.

"How are you doing with the sun?" I asked.

"As long as we stick mostly to the shade, I'll be fine," he said, reassuring me.

We eventually came to a thriving town nestled against the blue waters of the sea, a wonderful breath of comfortable, bustling civilization. It was a modestly affluent community with paved streets, groomed lawns, and waving palm trees.

"Wait here." Dashing into an empty backyard, I snatched some clothes drying on a line, sending a silent apology to the owners.

We dressed: Dante in a T-shirt and baggy shorts, and a pair of loose trousers and a fresh shirt for me. I rolled up the sleeves and knotted the loose ends of my borrowed shirt at my waist. There. American tourists. Although the bare feet did look a bit odd.

Dante bespelled the first fellow tourist we came across, his blue eyes lightening into true silver as he captured the man's will with a glimmer of power. "What town is this?"

"Corozal," the man replied.

"In Mexico?"

"No. In Belize, Central America."

"How far to the Mexican border?"

"About nine or ten miles north."

A murmured request from Dante, and the man pulled

out his cell phone, dialed the number Dante gave him, and handed him the phone.

"Hello?" answered a voice.

"Dad, it's Dante."

After eliciting twenty dollars—they accepted U.S. currency here—Dante thanked the man and sent him on his way with instructions to forget meeting us.

"Aquila will be here in an hour," Dante said. "The rest will be along as soon as they can."

"Is Aquila the bird man?" I asked.

"Bird man? Ah, you mean the eagle shifter." He eyed me pensively. "You still have no remembrance?"

"Only a few things. I'm not sure if they're true memory or something I dreamed up. I wanted to ask you about them, but not here," I said, looking around the crowded street. "So what will it be? Shoes or something to eat and drink?"

Our stomachs won out over our tender feet. We chowed on fish, rice, and beans at the nearest restaurant and quenched our thirst with a pitcher of water, so hungry we didn't speak at all until we were finished eating.

"Eleven dollars left," Dante said, sitting back, replete. "I think we have enough to buy you some shoes. Shall we?"

We were able to pick up some cheap sandals for both of us, and made our way more comfortably to the waterfront where we sat on a stone bench overlooking the bay, watching the sun set in a majestic splash of color beneath the shade of a rustling palm.

"It's hard to believe that hours ago we were running for our lives," I murmured, head resting on his shoulder. "Humans seem to be much more civilized than the Monère."

"We can be a primitive bunch," Dante agreed, arm draped around me, fingertips stroking the bare skin of my arm. "But I beg you not to judge all Monère by what you saw of Mona

Sierra and her people. That was, indeed, truly primitive. We have more ruled order in America, and our conditions are not as meager as what you saw here."

It was the perfect segue into what I had wanted to ask him. "Is it? In one of my . . . I don't know what to call it . . . flashbacks, maybe, I saw a young teenage boy starved even more than those hunters were, and appearing even more wild. He was shackled to a wall and wore only torn trousers. His body was unwashed. His hair was so matted with filth I couldn't tell its true color, and he smelled of urine, like he'd been chained there for days. Was that something that really happened?"

"I cannot say for sure, but there is a young Mixed Blood boy I saw you with, whom you said had been abandoned in the bayous and grew up feral. When I saw him, however, he was clothed, his hair washed and combed."

I chewed over his words. Nothing conclusive, but disturbingly possible. I moved onto my next vision. "Then there was you. Pretty much like how I described the boy—half-naked, wild, shackled to the wall."

"Ah," said Dante. "That was true memory. You saw me in my maddened state."

True memory. The words jarred me. I had suspected, but to have someone confirm them as truth was still a shock.

"Do you remember anything else of our encounter?" he asked.

"No, just that brief glimpse. It was triggered when I came to rescue you from Roberto and found you chained up."

"And enraged. Similar to how you saw me before. Any other memories?"

"Yes. This one, though, was the most disturbing. The moon . . . I was pulling down light from the full moon. Pulling it into myself. Drinking it down like this amazing cocktail of energy. Was that real?"

"Very real. You are describing Basking, what you and other Monère Queens are able to do: pull down the moon's renewing light and energy. Take it into yourselves and share it with others around you. Only Queens can do this. That's what makes you so valuable to our people."

"So Mona Sierra has this ability also?"

Dante nodded.

"Why is that so valuable?"

"Because it renews us and allows us to live a full span of life—three hundred years."

"Three hundred years!" I squeaked. "You're kidding me."

"No, milady. I kid you not. Without Basking, we age faster and our lives are shortened to a human life span, which is why my brother and I are more physically mature than other Monère boys our same age. We were raised up among humans and never Basked in a Queen's light until you."

The questing brush of another's presence, distant yet, interrupted my next question. My head lifted from his shoulder as I felt Dante's own power flare out in response.

"Your friend?" I asked.

"It is Aquila," Dante replied after the briefest pause.

"Why did you hesitate?"

"Because Aquila is not my friend," Dante said, looking out over the water.

"Why? Do you dislike him?"

"No."

"Then why?"

"Because I left you."

We had danced delicately to this point once before. "Why did you leave me?" I asked.

"Because you desired that I go."

"Why, Dante? I can't remember any of it. You'll have to tell me."

"We . . . hurt each other," he said after a moment's reflection. "Both of us had the finest intentions, but we wanted different things. And then another matter crept between us, and after that yet another incident."

"Dante." I waited until his face turned to me. "You're saying a lot of things, but you're telling me nothing."

Aquila's presence grew stronger. He was visible now in the sky.

"I'm afraid to tell you," Dante said in a low voice. "Afraid to help you remember. Afraid that I'll lose you again when you do."

Whatever it is, now wasn't the right time to probe further, I noted in frustration as an eagle, large and graceful, clutching a cloth bundle in its talons, landed behind a building a hundred feet away. "It never seems to be the right time. But you'll have to tell me soon."

"Soon," he promised.

"I'll hold you to that," I said as a man emerged from behind the shed, his feathers exchanged for clothes. I looked with interest at the neat, thin mustache and the Vandyke beard, wondering if it would trigger any more memories, but no flashbacks occurred.

"Aquila, I presume," I said as he approached.

"My lady, are you well?" Aquila asked, both relief and consternation on his face.

"Much better than how I was faring a few hours ago."

"Dante says that you do not remember any of us."

"Nope, sorry. Hit my head real hard and can't remember anything of the last several months." Despite the easy way I spoke, I was far from blasé about it. "How long before the others arrive?"

"They should be along shortly. They'll be arriving by helicopter."

"Do you have any money?" I asked.

"Yes, milady." He pulled out a small wad of cash, to my vast delight.

"Good. Let's go do some shopping, and we'll fill you in on what happened."

We gave Aquila a brief rundown as we purchased some better-fitting clothes, along with bra and underwear for me—luxury items I'd never take for granted again. We also got sneakers for the both us, even more essential than a bra and underwear.

"The better to run in if we need to," I quipped, lacing them on.

Aquila looked quite pale after hearing us recount our adventures, and remained sharply alert when I returned our borrowed clothes back to the clothesline. The twenty dollars from the tourist looked like it was going to be a permanent donation, however. There was no sign of him.

The *whop-whop-whop* of a helicopter headed us back to the waterfront to await its arrival, drawing a crowd of curious onlookers as it landed like a giant metal gnat on the rippling green lawn.

"Quentin's here," Dante said. Even though he spoke in a normal tone of voice, I was still able to hear him over the noisy whirling of the helicopter blades.

"Who's Quentin?"

"My twin brother." With a broad smile, the first time I had ever seen Dante smile so openly, he stepped forward to greet his sibling. The young man who jumped out of the landed craft was seriously good-looking, I noted, with a face like a male model. They embraced with a quick, hard hug.

The wattage in the young man's grin rivaled the brilliance of the sun. "Milady. Aquila," Quentin said, greeting us easily. "Let's get on board."

Dante's father and another man I didn't recognize were seated in back. I climbed in and took the seat next to the stranger while Dante slung himself into the last seat beside me. Quentin and Aquila sat in front next to the pilot.

As soon as we were all buckled in, we lifted back into the air.

"I know you're Dante's father," I said to the large man sitting on the end, deliberately leaving the headset off so the pilot couldn't hear us. "But I don't remember your name."

"I'm Nolan, milady. Nolan Morell."

"Where's the other guy? The one who could turn invisible?"

"Chami's waiting for us back in Mexico," Nolan said. "The helicopter could only fit six besides the pilot."

I glanced at the man next to me who had been watching us silently. He had dark hair and eyes and his skin was deeply tanned like the Mexican natives here. His dark coloring was offset by the white silk shirt and the tan leather gloves he wore, lending a quiet, subdued elegance to his otherwise average appearance.

"I'm sorry," I said in a loud voice, thinking him human like our pilot, as I peered more closely at his face. "You seem oddly familiar. Do I know you?"

It seemed as if all breath suspended inside the craft for a moment.

"My name is Halcyon," came the quiet reply, as if the man knew he didn't have to raise his voice above the noisy thrumming to be heard by me.

Halcyon . . . I had heard that name recently. Then it came to me—when and where, and why he had seemed familiar. "This Halcyon?" I asked, lifting out the necklace I wore around my neck with the cameo that bore the face of the man sitting next to me. The face I had seen briefly in flashback.

"Yes."

His confirmation threw my world spinning topsy-turvy once more.

I wanted to make him clarify exactly *what* he was confirming—that he was what Dante had called him, a demon. But I couldn't, not with Dante's other words echoing in my ears.

The woman before you is the High Prince of Hell's chosen mate.

"The woman" being me.

I swallowed with a mouth that was suddenly dry as I turned to Dante and asked, "This is the Halcyon you were talking about?"

Dante nodded. "Yes."

"I thought you were making all that stuff up to try and scare Mona Sierra."

"No," Dante said, all his joy over seeing his brother draining away into familiar grimness. "I made nothing up. Everything I said was true."

SEVENTEEN

I SAT THERE in shock, surrounded by my lover, and what—a demon?

What exactly did *chosen mate* entail? And that was just the first wave of confusion. More came as I remembered everything else Dante had said . . . everything he had been called.

Queen killer.

I had ignored Dante's words during our capture, putting it down to the most outrageous and creative bit of lying I'd ever heard.

Everything I said is true.

I remembered his other wild, incredible claim: that I was this supposed Mona Lyra reincarnated. And that *he* had been the one to kill Mona Lyra.

Queen killer . . .

And that I—Mona Lyra—had taken his father's life and cursed Dante with my dying breath.

It was a tale crazier than the most bizarre Greek tragedy. Unbelievable.

Everything I said is true . . .

"Do you wish me to leave?" Dante asked, snapping me out of the long silence I had fallen into.

Why did you leave me? I had asked him. And his answer: *Because you desired that I go.*

"If I say yes, what will you do?" I asked. "Jump out of the helicopter into the sea?"

"Yes, if you wish."

"Don't be ridiculous, Dante." My slight smile seemed to surprise him. "I'm not giving you up after all the trouble I just went to. The only way I'll let you leave is if you want to. Do you?" I asked quietly.

"No."

"Good, because I'm not sure I could give you up even then." I wrapped my hand around his and felt his broad fingers close around my slimmer ones. "We'll have to talk more about all those things you said, and fill in all those gaps in my memory, but going by my actions, I don't think they'll be insurmountable. In the end, I came after you, didn't I?"

"How much memory did you lose?"

The question, and voice, drew my attention back to Halcyon. "A pretty large gap. The last thing I remember is working as a nurse in Manhattan. Nothing after that. Not even moving out of the city."

"How do you feel?" Halcyon asked with calm, focused intensity.

"Fine—no injuries. Everything's healed." I was more aware of him now. Aware of a faint sensing of his presence, and an odd lack of sound and movement that I suddenly accounted for with a rapid skittering of pulse. He wasn't breathing. Nor were there any heartbeats, none that my sensitive ears could discern. I sat there listening for a long time in vain. I was incredibly tired but on edge, finding, despite my lethargy, that I was simply unable to fall asleep next to someone who didn't have a heartbeat.

We landed at the heliport in Cancun International Airport and found Chami awaiting us there.

"Milady, forgive me. I know you don't remember us but . . ." The slender, curly-haired fellow who had displayed the alarming knack of turning invisible swept me up in an unexpected hug. "It's good to have you back," he said, releasing me. The man was much stronger than he appeared.

It was an odd thing being embraced so warmly by someone who was essentially a stranger to me. A stranger I had inadvertently caused harm to. "I'm sorry about before," I said awkwardly. "About getting you injured."

"No matter," Chami said, brushing it easily aside. "You are here now. Safe."

"Any sign of Roberto?" I asked. "The drug lord who took me?"

"Nope. More's the pity," Chami said, his eyes flashing with heat. "Would have liked to have gone a second round with that bastard."

We made our way to the terminal for private jets and boarded a comfortable jet without difficulty. Without passports or any form of identification, in fact. Trusting in the men's ingenuity and talent, I left all the details of finessing and compelling to them, too tired to do anything other.

With effort, once aboard the plane, I pushed back the drowsiness that clung to me like a sticky web. At Nolan's simple question of "What happened?" I filled everyone in on what had happened up to our escape from Roberto. Dante took up the rest of the tale after that, while I lounged back in my seat and listened with half-closed eyes.

Even tired as I was, I was aware of everyone's surprise on hearing about my nifty energy-blast trick. That seemed to be a new ability for me.

"What about you, Quentin?" Dante asked, turning to his brother. "Why are you up here instead of with your Queen?"

"Dad called me when things got screwed up, and I came down to save your ass."

"Did you have your Queen's permission to leave?" Dante asked.

"Quit playing the older brother. You're only older than me by six lousy minutes. Of course I got Mona Maretta's permission, but she's not my Queen anymore."

By Dante's sudden stillness, I gathered that this was more significant than it sounded to me.

"You were only with her for several months," Dante said. "What happened?"

Quentin shrugged. "Got homesick, I guess."

"Did she abuse you?" The question was asked in a dangerously quiet voice.

"With you as my big brother?" Quentin said mockingly. "Don't be stupid. She's not that dumb. Nah, she was actually pretty nice to me. Just wasn't what I thought it would be. Maybe I was too sheltered. Or maybe I just grew up with too much human value. She treated me well, but I didn't like how she treated other people. Plus, I think she was starting to get tired of me in bed."

"Already?" Dante said. "Maybe Dad should have concentrated on teaching you how to use your other sword more adeptly."

Quentin mock-punched him in the arm with enough force to sway him back several inches.

"Hah! I'll wager I'm more adept with that other sword than you are now. No disrespect intended you, milady,"

Quentin said, casting a quick glance at me, "or any slur on what you may or may not have taught this lout yet. We're just joking around."

The sudden apology—and mention of intimate matters between me and Dante—caused a flush of embarrassment to sweep over my face. I waved my hand in a *never-mind, just-go-on* manner. Thankfully Quentin did, pulling attention back to him.

"You know the saying—two's company, three's a crowd? Well, Mona Maretta didn't feel that way. To her, the number three was just a starting point."

The choked sound I made drew a few concerned glances my way. My cheeks had to be brilliant red at this point. I fluttered my hand again, encouraging all to ignore me.

"Anyway, I was starting to grow tired of just being her appetizer, and only a small part of it. And I think she was starting to tire of my declining to join in on the more adventuresome bed sport she favored."

"She was kind to give you a choice," Nolan noted impassively.

"I know," Quentin said. "She could have forced me with a simple command. Probably would have, in fact, had I been anybody else's brother." He waggled his finely arched brows at Dante. "Anyhow, I didn't like living like that, by her whim, watching her treat her people as if they had no rights other than what she allowed. Like I said, she wasn't that bad, just uncaring at times. I'd already made up my mind not to renew my one-year contract with her. When Dad called, it just expedited things. Having it involve *your* reappearance"—Quentin flashed a sardonic smile at his twin—"was just extra icing. When I asked to be released from her service to come to my family's aid, Mona Maretta dropped my contract faster than a hot potato."

"Why would she fear Dante?" I asked. That had been what he'd been implying.

Quentin glanced at his brother's austere face. "Let's just say he established quite a reputation at the last service fair."

"What did he do to earn such a reputation?" I persisted.

When no one answered my question, I turned to Dante. "Tell me," I urged softly.

"A Queen caused you a grievous injury," Dante said, his face carefully free of expression. "I killed her men in retaliation."

So it was partly my fault, I thought. "Men, as in plural, more than one," I noted.

Dante nodded.

"How many men?"

"Thirty in total."

I absorbed the information in shocked silence. "So many?" I whispered. "Just yourself, against so many?"

Dante dipped his head. "It was a serious harm done against you. Done with malicious intent."

Serious enough to kill thirty men for? "What did she do to me?"

"If you do not remember it, I would rather not speak of it now," Dante said. He bowed his head. "Please, milady."

"He is correct," Prince Halcyon said quietly. "You can talk of such matters later. She is clearly exhausted. You should allow her to rest."

Everyone deferred to the Demon Prince's wishes and all conversation ceased. Dante moved across the aisle to sprawl his length across the bench seat and stare out the window, while Quentin and Nolan busied themselves reading magazines. Chami took out a cloth and began cleaning a wickedly sharp-looking blade; Aquila nodded at me gravely and looked away. Prince Halcyon simply closed his eyes, setting an example of the rest he wanted me to get.

Everyone was cooperating except for me. I tried sitting back and closing my eyes, but my tired brain continued to whirl with Quentin's words . . . *Could have forced me . . . with a simple command. Probably would have. . . had I been anybody else's brother . . .*

Were all Queens like that?

They said I was a Queen . . .

I succumbed to another yawn. My body wanted to sleep, but my mind wouldn't shut down. Plus, I'd always been a nervous flyer.

After fifteen minutes of torturous pretend sleep, I opened my eyes and looked across the small cabin. My gaze touched on Quentin, his young and open face, the most normal, affable one among them. From there it went to Nolan, Chami, and Aquila, who had all come to my aid, who were supposed to be my friends.

My glance fell upon the dark, resting countenance of Prince Halcyon and skittered away, uneasy, nervous, despite the fact that I was, allegedly, the Demon Prince's chosen mate . . . maybe especially because of that. How could I accept as fact this supposed betrothal—to a prince of Hell, no less—when I had no recollection of the feelings that had led up to it? The whole story seemed like empty fiction, make-believe.

As to the others, despite all their helpful aid and assistance, I didn't know them. The only one I trusted here, the only one I knew, was a confessed killer—of me (or, rather, me in a former life!) and thirty other Monère men. Again, knowing something but not remembering it made it seem unreal. The only real thing was what I had experienced with Dante. Absurdly enough, he was the only one I felt safe and comfortable with.

I left my chair and made my way across the aisle. Dante swung his feet down, and I settled into the freed-up space beside him. Ignoring the closed expression of his face, I rested my head against his shoulder. "I'm totally wiped out, but I can't sleep," I whispered.

Dante's stiff, surprised body slowly loosened and relaxed. His arm came around my shoulder, and his other hand stroked my hair in a tender, soothing caress. "That's all right," he murmured. "Just close your eyes and rest."

Held by him, surrounded by his comforting scent, I did. I closed my eyes and felt the tension in me ebb and float away.

HALCYON WATCHED HIS mate fall asleep in Dante's arms, so exhausted she didn't stir as Dante lifted her up, turned sideways, lifting his legs back onto the seat, and settled her in a more comfortable sprawl across his chest.

The two were lovers again; their intermingled scent clinging to each other's skin. He didn't begrudge the comfort sought and given, then or now. Indeed, Halcyon was grateful for it even while still bleeding from the sword thrust of her innocent question. *I'm sorry. You seem familiar. Do I know you?*

Oh, my love . . .

It hurt even more than Mona Lisa's wariness of him. To be forgotten—everything they had shared. That brief, warm touch of her love on his lonely existence.

Halcyon could likely, in all probability, restore her lost memory. A simple compulsion, a command to remember. But his demon presence had not stirred up the demon essence—*his* demon essence—in her. A curious thing.

There was no sign of demon bloodlust at all. Was it because she didn't remember?

Memory—belief—were powerful things. Did she no

longer react to him because of that lost memory? Or was she truly different now after Mona Louisa, the other dead Queen who resided in her, had been ripped out of Mona Lisa's soul, and then remeshed together when the two of them, separate and apart, began dying. Had the experience physically altered Mona Lisa that much, so that the demon essence no longer held sway over her anymore? Was she no longer *Damanôen*, demon living? Or would that affliction return to her if she regained her memory? Or, another thought, if Halcyon used his demon powers on her, would that cause the weakened essence to grow strong within her once again?

Mona Louisa's dead, entwined spirit had trapped Mona Lisa in NetherHell, the cursed realm of the guilty dead. Tearing Mona Louisa out of her had been the only way to save Mona Lisa. It had even been her choice. But it had been Halcyon who had had to inflict horrendous pain to do so. He still remembered Mona Lisa's screams. Indeed, they replayed all too vividly in his nightmares. He had saved his lady and then lost her, because afterward she had feared him. Feared the remembered pain associated with him from that point on.

No. Even with the quietly bleeding wound of Mona Lisa not knowing him, not remembering what they had been to each other, Halcyon would not tamper with her damaged memory. She was wary of him, yes, but not fearful.

Dante, however, *could* restore her memory, his powers of compulsion almost as strong as that of a demon. Interesting that he, too, had chosen not to do so. But then, his advent into Mona Lisa's life and his leaving had been filled with violence and tragedy, both then and now. He almost pitied the poor bastard even though he held treasure, the woman they both wanted, in his arms now. The tide could turn, not if but *when* she remembered. Halcyon had hurt her. But Dante had killed her.

And not just her but everyone she had once loved.

EIGHTEEN

I SLEPT FOR hours, so deeply that I didn't wake until someone roused me. "We're home," Dante murmured, touching my face.

I slowly blinked awake, drifting up to that familiar voice, that pleasant touch. "Where's home?" I asked drowsily. It took another lazy blink to realize I was draped on top of him like an intimate blanket of arms, body, and legs across the seat we occupied. And that we were in a plane full of other people, who carefully kept their faces turned away from us as they left the plane.

"Louisiana," Dante said, helping me sit up. "We're at Lakefront Airport. It'll take another fifty minutes to drive to your house."

Outside, we were met by a teenage boy—an older teen. His ginger red freckles were framed by flame-bright russet curls. "Mona Lisa!" he cried, pulling me into a hug. "We were so worried. Dante, good to have you back. Thaddeus wanted to come, as did my mom and sister, but Amber said not to overwhelm you. Is it true that you have some sort of amnesia? That you don't remember us?"

I nodded, a bit overwhelmed as it was with all the names he'd pelted out of all the people I apparently knew. Who were they? Neighbors?

"It's okay. You'll get your memory back. I'm Jamie, your friend." He bestowed a sweet smile as bright as the color of his hair, and continued his excited stream of words. "Any more bags or luggage? No? Man, I can't wait to hear what happened to you guys. The car's parked over here."

The car turned out to be a Suburban that all eight of us were able to squeeze into with surprising comfort. All the while, I puzzled over Jamie. Who—or exactly, *what*—he was. He didn't have the full, rich presence of a Full Blood Monère or even that of a three-quarters Mixed Blood like me and Roberto—his power signature was noticeably dimmer, though not as muted as Prince Halcyon's.

"Are you Monère, Jamie?" I finally asked.

He glanced over his shoulder at me as if surprised by the question. "Partly. I'm a Mixed Blood like you, as is my sister, Tersa. But we're a half-half mix. You're three-quarters Monère, one-fourth human, like your brother Thaddeus."

It was the greatest shock. "I have a brother?"

"Yeah . . . I'm sorry," Jamie said, growing more subdued. "You didn't know?"

"I have a brother?" I asked, turning to Dante.

Dante nodded confirmation.

"How?"

"I was not with you then," Dante said. "The others will have to tell you."

"You found him right after you became the acknowledged Queen," Chami said, sitting between me and Dante in the second row. "He grew up like you, thinking himself human.

After his adoptive parents were killed, he came to live with you."

"How old is he?" I asked, trying to contain my emotions.

"He's seventeen."

"Oh!" Tears blurred my vision. "I have a brother." I wiped my eyes, then laughed tremulously as Jamie passed a box of tissues back to me. "I'm okay," I told him. "That's good news. Wonderful news, in fact."

Dante's arm came around me. "You're trembling."

"It was quite a shock. But a nice one."

"Perhaps it would be best if we tried to keep the shocks to a minimum," Dante said, catching Jamie's gaze in the rear-view mirror.

"Yes, sir. I'm sorry."

"Don't blame him," I said, elbowing Dante.

"I don't," Dante said. "But the idea of easing you back into things is sound."

"What about the other people I'll be meeting? Maybe you better tell me about them so I don't embarrass myself."

"You will not embarrass yourself," Dante said, reassuring me. "They are all your friends, who care about you, and are aware of your memory loss. Meet them first, see if it triggers any memories."

I had a feeling what Dante really intended was to space out the shocks. The first one came as we pulled into a long, private driveway. The house that loomed into view was a huge plantation home. The grand, white-columned building was so resplendently well maintained that one could almost be fooled into thinking it a new construction if one didn't notice the live oaks, draped in lace-like Spanish moss, so thick around it would take two men to hug their girth, proclaiming that this was the real deal, something built a couple of hundred years ago.

"What is this place?" I asked in awe. "A hotel?"

"No, milady," answered Aquila. "It's your home."

Shock number two was the number of people that came running down the front stairs, calling my name. Not Lisa, but the other one—Mona Lisa.

There was an onslaught of quick impressions and then I was surrounded by a happy babble of voices. There were two men, two women, and two younger people about Jamie's age—a petite girl and a lanky boy matching my height. As one of the ladies ran with a glad cry to embrace Dante—his mother?—my eyes fixed on the lanky boy. He looked like any other seventeen-year-old kid with dark hair and eyes—unremarkable if you could not feel his presence. I searched his pleasantly attractive features for likeness, similarity.

"Thaddeus?" I said, my voice lifted in question.

Everyone quieted.

"Yeah, it's me," the boy grinned. "Hey, I thought you didn't remember us."

"I don't. Jamie told me about you in the car."

"Oh. So I'm like a stranger again to you, huh?" There was kind intelligence in those brown eyes so like my own. "Must be weird being greeted by a bunch of people you're supposed to know but don't."

I laughed. "Yeah, a little."

"That's okay," Thaddeus said. "What about the others? Are you pulling a blank on them, too?"

Only then did I focus on the others, the sweet-looking woman who stood between Dante and Quentin, an arm around each. "You must be Dante and Quentin's mother," I said, "though you hardly look old enough to be the parent of two full-grown sons."

She flashed me a bright smile, holding tight to her boys.

"I'm Hannah Morell. I serve as your healer here. Thank you, milady. Thank you so much for bringing Dante safely back."

"No need to thank me," I said, looking at Dante. "We brought each other safely back."

I turned to the petite girl with the russet hair, quiet manner, and subdued energy signature. "You must be Tersa, Jamie's sister."

A brief, shy smile. "Yes, milady."

"And is this your mother?" I asked, glancing at the large Monère woman beside her.

Tersa nodded and the large woman dipped her knees in a curtsy. "I'm Rosemary, milady. I run this house for you."

"Thank God," I said in happy relief. "Good to know someone else is in charge of taking care of this huge place besides me. Who owns this property?"

"You do, milady," Rosemary said.

My eyes bugged out. "You must be mistaken. I could never afford a place like this."

"It was given to you when you became a Monère Queen," Thaddeus told me, his dark eyes twinkling. "Pretty cool, huh?"

"More like mind-boggling. Someone's going to have to explain this Monère Queen business to me later," I said fervently. My eyes swept to the last two men standing behind the others and I blinked. One was a blond Adonis, literally breathtaking, so handsome he was. The other was one of the largest men I had ever seen, both in height and muscled mass. Put a war hammer in his hand and he could have passed as Thor, the god of thunder. Their presence proclaimed them both powerful Monère males, but the bigger one gave off an extra crank of power in his energy signature.

We searched each other's faces as I made my way over to them.

"Do you remember me?" the blond Adonis asked. It was a bit unnerving to be held under the intent regard of his dazzling jade green eyes. As if the rest of his looks were not enough to knock you off your feet already.

"No, I'm sorry. I don't," I said after searching his face.

There was no change in expression, but I had the sense that my words had left him vastly upset and perturbed.

The big giant took my hand and gently turned me to him. I got the impression of careful strength as his large hand swallowed mine. At five foot eight, I wasn't used to looking up; I met most men at close to eye level. But I had to tilt my head back at a neck-craning angle in order to meet his gaze. This guy had to be at least six and a half feet tall, but it wasn't just the height that made him so intimidating; it was the sheer breadth and mass of him. If he accidentally fell on top of me, I'd be squashed flat like a bug. His features were ruggedly powerful, his eyes a striking dark cerulean blue. He wore a beautiful gold medallion necklace, and his voice, when he spoke, was a deep, soft rumble. "And me," he asked, "do you not know me either?"

"Sorry," I said, shaking my head. "Who are you?"

Again, I got the distinct impression that my softly worded apology had eviscerated the big man.

My hand was gently, carefully released as we fell into acknowledged stranger status. "I am Amber," he said, introducing himself. "I serve as your Warrior Lord."

The blond sun god introduced himself as well, his smile woefully strained. "And I am Dontaine, your master at arms."

What the heck was with the titles? "Do I have an army?" I asked, my question meant to be more flippant than serious.

"Not an army, milady," Dontaine replied, his smile dropping away, "just guards—over a hundred trained warriors."

Right. As if things were not surreal enough without try-ing to confuse me more with that incredibly lame joke.

Deciding to ignore the trivial stuff, I concentrated instead on what I had sensed, the strong emotions I had felt emanat-ing from these two, prodding me to ask with shy hesitance, "Are we close friends? Or more newfound relatives, perhaps?"

"They are your lovers," Dante said behind me.

Pin-dropping silence followed his words.

"Don't joke like that," I said, my face flushing, pained embarrassment making my voice sharp and brittle. "It's not funny at all!" Close friends? Possible. But sex with these guys? No way! Last I knew, I had been more frigid than a Popsicle. Dante was more than I ever dared hoped for, dreamed of. But imagining myself breaking out of my sexual Siberia with these two striking and intimidating men . . . no way. I knew what I looked like.

A blanket of uneasy dismay fell over everyone, as if no one knew what to say to my strong reaction.

"Let's all go inside," Halcyon suggested into the sudden silence. The guy didn't speak much, but when he did, people listened.

We trekked into the house, and if the outside was over-whelming, the inside was even more so. Everything was done with taste and class and lots and lots of money. The gold-leaf wallpaper, in fact, smelled like the real deal, metallic gold. And over my head was one of the hugest chandeliers I'd ever laid eyes on.

I wondered if I had wiped my feet. Probably not, didn't remember doing so. I stopped and kicked off my shoes, not wanting to dirty the pristine black-and-white marble floor.

"Oh, that's not ne—" Rosemary bit off the rest of her words as Dante removed his shoes also. "I'm sorry," she said, flustered. "We don't have any slippers on hand, milady. I'll be sure to get some tomorrow."

"No need. Just didn't want to get your clean floor dirty. I'm fine walking around in my socks, if you don't mind."

"Oh, no, not at all. Whatever you wish, milady."

She was clearly uncomfortable, and my own uneasiness was starting to rub off on the others.

I looked like someone they knew but didn't act like that person. And their not-knowing-what-to-do was cranking up my own anxiety in a vicious circle.

A pile of shoes collected at the front entrance as the others all silently removed their shoes, plainly not something they were accustomed to doing.

I cursed my self-consciousness. It was only magnifying the growing awkwardness between us. This whole meet-and-greet felt like one of those horrible blind dates that spiraled calamitously downhill the moment you introduce yourselves, shattering the buildup of pleasantly hopeful anticipation.

How wonderful. The idea of myself as someone's nightmarish date from hell.

I felt my pulse quicken, my breath coming a bit too fast as I glanced around, my eyes unnaturally wide. "Are you sure you guys have the right person?" I asked with a small, nervous laugh, more serious than not. "This . . . everything—" The mansion that was supposed to belong to me, all these people who seemed to care about me when I had been so bitterly alone all my life . . . "It's just not me."

So, *so* not me.

I didn't know what to believe. Whether I *should* believe anything they told me because the life I knew, the *person* I knew myself to be, was completely different from what they seemed to be expecting.

"Maybe it's just a horrible case of mistaken identity,"

I found myself babbling. "Or maybe I'm just dreaming or in a coma or locked up in some mental institution and this is all just an elaborate fantasy I'm making up in my mind: dream lovers, friends and family, this mansion, all this talk about being a queen, about demons and princes, reincarnation, curses, and being reborn . . ." I paused, gulped for breath, and finished feebly, "That doesn't happen in real life."

By everyone's shocked expression, I could tell they thought I was in the middle of a breakdown. It made me laugh, because if I hadn't been in the midst of one, I sure was having one now.

"It's real," Dante said into the fraught silence. "You're not dreaming, not making all this up in your mind."

The hand he laid on my shoulder certainly felt real.

"This is all just too much," I whispered, flinging out my hand to wordlessly encompass everything, including the two spectacular men who were supposed to be my lovers, the Demon Prince who claimed to be my mate, even Dante himself . . .

"Too much . . . too good to be true," I muttered as tears welled up and start to overflow their fragile tension. "It can't be real."

"Hush," Dante soothed. His eyes captured mine, and I watched with dazed bewilderment as those pale blue eyes turned a mesmerizing silver and started to glow.

"Can't be real," I said, shaking my head.

"Close your eyes, my love," he murmured, "and sleep."

And all my panic, doubt, and sadness drifted away as I succumbed to another's greater will.

NINETEEN

I WOKE ALONE in bed. At first I thought I was back home in my Manhattan apartment and that everything had been a bizarre dream.

It was the smell, the different scents that flashed my eyes open. That's right, *scents* as in plural, not singular. My own scent was strongest, mixed with the fainter smell of—what were their names? I thought for a moment and recalled them: Dontaine and Amber. The smell of them both, here on the bed, on the red silk sheets. In one of the largest bedrooms I'd ever seen.

Oh . . . shit.

I looked around. Everything strange. The only thing familiar being that everything was *not* familiar. I pinched myself on the arm and felt a painful sting, but no altering of reality.

Sitting up, I noted that I was still fully dressed. How long had I slept or, more accurately, been knocked out? I rubbed my eyes and blinked. Had Dante's eyes really turned silver and started glowing?

I got up and wandered around, inspecting the room. The hairbrush on the dresser had strands of hair that matched my own new color. Old, familiar T-shirts were mixed in with newer ones I'd never seen before, likewise with my pants, underwear, and socks; unsettling, the mingling of the comfortable old with the new and unremembered. The walk-in closet was the same, containing an array of my old stuff mixed with expensively styled new clothing and shoes.

I walked through an open archway into the large connected bathroom and gazed at my reflected image in the long stretch of paneled mirrors ribboning one entire wall.

Who had I become? Had I lost the new me with this large gap in my memory?

It was probably what everyone else was wondering.

I took a shower and felt much better afterward dressing in my old, comfortable clothing—T-shirt and jeans, a battered pair of sneakers, with my hair up in a ponytail.

Self-armored, I left the room and came to a door halfway down the corridor—two doors, actually, directly across from each other. Both rooms were empty, no heartbeat. I turned the brass-handle doorknob and found myself looking into a bedroom: Amber's room by the scent, large and roomy and tall-ceilinged like the rest of the house. My perusal paused a moment on a standing mirror, a tingle traveling down my back as the sight of it touched a strand of a memory that seemed almost tangible but wasn't quite—something to do with that mirror. I waited but nothing more came.

His closet was mostly empty with only a few articles of clothing hung within. The dresser drawers were likewise scantily filled. I retreated back into the hallway, closing the door quietly behind me, apologizing silently to the big man for intruding on his privacy but needing to know something more of this house and its occupants—who these people were and who I was to them.

The other bedroom was imbued with Dontaine's scent. His drawers were all full: socks, T-shirts, underwear—silk boxers. The latter made me hastily close the drawer. His closet was packed full of clothing as well, all carrying his scent. It was looking at those articles of clothing that caused a vision to come upon me.

I stood in the same closest but was looking at a different set of clothes, much fewer, filling only a small portion, and the scent was different, belonging to someone else . . . I was sad . . . so sad.

The memory of that time came to me with a clarity that was sharp and stunning, and my hand spread across my stomach, now as it had then. *My empty womb*, I remembered thinking and feeling. I had just finished my monthly flow, my red blood spilling down the toilet along with my hopes and dreams of a child from this man whom I was . . . what? . . . Desperately, I grasped onto that last thread. Those feelings . . . that scent . . .

Who was this man to me? Someone important . . .

At that question, that certainty, a face came to me, swirling me back to yet another time . . .

A face like a fallen angel, heartbreakingly beautiful. Skin luminous white and hair as dark as sin. Lips red and full, pulled tight with pain.

He was injured, lying on a stretcher in the emergency room.

And with that image, that remembrance, everything inside me unlocked, and all the memories came flooding back in a gushing cascade.

Gryphon—my first love, my first lover. My first rending loss . . .

I found myself on the floor, curled up in a ball, not daring to move or make a sound lest it stop. But it didn't. It kept coming and coming in an overwhelming outpour, the flood-gates too open now to stop.

Tears poured down my face, and my heart ached in silent, joyful memory. I remembered everything . . . including the baby I had lost—Dante's and mine.

I don't know how long I stayed like that, huddled on the floor, my hands clamped over my mouth to keep the screams locked within me. Minutes might have passed, hours. It felt like days . . . like an eternity.

My head ached. So did my heart. And my skin felt pain-fully raw and tight, newly formed, as if it had been physically stretched to contain the new expansion of myself.

How sweet and sad, wonderful and awful, to remember.

I staggered back to my room to splash water on my face and change out of my sweat-dampened clothes, grabbing the first thing that came to hand—old or new, they all were familiar to me now.

My hands were trembling, I noted vaguely as I sat in front of the mirrored dresser, gazing at my reflection. I looked the same, but the woman staring back at me was different from the woman who had sat there just a short while ago.

I was complete now.

Downstairs was silent but for some bustling in the back kitchen area. Empty, I thought at first, until I heard a page rustle in the front parlor. Following the sound, I came upon Halcyon seated gracefully in a wing chair, a book on his lap. He had to have known I was there—my beating heart announced my presence to him as loudly as a knock—but his gaze remained down, giving me the chance of polite escape.

My Demon Prince. Whom I had not recognized. Who I had thought human at first. Who I had been so carefully avoiding with nervous dread since the words *demon* and *Hell* and *chosen mate* had been uttered. Who sat there as solitary and alone as when I first saw him in a sun-dappled meadow.

"Halcyon," I said, speaking his name softly, emotions welling within me like a soft, rising tide as I went to him.

He stood with polite, guarded containment. It changed to clear surprise when I didn't stop a careful distance away but kept going until I was flush against that slender, hard body, embracing him. "Oh, Halcyon."

"Mona Lisa?"

"Yeah, it's me," I said against his chest.

A moment of stunned silence, and then his own arms coming up to hold me in a suddenly tight grip. "You remember?" he asked.

"Yes."

"How much?"

"Everything. I remember everything, Halcyon."

He eased me back gently so he could see my face. "Do you remember how we last parted?"

"What? Me acting like a skittish idiot after you saved me and brought me out of NetherHell?"

"After I hurt you," he amended.

"In order to get me out of that awful place."

"If you remember, why are you so glad to see me now?"

"Because I almost lost you. Because I *did* lose you for a little while. I'm so sorry—it must have hurt when I didn't know you."

He drew in a deep, shuddering breath. "It was like a samurai sword being thrust right through me. And then, like a fool, I felt glad . . . happy that you'd forgotten your fear of me. Only it wasn't any better. You were still skittish, still afraid of me. Why?"

"Because your name belonged to this demon who

supposedly ruled Hell and had some sort of claim over me. Of course I was afraid of you after hearing that; human perceptions of demons are quite different, you know. Dante said that you'd given me the necklace I was wearing around my neck, and it had freaky properties like allowing you to know when someone who intends me ill touches it. It burned the fingers of Mona Sierra, by the way, a Queen who has this, like, long family grudge against Dante. Was it true?"

"Which part?"

"That the necklace gave you some sort of vibe when it burned her fingers?"

"Yes, it told me you were in danger. It's why I'm here now. How do you feel?"

"Fine—better than fine. I feel normal."

"No agitation or reaction to my demon presence?"

"Oh, that." Before, in the past, I had been quite stirred up by close contact with Halcyon.

I had been in the process of becoming *Damanôen*, demon living. Now, though, there was nothing. No rising bloodlust or red eyes or demon claws.

The relief of that nonreaction was almost as jarring as getting my memory back. Halcyon's arms came around my waist as I sagged against him. And even with physical contact, there was still nothing.

"Oh my God, Halcyon, I'm totally fine. Even when you touch me." I laughed, happy, exuberant. "It must be what you did to me to get me out of NetherHell, tearing Mona Louisa out of me, separating us."

In the damned realm of the cursed dead, Mona Louisa had grown as strong as my own self, our shared body taking on the physical shape and facial features of whoever was dominant at the moment—talk about weird. It had taken multiple personality disorder to a whole different level.

She might have even permanently overpowered my own personality had we stayed longer in that realm. But we hadn't. Our integrating souls had been physically separated, leaving a gaping wound that had been slowly killing us both. She had almost faded completely from existence when I had absorbed her back into me.

"She was greatly weakened when we merged back together again," I said, speaking my thoughts aloud. "Maybe that's why I'm so calm and nonreactive to your presence now. The question is whether this calmness will last or whether she'll grow strong again." And turn me back into a living demon schizoid, who might attack anyone close to me.

"You seem to be fully integrated now," Halcyon observed. "You said you were able to shift into her vulture form."

"That's right, I did." A bright, optimistic thought— especially what it implied. That I might be stable, at status quo now, and wouldn't start changing and evolving back again into that frightening living demon thing I had been becoming before.

The sound of people, the feel of them, told us that we were no longer alone. Turning, I saw a crowd of faces gathered at the doorway.

"You remember us now, milady?" Rosemary asked.

"Oh," I gasped as I not just saw them but *recognized* them. Knew them. "I can't believe I forgot you guys."

It was Happy Reunion, Take 2. This time without any awkwardness or freaky meltdown to spoil things. I hugged Tersa, rumpled Jamie's carrottop head, squeezed Rosemary's ample waist, and exclaimed to a grinning Thaddeus, "My God, you're as tall as I am now. When did you suddenly shoot up?"

"He's been growing like a weed the last several months," Chami said, grinning. "You just didn't notice, seeing him every day."

"Where's Tomas?" I asked, naming one of my other guards.

"He's over in Amber's territory, helping run things while Amber was here," Aquila informed me.

"Amber didn't leave . . . he didn't go back yet, did he?"

"No, I am still here," Amber said, his voice coming from behind the others. Dontaine was beside him, I saw as the rest of them made room, allowing them to come to me.

They were still both striking men but no longer intimidating, no longer overwhelming. I saw them now through eyes filtered by love and shared experience. Amber, rugged giant that he was—indeed, one of the most physically imposing men I'd ever come upon—had been frighteningly vulnerable when I first met him, literally crawling in the dirt before his former Queen, begging for mercy she had not shown him. And Dontaine—beautiful, stunning Dontaine. I still remembered him with his throat torn, bloody and helpless while I washed the gore from his body and cared for him. They had earned my love, and even more important, I had earned theirs.

"Oh, Amber." I flew into his big arms and careful embrace.

"How did you remember? When?" Amber asked in a deep rumble.

"After I woke up. I wandered into your room and Dontaine's upstairs and had one of those flashbacks. I remembered Gryphon—he was the key. Everything came flooding back once I remembered Gryphon and how it all started."

The loss of my first love was a gentle sorrow I shared in my glance with Amber, who had known him best of all those here. But it was a gentle loss because Gryphon was not truly gone, just existing in a different realm now as demon dead.

I released my big giant and turned to my other lover.

"Dontaine." I didn't make him come to me as I had done so often in the past. I walked to him, to where he stood in cautious wait.

I went to him, held him, exhaling softly against his chest. "Oh, Dontaine, I'm so sorry . . . so sorry I forgot you. You pack one heck of a second first impression."

The stiff wariness I had taught him melted away and his arms came around to embrace me also. "As long as you're not rejecting me," Dontaine said against the top of my head.

"No," I murmured.

He pressed a kiss to my crown and I pulled back to smile up at him, but I wasn't done yet. There was one last important man in my life. One last lover I had yet to look upon with eyes filled with memories, to ask questions of.

I ended up driving. Such a simple, normal thing to do— drive a car. And for only a short distance. The Morells lived in a small house just down the road, within the vast property of the estate. Close enough, and more important, safe enough for the others to let me travel to by myself. After this latest scare, I had a feeling they were going to keep a really close eye on me, and I was going to happily let them. I had almost lost everything, not through another's fault or treachery, but through betrayal of my own mind.

Dante came out of the house as I pulled into the driveway. The rest of the family was still inside, giving us token privacy. He had that grim look on his face once again. "I apologize for using compulsion on you—" he began.

"I remember," I said, cutting across his words.

His body didn't stiffen, but his focus sharpened on me, stiletto sharp. Then he blew out a breath, releasing the tension, his eyes growing unreadable. "Come walk with me," he suggested quietly. He didn't hold out his hand, nor did I take his. We walked, as he had requested.

Soft moonlight trickled down through the trees as we went deeper into the forest until we came to a wide clearing. Here was where we gathered every month, each full moon, to Bask. Here, also, was where my men came to train and practice each evening, just before dawn—the place where Dante had first revealed the twisted past between him and me, our cursed enmity, and stood there waiting to be killed.

"What do you remember?" Dante asked, as we stood with the thrum of old power faint and soft in the soil beneath our feet.

"Everything." Every last wretched, painful thing. "Oh, Dante . . . our child. I lost our baby."

Tears—both his and mine—bridged the distance as no words could have, and I found myself suddenly held by Dante, sobbing softly into his neck, feeling his shared grief in the wet drops that moistened my temple.

The loss was mingled with remembered guilt, and the double loss of Dante immediately after like a one-two blow. But it was old grief that twinged anew, not fresh grief. Eventually my tears lessened, subsiding into an occasional hiccup, the quick ebbing of it hastened by the man who held and comforted me now.

One loss irrevocable, the other not so. Or so I hoped.

I said now what I had wanted but had not the chance to say before. "I'm sorry, Dante." And the added plea. "Don't leave me again. Stay, please stay."

He smoothed back my hair, searching my face. "Do you remember that time before, when I took your life and you cursed me?"

I took a deep, ragged breath. "Yes."

"Then how can you want me to stay?"

"Our present life eclipses our past," I said, gripping his arms. "We're in the middle of our second chance, and second chances are rare and precious. I happen to be freshly reminded of that." More gently, "Say you'll stay."

He squeezed his eyes shut. Opened them. "Yes," he said simply.

My heart leaped in joy. "Mona Sierra," I said, pressing while I yet had the advantage, "you won't go back to South America to punish her?"

Diamond blue eyes darkened. "I promised her my vengeance—"

"Which you will have," I hastened to point out. "She'll be fearful and uneasy for the rest of her life, always looking over her shoulder, waiting for you to strike." *Waiting for you to slaughter her and all her people*—which I didn't say out loud. "That waiting, always being on edge . . . let that be vengeance enough," I begged. "Please."

A light shudder ran through him. He bowed his head. "As my lady wills . . ."

"Thank you."

". . . as long as she bothers us not."

"Roberto, too."

He swallowed tightly. "Agreed."

"Agreed," I said in soft echo.

We sealed the deal with a kiss.

TWENTY

A MBER LEFT THE next day, returning to his territory; Halcyon departed the day after to his realm, both leaving with the promise to return soon. Things settled once more into routine, with a few changes. Dante and Quentin joined my daily fencing lessons with Edmond, under Nolan's tutelage. Needless to say, the Morell twins were in the advanced class; Edmond and I were, if not quite novices, then more along the lines of being orange belts to their black belt status. Most of the time, we worked in our evenly matched original pairings, but occasionally Nolan had us change partners, allowing Edmond and me to test ourselves against more superior opponents.

When the hour of sword practice was complete, Edmond left, and I continued on for yet another hour to work on new, additional skills—practicing the weird stuff, as I dubbed it. The extra hour had been suggested by Dante and agreed upon by Nolan. The first part was using the Goddess's Tear in my left hand to generate a blocking shield of energy. When we first tried this, of course, no one stood in front of me or my power-generating mole. Good thing, too. I knocked over a few trees and blasted the heck out of some bushes before I finally got the knack for calling up energy in a more controlled and modest quantity—a light tugging, not a ferocious pull. And not tossing out the energy but continuing to hold it steady a few inches away from my palm in a light, invisible thrum shaped into a small oval shield the size of my hand.

The last part of the session, I worked on what was the far easier stuff for me, pure blasting power.

When I let loose and just threw out power, I was able to send a spreading wave of energy that stretched to a twenty-foot radius that could travel a distance of fifty-two feet, measured by the violent rattling of trees and bushes.

Close-up work with projectile energy was even more notable. The first time I tried it, I blasted a head-sized hole through a heavy tree trunk, which was both frightening and impressive, since that hadn't been my intent.

"Remind me never to piss you off," Quentin said, whistling as the exploded wood chips dropped in pieces to the ground.

It had to have brought back dark memories for Dante, but he only asked, "Did you mean to do that?"

I shook my head. "No, I thought it would just knock over the tree."

"We'll have to work on control," was Dante's judicious comment.

Nolan nodded solemn agreement. "Yes. We want to make sure you're doing that on purpose and not by accident."

"Definitely," I said faintly, blanching at the idea of taking a life by clumsy accident rather than by sure intent.

By the time Halcyon returned on the fourth day, rested and regenerated from his stay in Hell, I had enough control to maintain a left-handed shield widened out to the size of a basketball. It was no doubt an odd sight to see me blocking Dante's wooden sword with no visible barrier other than my upheld hand.

"Very nice trick," Halcyon observed, watching from the side.

"Oh yeah?" I said, quite pleased. "See that pine tree over by the left edge of the lawn, about forty paces away? Keep an eye on the lowest branch." Aiming my right hand, I emitted a stream of energy I had managed to narrow down to a plate-sized diameter. The energy beam hit its target, sending four pinecones flying from the lowest branch.

"Not bad range and control for—how many days of practice?" Halcyon asked.

"Four."

"Hmm," he mused, glancing at the pine tree. "It's been a while since I practiced . . . but you see that single pinecone above the cluster you just hit?"

"Uh huh."

He sent out a flick of mental energy and dropped the single cone—without even swaying the branch.

"Oooooh." I grinned with delight at the competitive challenge. "Neat trick, yourself."

Pitting myself against Halcyon over the following weeks, I honed my skills to an even finer degree, narrowing my beam down to a two-inch diameter, pushing myself until I was able to almost, but not quite, match Halcyon's pinpoint accuracy. Control was the issue with me—not power but rather harnessing that power, learning the breadth and range of it. And, as was often the case when pitting yourself against someone better, I improved, developing a finer degree of control—certainly more than I would have had I been practicing alone. Even Amber joined in the fun on the days he came to visit, alternately cheering for me, other times for Halcyon, the big twerp, which I would punish him for later in a sweaty, wrestling romp in bed, tickling him without mercy.

In defensive maneuvers, I was eventually able to stretch the size of my shield out to a radius large enough to cover my entire body, good at deflecting swords and daggers and even bullets, sort of. The first time we tried it, the bullet punched right through my shield. It took six more tries before I finally found the right level of energy to produce. Even then, Nolan always aimed to the side, never directly at me, no matter how I urged him to do otherwise, assuring him I had it now. He chose prudence, and I couldn't really blame him. It would be bad form to shoot your Queen, even if it was her own idiotic fault.

On his fourth visit, when Halcyon left, I went with him back to his realm.

Hell was different, viewed with its powerful ruler strolling by your side. Needless to say, you didn't feel as threatened, even when your heart was the only living thing beating down there, calling out like a dinner bell to all occupants.

It took only one of Halcyon's powerful mental flicks, sending a wolf—Hell's nasty version of one, at least—tumbling away from us, to warn off other carnivores . . . and down here everything was a carnivore. Even their bunny rabbits had fangs sharp enough to bite your fingers off with.

"I wonder if I can do that now," I said.

Halcyon lifted a brow. "By all means. The next one is yours."

The next one didn't come until ten minutes later, a flying serpent that was strangely beautiful, like a large dragonfly, its iridescent red and brown scales gleaming under Hell's hot midday moon. It zoomed straight for us, hissing, venomous fangs on full display.

I lifted my left hand, shot out a careful pulse of power, and whoops . . . missed!

"Um . . ." Halcyon issued tentatively.

"I got it," I muttered. Taking quick aim again, I loosed a second pulse from my palm. This one connected with its target just in time, dropping the serpent less than ten feet away from us to writhe in a ropey mass on the ground, lightly stunned, looking more like a regular snake with its delicate wings folded onto its back.

"If I may," Halcyon said, politely offering his services as the serpent hissed at us and spread its wings.

"By all means," I replied easily, much more agreeable now after having proved my marksmanship on, if not the first, then at least, the second shot.

With a light mental flick, Halcyon sent the coiled serpent tumbling away from us.

"I should come down here more often to practice on moving targets," I said.

"Your visits would be more than welcome," Halcyon said with a smile, "and for more than just target practice."

"By the way, it was nice of you to shield me in the portal, but not necessary."

He looked at me quizzically. "I did not shield you."

"You didn't? But it didn't hurt, at all." Normally, transporting myself through the portal involved severe and biting pain, as if tiny blades were crudely hacking away bits of my flesh. "Why is that? What's changed?"

Because something in me obviously had.

"If I were to guess, I'd say that your body has altered since reabsorbing Mona Louisa's essence back into you, incorporating enough demon essence to make traveling the portal painless. And yet, curiously, you have been stable since then, with no other ill effects. Have you had any flaring of demon bloodlust?"

"No, none," I said, considering what he had said. "So you're saying the physical nature of my body has changed. Maybe the change occurred when you tore her out of me. Or when I was pulled down to NetherHell."

"Or when her separated spirit, substantially weakened, reintegrated back with yours," Halcyon said. Like a bandage slapped on just in the nick of time. Both of us had been trickling out vital energy like invisible blood, everything going out and nothing coming back in. "You said the touch of the gargoyle lord kept Mona Louisa from fading completely away," Halcyon said thoughtfully.

"A gargoyle," I said, continuing Halcyon's line of thought, "who has the ability to turn anything it touches into stone, one of the most solid and stable substances." And Gordane, the Gargoyle Lord, had been pumping heavy doses of his solidifying power into Mona Louisa there toward the end to keep her from fading completely away. "Do you think that's why I've been free of demon symptoms?" Symptoms that had been growing progressively and distressingly worse until Halcyon had feared having to kill me if I lost control completely and began slaughtering people and drinking their blood. I had come perilously close to that edge before being yanked down to NetherHell, and all that had followed afterward.

"If that is the reason," Halcyon said, "then NetherHell was a blessing in disguise, and everything, including your fear of me afterward, was well worth it." That had upset Halcyon in a way I'd never seen before, my rejection of him, my fearful recoiling away from his touch after experiencing that tearing, excruciating pain he had caused ripping Mona Louisa's dead spirit out of me. And yet, without that necessary action, I would still be trapped down in NetherHell, not only dead, but likely dead and truly gone by now. It was not easy surviving in the harsh realm of the damned dead.

As for why it no longer hurt traveling the portal down to Hell, the realm of the living dead, it could be that there was a part of me that was truly lifeless now—the part of me that was Mona Louisa, fully integrated into me. Or again, it could be the lingering aftermath of Gordane's gargoyle touch, or from a subtle change after being down in NetherHell.

I didn't know or really care. I was just grateful.

We reached Halcyon's home unmolested, though not from lack of trying. I had two more opportunities for target practice, and Halcyon three.

"I would not suggest you come down to visit on your own," Halcyon said after dispensing with a particularly nasty-looking creature I didn't even have a name for.

"Don't worry," I assured him. "Not even tempted." Cool, neat weapon that my mole-emitted beams were proving to be, without Halcyon's powerful presence by my side, the attacks on us would have been likely triple what they had been, or even more. The most dangerous predators, the demon dead themselves, had not ventured anywhere near us. That, I was sure, wouldn't have been the case had I been walking alone with my loudly beating heart calling out to all the blood-hungry denizens.

Halcyon's house was a far more modest abode than his father's dark, towering fortress, quietly elegant, solid and powerful like the man himself. Tuck and Keven, two elite demon guards patrolling the grounds, met us at the property line. We exchanged greetings and made our way to the house.

The door opened before we could turn the knob, and a querulous voice said sourly, "I'll get it. Stand back, you lout. 'Tis my job, not yours."

I had to adjust my gaze significantly downward to meet the eyes of the small female demon that stood there: Jory, a dour old demoness who oversaw the smooth running of Halcyon's household.

"Welcome, my prince, my lady," she said blandly.

"Thank you, Jory," I returned, and lifted my gaze to the demon lout she had been scolding.

He stood waiting a few steps away in brimming impatience.

I felt my heart kick hard at the sight of him and his name left my lips in soft utterance. "Gryphon."

TWENTY-ONE

GRYPHON HAD HEARD her heartbeat a distance away, and his own dead heart thumped, not with sound or movement but with emotions. Joy and dread and torturous love.

She's here! She's here!

The two words beat loudly within his mind, his chest, filling him with a maddening surge of dizzy excitement that hazed his vision red and changed the color of his eyes. It took a moment of conscious control to bring himself back to the calm a demon needed. Another few precious moments to gulp down a cup of challo, blood wine, and chase that down with swallows of water to rinse away the smell of blood. Then a quick chew on a sprig of mint, running the comb through his hair, and a mad dash down to the front door that Jory beat him in opening.

Gryphon's eyes were blind to all else but the lady who stood there. His ears deaf to everything but the sound of what fell from her lips. His name.

"Mona Lisa," Gryphon said in a rasping sigh. He held still, letting her come to him, conscious, so conscious of that careful control he had to maintain. Then she was in his arms and he was breathing in her sweet, living scent, feeling the thump of her heart against his own silent chest.

"Dear heart," Gryphon murmured, relaxing and gathering her up against him when he found that it was not as hard as he had feared, holding her like that, warm and precious. His demon hunger for her blood was tamed, held in abeyance for the moment, superseded by another appetite that suddenly roared forth, stiffening against her. "Oh, my lady," he groaned, clutching her to him, "it is so good to see you again."

"As I can see," Mona Lisa murmured in an amused, soft undertone, ". . . and feel."

"Forgive me," Gryphon said, scooping up her legs.

She squealed, laughing. "Put me down. I can walk."

"Quicker this way." He threw a quick glance at Halcyon. "Your room?"

At the answering nod, he moved, unbelievably fast.

They were suddenly in Halcyon's room, and Halcyon was pulling the door closed behind him—not *outside* the room but *inside* as Gryphon set Mona Lisa down on her feet.

"You're staying?" Mona Lisa asked her Demon Prince.

"It's what we agreed would be most safe," Halcyon said, steady and calm. Something in his eyes, however, prickled the small hairs on Mona Lisa's arms, standing them up with a dark, dangerous thrill of excitement.

"Let me," Gryphon said, gripping the edge of her shirt.

At her answering "Yes," he lifted her top in a slow, reverent unveiling.

The next article of clothing was removed by the brush of

invisible fingers. One bra strap delicately pushed down, then the other. "Was that you?" Mona Lisa asked Gryphon with startled eyes.

"No," answered Halcyon. "It was me."

Mona Lisa gasped as she felt those phantom fingers deftly unhook the back clasp. Both men watched as her bra fell away, revealing the soft, white mounds of her breasts.

Tension heightened a notable notch as Halcyon began unbuttoning his shirt, walking slowly toward her. "May I join you?" he asked, as politely as could be, but his eyes . . . the heated smolder in his eyes played contrary to the casual ease of his words.

Mona Lisa swallowed hard, felt her pulse skitter. Felt it pound even more as Gryphon leaned down to brush his lips against the hollow of her throat, slide his mouth over her pulse point. Dangerous, dangerous delight.

She had never been with both of them together before— that is, openly agreed upon, *beginning* that way. It was, she found, startlingly different.

"By all means, yes," Mona Lisa said in a breathless whisper.

Everything suspended and became truly breathless as Halcyon began disrobing in a deliberately slow and graceful striptease.

Just those two things: the feel of Gryphon's lips and the sight of Halcyon moving, acting, in a way she'd never seen before—knowingly, sensually, blatantly sexual.

It was unbelievably arousing.

Her breath came faster, and the unsubtle scent of her arousal filled the air.

"Take off your pants, love," Gryphon murmured, licking his way up her neck to nuzzle a particularly sensitive spot behind her ear that curled her toes and pulled a soft moan from her. The light touch of Gryphon's palms running down her shoulders, grazing the sides of her breasts, made her shudder.

There was nothing like a lover who was intimately familiar with your body . . . unless it was two lovers who knew your body's every secret and erogenous zone.

With teasing slowness, Halcyon slid his pants down. Mona Lisa's movements were more hasty as she kicked off her shoes and lowered the zipper of her jeans. Her body quivered under Gryphon's physical touch while her eyes hotly devoured the sight of Halcyon deliberately revealing his body in a blatantly carnal dance. She pulled in a soft breath as his hard organ sprang free. Let loose a gasp as Gryphon's rough palms pushed her jeans down her legs. He crouched, kneeling at her feet, his mouth so tantalizingly close to the soft feminine juncture where her thighs met.

She felt his breath puff upon her there, ruffling her curls, and gasped in a breath.

Gryphon lifted his wicked blue eyes to her. "Lift your feet," he commanded softly.

She did, one at a time, feeling his hand brush down her calf, her ankle, the top of the foot—areas more sensitive than she would have imagined. He eased her clothes away so that she stood revealed, naked and vulnerable in front of her two lovers, one as beautifully bare as she was, the other still yet fully clothed.

Like two dancers following choreographed steps, they switched positions, Halcyon coming to stand behind Mona Lisa, caressing her with the delicious brush of bare skin to bare skin, while Gryphon stood up and began his own languid and erotic disrobing.

The Demon Prince touched Mona Lisa with his hands, traveling the same path down her body that Gryphon had followed, while Gryphon stroked her with words, with the heat of his eyes, telling her what he was going to do to her in explicit, detailed, and blunt language. . . what they were *both* going to do to her.

She found herself throbbingly moist, fully aroused by the time Gryphon parted with his last article of clothing and closed the distance between them to stand in front of her, not touching. Halcyon's hands fell away, too, so that the two men surrounded her, front and back, for a moment, a walled enclosure of strong, naked male bodies.

Gryphon backed slowly onto the bed, holding her gaze. "Come here," he said in a rough, sensual demand, lying back against the pillows like a pagan lord.

Had they deliberately planned it this way? she wondered. The last time she had been with Gryphon—the first time making love to him since he had become demon dead—had been difficult. Afraid of touching her with his sharp demon nails or his fanged mouth, Gryphon had been unable to prepare her adequately. Now, though, her body was more than ready for him after the show the two of them had put on, or more accurately, put her through.

Well, if two could play the same game, so could three.

With a gentle sway of her hips, Mona Lisa stepped toward the bed, at an angle so that both of her dark, teasing demons could see.

Her hands started at her neck and stroked slowly, smoothly, down the mounds of her breast, grazing over her nipples. The unexpectedly sharp jolt of sensation hardened the peaks and pulled one groan, and one growl, from her audience of two. They watched her with hot, avid attention. Followed the caressing glide of her fingers down her midriff as she swayed and sauntered over to the bed. Watched with glued eyes as she came to the edge of the mattress and ran her hands down her thighs and then back up, coming to a teasing halt just above her small triangle of hair.

She wasn't beautiful, but under their intent gazes, she felt more than beautiful: she felt like a wanton seductress, the slightest move of her hands hungrily devoured by their gleaming eyes.

Sinuously she crawled onto the bed.

Gryphon began to sit up and she used one finger to hold him still. "Oh, no," she whispered, "I haven't had my turn yet." Leaning in, she kissed the corner of his mouth, nibbled the curve of his lower lip. "You have the most gorgeous mouth," she murmured, pulling away when he began to kiss her back. Using both hands, she pushed him prone again, his body deliciously laid out for her enjoyment.

God, he was beautiful. A stunning, dazzling feast to the eyes.

Her gaze drifted to her dark Demon Prince. "Come here on the other side, Halcyon, so I can see and enjoy you both."

Her Demon Prince moved—no, not moved, that would be too tame a word for what Halcyon did. He *prowled* with dangerous grace to the other side of the bed, his erect sword leading the way, every fluid movement imbued with raw carnality. The sensual heat of his eyes was mixed with amusement. "Competitive little thing, aren't you?" he murmured.

"Oh," she purred, "you have no idea."

Kneeling beside Gryphon, with her eyes fastened on Halcyon, Mona Lisa put her left hand over the top of Gryphon's foot and stroked the delicately arched insole.

Gryphon twitched.

"Stay still," she murmured, and ran her hand up his leg.

Gryphon's staff, already thick and flushed, grew even duskier in hue as her fingers trailed closer. Halcyon's thickened pole bobbed and twitched as well, she was happy to see as she continued the upward sweep of her hand. Her fingers ran along Gryphon's hip, traced the muscles along his abdomen and chest with sweet, appreciative pleasure. And what she touched on Gryphon's body with her hand, her eyes swept in visual caress over Halcyon.

"Watch me," Mona Lisa said in soft command to her Demon Prince. Leaning over, with her breasts suspended over Gryphon, she began kissing her way down his chin, his throat, the upper pectoral swell, the hard, flat abdomen, and what lay against it in quivering attention.

She kissed her way down the length of his penis, one hand cupping and squeezed his balls, while the other grasped his twitching staff and held it still as she put her mouth over the tip, letting her soft breath caress him for a torturous moment of strung-out anticipation.

"Mona Lisa . . ." Gryphon spoke her name in a rough, needy groan.

In reward, her tongue flicked out and licked the fluid that had gathered at the tip. Eyes fastened on Halcyon, Mona Lisa delicately licked her way around the entire head until she came to the sensitive under-ridge and laved it with attentive care, probing there until Gryphon's hips arched up involuntarily. She slipped her mouth down over him for a briefly blissful sucking second, then released him, pinning down his hips with both hands. "Uh-uh. No moving until I tell you to," she chastised gently.

Her eyes flicked back up to her Demon Lord. "Up on the bed by the pillows, Halcyon. I want you to have a good view."

"As my lady commands," Halcyon murmured, moving with catlike grace onto the bed, his dark eyes growing even more brilliant and intent as Mona Lisa swung her leg over

Gryphon, straddling him. Using one hand to position him, she sank down on him in a hot, wet glide.

"Sweet Goddess of Light," Gryphon said, his voice taut and strained as Mona Lisa began to glow. "So tight . . ."

Mona Lisa didn't rush it. Just let her weight slowly sink her down, watching Halcyon, whose dark, glittering eyes focused on where Gryphon penetrated her, disappearing inch by inch.

Mona Lisa couldn't see it, but she could feel it, imagine it: Gryphon's thick length slowly spearing into her. Her own inner muscles tightly surrounding, engulfing him, swallowing him up until their mounds met.

She lifted herself steadily back up as if she were riding a carousel horse, rising almost to the end of his pole, feeling the hard slide of him out. Slowly impaling herself on him back down. But at the end of this cycle, instead of rising up, she leaned back until her spine brushed against Gryphon's thighs, bending his rigid staff at an acute angle, and rode him this way so that *she* could see now as well. So all of them, Halcyon and Gryphon and herself, could watch the hard, wet glide of him pushing into her and coming back out, hear the wet, sucking sound they made as his cock entered and exited, feel the angled tension of him rub and pull against her tight sheath.

"Move, Gryphon. Now," she gasped, quivering, and felt him take over the movement, the rhythm, driving harder, faster, into her. She closed her eyes, remembering the visual image coupled with the physical sensation of his glistening cock disappearing into her, both of their bodies lit, shining. . . Sweet Goddess, indeed. She wasn't going to last long.

"Halcyon . . . please," she cried, wanting both of them in her when she went. "Join us."

He moved so fast she didn't see him, one moment on his

knees against the headboard, the next moment standing there beside them.

"Open your mouth," Halcyon said harshly, his hands fisting in her hair.

Mona Lisa parted her lips and he pushed his way in. Sweet bliss.

She licked, sucked hungrily as Halcyon pumped in and out of her mouth, humming blissfully at the taste and feel of both of them within her.

Halcyon pulled out and was suddenly behind her, pushing her gently forward, down over Gryphon's chest. Gryphon lifted his head and took her mouth in a hot, raw kiss as she felt the tip of Halcyon's cock push into her from behind.

Gryphon's tongue speared into her mouth at the same time Halcyon entered her anus, and then they were both fucking her in slow, gentle push-pull rhythm, perfectly coordinated, in and out. In and out.

Mona Lisa felt Halcyon's phantom hands caress her breast, squeeze her nipples, stroke with devilish lightness over the nub between her wet, parted folds. Clever, invisible fingers tugging, pulling, stroking, and caressing her, feeling as real as the two hard cocks surging into her like dueling swords, rubbing alongside each other separated only by a thin layer of tissued membrane.

They increased their speed, their harmonized tempo, and everything built and tightened and tensed within her.

Mona Lisa broke their kiss as she felt Gryphon's teeth lengthen and sharpen, knew with a thrill the bloodlust he was feeling, felt a surprisingly corresponding need to be marked and pierced by those very teeth—something she had missed more than she knew.

Gryphon's rhythm suddenly faltered.

"No, it's okay. I want it," she said in hasty reassurance,

pulling his mouth to her breast, reaching back with her other hand to guide Halcyon's head to her neck. "Bite me, both of you. Drink my blood."

They didn't wait for a second invitation. Two sets of fangs pierced her.

They drank down her blood and thrust themselves inside her, driving themselves so deep and full within her. That the pleasure culminated and exploded in a visually blinding brilliant pulse of light. She convulsed. Felt the milking clench of her sheath and tightening of her sphincter set off their own spasming release.

"God," Mona Lisa gasped as she felt the withdrawal of their fangs, leaving behind a pleasant throbbing ache on her breast and neck. She twitched as she felt the twin laving of tongues over the puncture wounds, enhancing the tremors still running through her.

A heavy shiver as she felt Halcyon pull out of her. Another shudder as he lifted her off Gryphon and lay her down on the bed between them.

Three-way cuddling, Mona Lisa found, was nice.

Very, incredibly nice indeed.

TWENTY-TWO

THE DAY OUR world irrevocably changed began as a typical evening, breaking fast together with a main meal and then dispersing to our varied duties and chores, which for me was my two-hour practice session with the Morells.

Thaddeus was the one who brought it to our attention when we returned back to the house. "Hey, guys," Thaddeus called out from the living room. "Come here. You have to see this."

I stepped inside to see my brother glued to the television. The scene playing on it was indeed riveting: a news report of a tall apartment complex going up in flames. The caption *Breaking News* flashed along the bottom of the screen.

"It looks like a fire," I said, wondering what all the fuss was. "Is it local?"

"No. In Washington, DC, in one of the slum neighborhoods," Thaddeus said, raptly watching the news. "Wait, this is what I wanted you to see."

And the reason for his interest suddenly became clear as

a man came crashing through a window near the top floor. No, not a man, I realized as wings spread out in magnificent display. A Monère. Caught on film!

His arms—only his arms—were shifted into feathered wings. Wings that were burning, caught on fire. Clinging to the male was a teenage girl wearing pajamas, coughing but otherwise seeming unharmed.

The reporter gave a startled cry. "What in the world . . . are you getting this?"

The cameraman's excited affirmative was heard.

They flew for a moment, gracefully suspended in the air, an incredibly dramatic picture as the flames spread rapidly to the Monère's shirt, burning along his back, highlighting the man, his beating wings sharply outlined against the darkening night sky.

You could hear a faint cry as the flames reached his neck, and the girl let go, dropping away from him, falling, plummeting, her sleeves caught on fire.

There were gasps, cries of dismay from the news crew, from the crowd below. Then even more startled cries as the winged man rushed down after her in a hard swoop. The girl plummeted a sickening distance before the male caught her, shifting his wings in midflight back to arms. Burning feathers disappeared and became seared skin, his clothes licked bright with orange flames. Holding her tight against him, they dropped in freefall the last fifty feet.

He hit the ground hard, feetfirst, and rolled with his precious burden, taking the heavy brunt of the fall. Both of them were immediately sprayed with fire extinguishers by the waiting firemen before they even came to a stop. The footage ended with the male lifting the girl and staggering to his feet. He managed a few lurching steps before collapsing to his knees and slumping over the girl. The footage stopped there and switched back to the news anchor at the studio.

Thaddeus hit the mute button and flipped to other channels. All of them were running the same film segment. One channel had even clearer footage, a close-in zoom shot after the male burst out the window and first spread his wings. They froze it there, showing the burning feathers in clear, undeniable detail.

"I don't know how long they've been running this. I've just been watching the last ten minutes." Thaddeus turned to me. "Is it bad?"

"Yes," I said, dumbstruck. "It's *awful*. They have a zoom shot of him!" I turned to Nolan, the oldest Monère in the room. "Has anything like this ever happened before?"

Nolan shook his head. "We've never been caught on film like this before."

"What are the reporters saying?" Quentin asked Thaddeus.

"Everything but the truth. No mention of Monères so far." Thaddeus rubbed his face. "Some are calling it a hoax, claiming what we saw was just clever film editing and special effects. Although with three different news stations showing different live recordings, not much credence is being given to that. The most popular assumption is that he strapped wing-like contraptions on his arms and that they burned off." An ironic smile crossed Thaddeus's face. "One station is actually calling him an angel."

Dante snorted. "An angel?"

"Well, you have to admit, he sort of does look like one," Thaddeus said, shrugging. "A man with wings, flying. Hey, don't look at me like that; I'm just reporting back what I heard. But even without all that real-wings-versus-fake-wings argument going on, there's no getting around the fact that this guy jumped out of the nineteenth floor of a twenty-story burning apartment building and half flew, half fell down over two hundred feet without going splat. Hell, he was even able to stand up and walk afterward! Not something most humans can do. They're calling him a hero, whoever-whatever he is. So far, no one's come up with an identity for him or the girl."

"Do *we* know who they are?" I wondered.

"Luckily not our problem, though High Court must be going crazy," Nolan said. "Though I wonder if they even know this is being played on television yet."

I flipped open my cell phone, something my men had forced on me shortly after I became Queen, and now was grateful to have. "I'll give them a call."

I indentified myself to the person answering and asked, "Has the Queen Mother seen the news playing on TV?"

"Oh, yes, milady," the man said with feeling. "We've most definitely seen it."

"Good, just wanted to make sure she knew about it."

"Wait, please," he said before I could hang up. "The Queen Mother wishes to speak to you." He pronounced her title with careful reverence, as well he should for the sovereign of the Monère people here in the United States.

The Queen Mother's voice came on the line. "Mona Lisa, I was just about to call you myself. Have you seen the news?"

"Yes, I just saw it."

"Are you able to speak privately where no one can hear you?"

I looked at the others, all of them listening in on the conversation. "Uh . . ." Dante saved the day by removing the gold chain that hung around his neck, and holding it out to me. At the end of the chain hung a small gray stone the size of a robin's egg: the privacy charm I'd seen him use in the past. ". . . not yet. Give me a second."

"You can use my study," Aquila offered. He had drifted in, along with Rosemary, drawn by the commotion.

Dante and I hastened down the hallway to the study. Dante slipped his necklace over my head as soon as I sat down behind the desk, and activated the privacy charm with a small pulse of power. A ring of energy expanded, encircling us.

"Touch it with a small thrum of power to deactivate it," Dante instructed, and stepped out of the invisible circle, leaving only the sound of my own breath and heartbeat in that cone of silence. I couldn't hear anyone else, nor could they hear me.

"All right, I've got privacy now," I said, wondering what she had to say to me that could be so important in the midst of what had to be a critical situation.

"I've spoken to Halcyon. He's told me that you seem to be stable now," the Queen Mother said.

I glanced at the phone, then put it back to my ear. Whatever I'd been expecting, it hadn't been this chatty comment. "Yeah, it's been quiet. No one snatching me away or anything."

She gave a soft snort. "Yes. It's seems to have been one crisis after another for you ever since you've taken up the mantle of Queen. But what I meant was the demon blood you ingested secondhand through Mona Louisa. You no longer seem to be becoming *Damanôen*."

"Oh, that," I said after a moment of uncomfortable silence. "I, ah, didn't realize Halcyon had made you aware of that."

"Do you know how old I am, my dear?"

My brows scrunched together. Instead of saying, *What the hell does that have to do with what's going on?* I answered politely, "No, Queen Mother. I have no idea how old you are. No one does, was my impression."

"I am seven hundred and thirteen years old."

"Oh." I know, pretty lame, but what was I supposed to say? "I thought Monères only had a three-hundred-year life span."

"They do. Did you know that our original Monère society was clan based?" the Queen Mother continued. "Wolf clan, dragon, phoenix, tiger, and others, all maintaining separate courts based around their pure-blood clans and Queens."

"No, I didn't."

"A little over six hundred and fifty years ago, the clans unfortunately began to destabilize as fewer and fewer children were born among these separate groups. The few offspring who came were from those who had chosen a mate outside their own clan lineage, as Blaec did, Halcyon's father, when he married a woman from the phoenix clan, not his own dragon clan. We were a dying people, not only growing infertile but also killing off our numbers with a growing number of skirmishes and wars between clans. It was during this critical period in our history, as the old ways were falling apart and our people were in grave danger of dying out through their own foolish actions, that Blaec, the new young Demon Ruler of Hell, approached a young Queen and made a pact with her. He opened a vein in my arm and mixed one drop of his demon dead blood with my own."

For a moment, there was only the sound of my sharp, indrawn breath.

"With that one drop of blood," the Queen Mother said, "Blaec took a strong Queen and made her even stronger. With the High Lord of Hell's powerful backing, I changed and reordered things to what they are now, forming courts out of mixed-clan individuals. I created High Court and the High Queen's Council and established stable rule, putting a stop to all the squabbling. It was a secret Blaec and I have long kept. A secret shared only by his children, Halcyon, his son, who lends his support to High Court in Blaec's place now, Lucinda, his daughter . . . and now you."

"If no one else knows," I asked carefully, "why are you telling *me* this?"

"Because I'm old, my dear, old beyond my natural years." The Queen Mother was the only Monère who looked old among us, the only one who had wrinkles. White hair was common after hitting your second century, but not wrinkles; Monère skin remained relatively unlined, leaving you looking thirty-five until you died. The Queen Mother had been the exception to this rule. Now I knew why.

"I hoped you would be my successor," the Queen Mother said, astounding me even further. Before I could say anything . . . even *think* of anything to say, she continued speaking. "But then you began developing demon traits and my hopes were dashed. But now, my dear, it seems we both have a second chance."

"Queen Mother," I began with a calm that quickly evaporated, "there's no way in hell I can take your place."

She chuckled. "No way in hell . . . Ah, but you are wrong. It is because of your connection to Hell and its current ruler, Halcyon, that makes you the natural choice as my successor. What I accomplished would have been impossible without Blaec's strong backing."

"I don't *want* to be the next Queen Mother." It wasn't quite a wail, but it was real close. "You're not going to die soon or anything like that, are you?"

"Child," the Queen Mother said with gentle amusement, "I have been dying for many years now, but it is a slow, ongoing process, not imminent, if that's what you're asking. As to being the next Queen Mother . . . what if I gave you another choice? A choice to make your own path?"

"What choice?" I asked cautiously.

"What I chose for our people was the best solution for that time. But, alas, time has moved on, and the world around us has changed while we have not. We've been stable, but stagnant. Tell me, Mona Lisa. If you could change the rules, would you choose to do so?"

I cursed not being able to see her face. How honest could I be here? "Queen Mother . . ." I said, pausing.

"You may speak frankly with me," she encouraged.

"The rogues . . . how the Queens kill off their strongest men—that I wish most to see changed."

"And how would you change this?"

That was the kicker. "I don't know. If I could, I would offer them all shelter, but Lord Thorane warned me about—"

"Building up an army out of proportion to your territory. Yes, I asked him to warn you thus before you collected any more powerful men, as you seemed inclined to do, at quite a rapid pace. What, however, if the breadth of your territory suddenly expanded?"

"Beyond Louisiana? Did any of the neighboring Queens die?" I asked, alarmed.

"No, all the current territories and Queens are quite stable and in good health, at the moment. I am confusing you with this roundabout talk," she said, chiding herself, and paused a moment to gather her thoughts and words. "We always knew that one day we would be discovered. It was simply a matter of time with all this new technology. The choice we are faced with now is whether to use this opportunity to make ourselves known to the world or to sweep it under the rug once again, as we have always done, and continue on with our secret existence. I leave the choice up to you."

"Me?" My voice squeaked.

"Yes. We've determined the male to be a rogue by the name of Jarvis, who fled his Queen three years ago. The girl, however, appears to be human. I've asked the DC territory Queen to hold off taking any action for the moment, but that situation cannot hold for long. Both Jarvis and the girl are being taken to a hospital, accompanied, or rather surrounded, should I say, by human law enforcement. What I need to know is if you are willing to serve as our Monère ambassador."

"Wait . . . wait. You want *me* to introduce the Monères to the rest of the world? Why me?"

"Can you think of any other Queen able to do so?" Her tone was quite dry.

Okay, put that way, I could see her point. "All right, I agree most of the other Queens are too arrogant." Beyond arrogant, actually. "But what about the more reasonable ones, like Mona Carlisse?"

"Not as disastrous as the others," the Queen Mother granted, "but aside from the fact that she is still recovering from the ordeal of being raped and enslaved for over ten years by outlaw rogues, Mona Carlisse's contact with humans is too limited. She has only the most basic concept of human law."

"What about my mother, Mona Sera?" She was the territory Queen of Manhattan. "From what Gryphon told me, she has plenty of business dealings with humans. Some politicians, too, I gather."

"Mona Sera, who abandoned you at birth because of your mixed blood? Who drugs her people with aphrodisiacs and prostitutes them out for monetary gain and economic influence? To have *her* represent us? I think not," said the Queen Mother coldly. "I'd sooner trust our peoples' welfare to a rabid mongoose than to her."

That put paid to that suggestion plainly enough. "Why does it have to be a Queen? What about the Morells? They spent almost twenty years living among humans."

"As rogues. They'd be swatted down like flies, assassinated by the first Queen who didn't like our secrets being made public."

My voice thinned, became a little bit shrill. "And I won't?"

"You are the High Prince of Hell's chosen mate; his mantle of protection over you is more substantial than you realize. The threat of possibly endless torture and punishment during afterlife is a potent deterrent for even your most hateful enemy."

"That might cover the Monères, but what about the threat from humans themselves?"

"You will have to charm them."

I huffed out an exasperated breath. "That's not even close to being funny." It was ridiculous what she was asking me to do. To risk. "I have absolutely no training for this."

"You have the best training among us. You have lived among humans all your life, are familiar with their byways and laws, and—what no other Queen or Council member can claim—you are part human. Part human and part Monère. No one else can bridge our two worlds better, Mona Lisa." Her voice grew softer, though no less urgent. "No one else has a more valiant and generous heart. Trust me on this, when I say there is no other among us that can serve as a more fitting or more ideal representative."

"And if I don't? If I select the other option of sweeping this all under the rug?"

"Then the rogue and the girl will be discreetly killed, and a concentrated effort of eliminating other troublesome rogues will follow."

She gave me a moment to process this before continuing. "You have an opportunity to change things, my dear—our rules and laws and very way of living. Under the current individual court and territory system, there is no room for males who become too powerful for their Queens, other than to desert and become outlaw rogues, or risk being killed. A great waste of talent and strength, not to mention Monère lives. The problem before was there was no useful purpose for them to serve. But that can all change if the Monère come out publicly."

"How?"

"That is for you and I to decide and negotiate." The canny Queen Mother knew she had a hard-and-fast grip on my interest now. "I cannot risk the other Queens."

"Only me," I said, smiling wryly.

"I value you more than any other Queen," she said, her voice clipped. "That is the hardest part for me, to give you this choice. I am only willing to allow this risk for the greatest possible gain. Plus, you have proven to be a survivor. I am trusting in that. But enough. For practical matters, I can send only you and those of your people who are willing to tread this path with you out into the public eye. If none are willing, I will send some of my own men."

"So it's only going to be a handful of us."

"Not if you can entice others to join you," she offered ingeniously. "There are hundreds, maybe even thousands of outcast Monère living among the humans, outside of our society."

"You're talking about rogues," I breathed, suddenly seeing where she was going with this. "And how would I go about enticing these rogues to put their necks alongside mine on this chopping block of a public outing?"

"By granting them full pardon and allowing them to become part of an official court once again."

I laughed, amazed and appalled, excited and entranced by what she was proposing. "So you would have outcast rogues serve as Monère representatives. How utterly practical. Okay," I purred. "Let's bargain."

TWENTY-THREE

THE BARE BONES of it all fell into place within hours: an hour on the phone with the Queen Mother, another hour talking to my own people, one more hour to pack what we would be taking with us. Then we were on our way to the airport.

Amber met us there.

My greedy heart gave an exultant cry as our car pulled up next to his in the short-term parking lot of the airport. "I didn't know if you were coming," I said, stepping out of the car.

"When you asked me to build with you what my heart never dared dreamed for or imagined would ever be possible, how could I not?" he said as I flew into his arms.

We held each other tightly.

"The risk . . ." I said against his chest.

"Is one we are all willing to take for that glorious possibility of *maybe* . . . just maybe," he rumbled against me.

"Like, just maybe we can pull this crazy thing off," Quentin finished dryly.

"Hey, pup." Amber released me and swept his approving eyes over the rest of our group. "Glad to see you're coming, too."

"You kidding? Wouldn't miss it for the world," Quentin said, smiling. "My timing in leaving Mona Maretta couldn't have been more perfect. Makes me almost, like, prescient."

"Or just damn lucky," Dante muttered, messing up his brother's hair.

"How could I not come," Quentin said, eyes laughing as he ducked away and smoothed down his glossy locks, "after *you* jumped on board? Had to make sure my big brother stayed out of trouble."

"And where our two sons go," Nolan added, his big arm around his smiling wife, "Hannah and I go, too."

Dontaine's gaze met Amber's. "Like you, Lord Amber, my place is beside our lady."

Amber's eyes rested last on Chami, standing beside Thaddeus.

"Nope, I'm just the driver," Chami said to the silent question in Amber's eyes. "I'll be staying behind, watching over everything."

"Ah. The new master at arms?"

"That would be Tomas," said Chami.

Amber made a sound of approval. "A good choice."

Chami grinned. "My sole charge will be to keep an eye on our new young master here, Lord Thaddeus."

Thaddeus blushed and made a face. "Don't call me that."

"It will be your title," I said without sympathy. "Get used to it." It had been part of my agreement with the Queen Mother, after speaking with my brother. That Thaddeus would rule over the Louisiana territory in my place, and

Amber's as well, which would recombine back into the single original territory. It had been a shock to the Queen Mother, learning that a male could draw down the moon's rays and Bask. But a small shock, quickly absorbed, among all the other jarring changes about to occur.

"Until she can find a replacement," Thaddeus said now in clarification. "Then I can join you guys."

"Not allowed until things settle down and stabilize," I said firmly. That had been the one thing we had argued most about. "We're about to shake up the world, Thaddeus. It will be dangerous enough coming out as the first male able to Bask. First let the Monères get used to you, then we'll consider the rest of the world."

"How long do you think it'll take for things to settle down?" my brother asked wistfully.

"I don't know. A year at the earliest, if we're lucky. Heck, we might stumble at the first step—getting legal rights for the Monère people—and come crawling back here before you know it."

"Won't happen. You won't fail," Thaddeus said with the blithe assurance of youth.

"I pray not," was my soft reply. Gathering our luggage, we made our way down to the terminal for private jets.

I was taking Hannah and Dontaine away—a healer and my master at arms—but I wasn't leaving Thaddeus wholly bereft. My brother had some healing ability himself, his control of that useful talent coming along rather nicely after training under Hannah over the past months. Steady, faithful Tomas would be taking up Dontaine's mantle, a good responsibility for the older warrior who had been underutilized, really. I'd had an abundance of older, powerful Monère males—some of them had been rogues, in fact, like Aquila—who would continue overseeing the business side of things. Rosemary would capably continue in her role as chatelaine, with her Mixed Blood children staying safely here with her. Jamie had wanted to come, but as with Thaddeus, I had deemed it too dangerous at this initial stage. The strong pull of Wiley, the young and wild Mixed Blood boy Tersa had taken responsibility for, kept her anchored safely at home.

Last, but not least, there was Chami, my very talented, deadly chameleon. I trusted Chami to keep my brother safe. I knew that he, Aquila, and Tomas would guard Thaddeus with their lives—he was as precious to them as to me. Their unique hope.

The Queen Mother and Lord Thorane were already aboard the private jet, waiting for us. We knelt in the aisle and entryway in respectful genuflection.

"Rise," said the Queen Mother, her presence as commanding in the small airplane as if she had been seated on her throne. "Ah, a wise selection," she noted astutely, taking a quick inventory of my people.

"And very fortunate, on my part," I said, "that they are willing to venture forth in this matter with me. The Morells are already quite familiar with human society, as is Dontaine, my master at arms, who supervised most of the businesses in New Orleans under his former Queen's rule. And Amber—"

"As a Warrior Lord, is the perfect male to beckon forth frightened, disenfranchised rogues out of hiding, serving as the ultimate example of what they could be." The Queen Mother's eyes glinted with approval.

"So we hope. Amber has agreed to relinquish his current territory to head up the new District Court we hope to form."

"I do not know if that serves as an advancement or regression in status, Lord Amber," the Queen Mother said with a small nod.

"Advancement, most certainly, Queen Mother," Amber

replied, bowing his head low. "I wish to thank you on behalf of all the lost warriors out there for the opportunity to serve you in this extraordinary way—for the blanket pardon you are willing to issue them."

"It is a matter clearly close to your heart," she said with kind observance, "but do not thank me yet. It is good that you believe so fervently in this cause. Hold on to it tightly. It will sustain you during the hard road ahead as you carve this new path for us. Though we will not be visible, be assured that you have my gratitude and High Court's full support in this matter, as much as we can render." Her voice grew dry as she glanced at me. "Though I do wish you hadn't made us go through all the trouble of dividing your territory into two parts, only to recombine them once again, a few months later. Try and plan better in the future."

"Yes, Queen Mother," I said meekly.

"Chameleo," the Queen Mother said, addressing Chami by his full name.

Chami paled beneath the Queen Mother's scrutiny and gave a courtly bow. "At your service, Queen Mother."

"That was my next question, in fact—who will *you* be serving? Do you stay or do you go?"

"I will be staying with young master Thaddeus, honorable Queen Mother."

"Ah," she said. "A good choice."

Her glance fell on my brother, and I took the opportunity to introduce them. "Queen Mother, Lord Thorane, I would like to present to you my brother, Thaddeus Schiffer."

Thaddeus bowed, imitating Chami's courtly gesture. It came out endearingly clumsy.

"An honor and pleasure to meet you, Queen Mother, Lord Thorane," Thaddeus murmured.

"Everyone please have a seat," the Queen Mother said. She

gestured Thaddeus to the chair across from her; Lord Thorane, the only one she had brought for this secure and private
conversation, remained standing behind her. As a courtesy,
the rest of us took seats near the front of the cabin where Lord
Thorane could easily see all of us.

"I am glad we are able to meet, rushed though our time
must be," the Queen Mother said graciously to Thaddeus.
"Pray tell me, now, in your own words, how you came to
discover your ability to Bask."

She listened intently while Thaddeus awkwardly recited
the past events. His first experience with Basking had been
when outlaw rogues had snatched me to replace the Queen
I had freed from their enslavement. I had drawn down the
moon's rays.

Surrounded by Monères, feeling the tug himself, Thaddeus had instinctively pulled down the moonlight as well, to
the amazement of us all.

"You shared this light with others?" the Queen Mother
asked.

"Yes, with the rogues who were standing nearest me,"
Thaddeus answered.

"It was witnessed by Mona Lisa, Lord Amber, and myself,"
Chami confirmed, "along with six others."

"Have you Basked since that time?" she asked.

"No, milady. At that time, we decided it would be safest if
I hid that ability. I got the impression that the other Queens
wouldn't be happy to learn a male was able to do what, up till
now, had solely been a Queen's gift."

"And now?"

"Now," Thaddeus said, grinning widely, "it'll be only a
small shock compared to what Mona Lisa, Amber, and the
others here will be unleashing on everyone shortly."

"A much smaller threat, indeed," the Queen Mother said, smiling slightly.

"Plus," he shrugged, "the people here need me. It's no big deal for me to take my sister's place."

I added, "Thaddeus and Aquila have been pretty much overseeing all the business affairs without any input from me. As you saw from our tithe, we've been doing pretty well. He might as well have the official title to go along with the job he's been doing."

The Queen Mother smiled. "Ah, yes, the title. What shall it be, for the first Basking male in our history?"

"Well, you can't call me a Queen, that's for sure," Thaddeus said, grimacing.

I grinned. "What, you don't like Mona Thaddeus? It has a nice ring to it, don't you think?"

My brother shot me a quelling look.

The Queen Mother raised a hand to her lips, hiding her amusement. "I think in this matter we shall stay within tradition, nontraditional though it may be." At her nod, Lord Thorane drew a small case from the overhead compartment. Inside was a gold medallion chain similar to the one Amber wore.

At Lord Thorane's command to kneel, Thaddeus dropped to his knees before the Queen Mother. With graceful economy of movement, she took the heavy medallion chain from the case and slipped it over his head. "By the power of the moon, our ancestral planet, I hereby bestow upon you the title of Lord Thaddeus and assign you ruler of the territories of Louisiana and West Mississippi, recombined back into one whole land. Hereon, thereafter, all courtesy and respect are to be granted to you in accordance to your status by the laws of our High Council. May our Mother Moon always shine upon you. May her light always be your guide."

Thaddeus rose, dazzled by the brief ceremony despite himself.

It would take a little while before he started to feel not just the physical but the nonphysical weight of that medallion necklace, and all it represented.

Lord Thorane, then Amber, embraced their new brother, the only three living Monère males with that rare elevated status.

"If you have any questions, call me," Lord Thorane offered generously. "For now, we must hasten to depart."

"That reminds me—my gifts before I leave you guys," Thaddeus said, grabbing the three shopping bags Chami passed to him. Opening one, he handed three boxes to Lord Thorane. "Here, my lord, these are for the Queen Mother: I bought three disposable cell phones with prepaid minutes, which will expire in sixty days. Here's yours, sis," he said, passing the second bag to me. Inside were six boxes exactly like the ones he had handed Lord Thorane.

"This last bag is for the rest of you guys: Amber, Dontaine, and the Morells. Everything's labeled with your names. I bought this stuff while you guys were packing. Thought it'd be safer if you swapped your old cell phones for these new ones. I paid for everything in cash, that way no one can trace your accounts back to Louisiana. The phones already out of their boxes are for your daily regular use; each has a hundred prepaid minutes on them."

"I didn't think of that," I said, handing him my old phone.

"It's amazing you guys were ready to fly out to DC less than three hours after deciding to radically change your lives, and everyone else's in the world. You're not alone, sis. Don't forget that."

After collecting all the old phones, he handed everyone a

sheet of paper with all the new numbers, including the three new cell phones he had bought for himself.

"I used initials for everyone," Thaddeus said. The Queen Mother was QM. I was ML. "For the disposable phones, and I really do mean that—they're only meant for onetime use—I labeled each phone respectively as number one, two, three, four, five, and six. You should use the phones numbered one, two, and three in that order. For example, Lisa, if you need to call the Queen Mother, you use the cell phone labeled number one, place your call, then deactivate your phone after you've finished talking to her. Same with her."

He demonstrated by removing the battery and the small SIM memory disc from his own cell phone. "Throw away the phone and battery, and crush the SIM card. They won't be able to trace the call or pinpoint the Queen Mother's location that way. The next time—let's say the Queen Mother needs to call you this time, Lisa—she uses phone number two, and both of you destroy your SIM cards and throw away your second deactivated phones as soon as you're done talking. Use numbers four, five, and six to call me. And here's the name and address of the hospital where they took Jarvis and the girl," Thaddeus said, stuffing more sheets of paper into my hands, "along with a listing of hotels and motels nearby. Also some lawyers in the area specializing in criminal law. You'll probably need a lawyer to get Jarvis out of the cops' hands if he's still at the hospital, if you decide to go about it the legal way."

"Cops? Why would cops be there?" I asked. "He didn't do anything wrong."

"Other than fly out of a nineteenth-story window using wings, which he then transformed back into arms. All captured nicely on late-night news. Cops will be the least of it, sis," Thaddeus said. "You'll probably have FBI, maybe even Homeland Security swarming around, wanting to take him into custody."

I felt a sudden urgent need to be off, instead of being grounded here on the runway.

"Almost done," Thaddeus said, reading my tense expression. "There's a list of three large law firms I found in DC specializing in public law and policy, and American Indian law—the closest thing I could think of to our situation. I don't know if these firms are the best, just what I could find quickly on the Internet."

"My smart and brilliant brother," I said, impressed by his foresight. "I think all the brains went to you."

"Then you must have gotten all the guts. Go rock the world, sis," Thaddeus murmured, hugging me good-bye.

Over his shoulder, I exchanged a nod with Chami, passing my brother's care into his hands.

"My thanks as well, Lord Thaddeus," said the Queen Mother, wearing a pleased smile. "One of the most practical gifts I have ever received."

My brother ducked his head with embarrassed pleasure.

The Queen Mother handed Thaddeus a small business card. "Call this number and speak with my man, Raiden. He'll help you transfer things over into your name."

With a final wave of thanks and farewell, Thaddeus and Chami departed the plane.

Less than ten minutes later, we were airborne.

TWENTY-FOUR

"A MOST UNUSUALLY intelligent and gifted young man," the Queen Mother observed as our small jet lifted into the air.

"Yeah, Thaddeus is special. And he has good people watching him but . . . can you do what you can to keep him safe?" I asked.

"You have my word. Next to you, he is perhaps the most well suited to helping us bridge our two worlds."

"I'll be using my real name, Lisa Hamilton. Will they be able to trace that back to him and Belle Vista?"

"I do not know. Raiden will work quickly to eradicate your name from all records and scrub as many memories as possible before you bring the news of our existence to the public. By the way, when do you plan to make your announcement?"

"Today, after I secure Jarvis."

"What about on your end? Any acquaintances you made that will lead back to your brother?"

I shook my head. "No, only a few people at the new high

school in Louisiana, when I registered Thaddeus there, but they may not remember me; my hair's a different style and color now. And Thaddeus has a different last name than mine."

"Any credit cards or checking accounts that you opened up yourself?"

"Nothing but what you established for me."

"Then we should hopefully be able to keep Thaddeus sheltered from the public arena for now. But what about the Morells? Do you intend to use their real names?"

"If it pleases you, Queen Mother," Nolan answered "that would be preferable. My sons, Dante and Quentin, have birth certificates, Social Security numbers, and school records in their name. Legal citizens of the United States. The rest of us are, in their eyes, apart from Mona Lisa, illegal aliens."

Quentin grinned. "They may not consider me and Dante American citizens, not with us being Monère. Only you, Mona Lisa. You're part human."

"A quarter. Does that mean I only have a quarter of their rights? Never mind. That'll be a matter for whatever lawyer we hire. But the Queen Mother has a good point. Are there any records leading back to Louisiana, to Thaddeus?"

"Our cell phone records," Dante answered. "And my family's been out in the community—the supermarket, the mall. Someone might remember seeing us."

"Me as well," said Dontaine. "There are many people who will recognize me from New Orleans."

"Crap. I forgot your friends who did my makeover," I said, rubbing my temples. "Okay, so once they start digging, they'll likely be able to track us to New Orleans."

"But not to Belle Vista. Not to Thaddeus," Dontaine said, squeezing my arm in comfort.

"The threads are there," I said. "It just depends on how deep they dig into our pasts—and I have a feeling they're going to be willing to dig as far as China." I blew out a breath. "Thaddeus knows the risk, that he might be pulled into this. But I'd like to keep him out of it for as long as I can." I looked at the Queen Mother and Lord Thorane. "The location of High Court must remain secret as well. But in all other things, I wish to speak plainly about ourselves."

That launched us all into heated discussion for the next three hours of our flight as we ironed out the parameters of our mission and what we would and would not be revealing to the rest of the world.

"You wish to expose our weakness?" Lord Thorane exclaimed, his brows beetling together. "How to capture us, kill us?"

"Our weaknesses as well as our strengths. The truth," I insisted. "We cannot lie to them."

"How much of the truth?" asked the Queen Mother.

"Everything about us. But we leave out mention of other realms. No demon dead, no Hell, no NetherHell. Oh, and no mention of reincarnation or curses, either. We'll introduce those concepts to them later," I said, and refrained from glancing at Dante. "For now, it will be enough for people to swallow down what a normal Monère is capable of. But everything else is fair game. We tell them all the good and bad about us, and how we are trying to change. I know—I'm pushing the boundaries. But if we fail, I want to fail big. Not from lack of trying. And definitely not from misinformation."

The Queen Mother considered it for a long, quiet moment, then finally nodded. "Very well, tell them the truth about us. I agreed to try and let you carve out your own path. We shall see where it leads us. I only request that you keep our weaknesses secret for now. You can reveal them if and when you are questioned before their legislative courts or government—when you have a serious chance of gaining us rights. Not before. No need to make it easier for them to kill you before then."

It was far more than I had expected. A part of me was euphoric. Another part was terrified now. We would either win . . . or mess up big-time.

"Your brother provided you with much of what you will need," the Queen Mother said, smiling fondly in remembrance of my brother's gifts. "This is our contribution."

Lord Thorane retrieved another briefcase from the overhead bin. "The combination is three-six-seven," he said, setting it on my lap. He opened the briefcase, revealing more money than I'd ever seen in my entire life. There were stacks of twenties, one bundle of fifties, and another of one hundreds. The bottom row were all in much higher currency denominations—five-hundred-, one-thousand-, and five-thousand-dollar bills. I fanned through the last stack and found several ten-thousand-dollar bills. "I didn't even know they made these. Is this money real?" I asked.

The Queen Mother chuckled. "They are not counterfeit, if that is what you are asking."

"My God, how much is this?"

"A million dollars," was her answer. "I am sorry I could not give you more seed money to start with. It was all we had available—all that we can give you for now, and probably even after you gain our people rights."

It was nice how she stated that as a foregone conclusion: that I would succeed in gaining us those rights.

"I understand," I said. "You'll have to limit your contact with us to keep the location of High Court secret.

Don't worry, this is more than enough—much more than I expected, actually."

"It will help fund the legal fight you have ahead of you. But money, you will find, goes rather quickly. Use it well. It will not be enough to establish your first District Court."

"It may go further than you expected, Queen Mother," Quentin said, examining the higher currency bills. "Some of these are dated from the early 1900s. They may be worth more than double their printed value to currency dealers and collectors."

"Part of the money was from a reserve we kept for emergency use," Lord Thorane said. "Money that has been sitting in our vault for a long time."

"Are you saying this is the Monère's first real emergency?" I asked. The plane began to descend, setting off a flutter of nerves—both a physical response and in emotional anticipation of our imminent arrival.

"Not so much emergency as a chosen strike," corrected the Queen Mother. "A deliberate move on a chessboard, grasping an ideal opportunity that has presented itself."

"Well, let's hope all our pieces don't get knocked over," I muttered, gripping the armrest.

"Especially the Queen," rumbled Amber.

I glanced at my watch. "It's almost eight in the morning. Quentin, can you turn on the screen and see what the news is saying?"

The morning news was saying plenty. Every one of those channels was featuring updates on Jarvis, who was listed in critical condition.

"It's been ten hours," Hannah, our healer, observed. "He should have healed his most severe burns by now."

"That's probably how they admitted him," I said. "I bet

the hospital isn't talking to reporters yet, and they're just going with his last known status."

"I'm surprised he hasn't flown the coop by now," Quentin murmured.

"And go where?" asked Dante. "He knows there'll be Monère warriors waiting for him as soon as he steps out of the hospital, after all the public attention he's drawn. He broke our number one rule: to keep our existence secret from humans. The poor bastard's probably wondering why someone hasn't already come to kill him."

The busy reporters had finally managed to dig up some names. Kelly Rawlings for the girl. Eighteen years old. An orphan who was adopted but ran away from home at fifteen to live on the streets. For the winged wonder, they had the name Jarvis Condorizi.

"He was a quiet guy. Never said a word," said a neighbor, glancing away from the reporter into the camera. "The two of them kept to themselves."

"She's a waitress at my restaurant," said another nervous, bald man they interviewed. "Jarvis bused tables and washed dishes. They work part-time, during the day; wouldn't stay once it got dark."

Quentin flipped to another channel where a reporter was speaking to a fireman who remembered seeing Jarvis coming on the scene. "He just dropped this bag and then was suddenly gone. Must have ran past me up into the building, but I didn't see him or I woulda stopped him." The camera zoomed in on an old burlap bag opened to reveal two dead mallards inside.

The poor guy had probably dropped off the girl at home, then gone out hunting, returning to see his building up in flames. It was easy visualizing the rest. After determining Kelly wasn't among the crowd outside, he must have run inside the burning building and made his way up to the nineteenth floor only to find the girl trapped, with the fire blocking their way back down, though not for him. Jarvis could have survived the fire, the lack of oxygen, had he zipped back down through the flames, but not a human. A human would not have been able to survive.

"I wonder what the girl is to him," I said thoughtfully.

"Not lovers," Dontaine said with certainty. "She's human."

"Not necessarily true," I said, shaking my head. "She might be a Mixed Blood. They said she was an orphan, remember." Like I myself had been. Left on the doorsteps of an orphanage. "The other Monère watching him wouldn't be able to sense that unless they got in close to her. If she's a Mixed Blood, it wouldn't be unpleasant for him to mate with her."

"Whatever they are, lovers or friends, he risked a hell of a lot for her," said Dante grimly.

It seemed like forever before we finally touched down. And then, once we did, it suddenly seemed as if time had flown by much too quickly, and much too soon we were bidding farewell to the Queen Mother and Lord Thorane—my last physical contact with them in who knew how long.

"May the Goddess bless you, keep you, and guide you," said the Queen Mother in warm benediction. One last quick embrace, and then we were on our own, armed with disposable cell phones, a list of names, and a million dollars in cash.

Our first expenditure was renting a passenger van with a portable GPS navigation system, the type you stick on the front windshield via suction cup.

Quentin punched in the address for the Residence Inn that we decided would be the best place to stay. It was two miles away from the hospital, and less crowded than a hotel, easier for us to exit. I flipped open my new cell phone while he drove, and dialed the first number my brother had printed out on his list.

"Adams, McManus, and Kent. How may I help you?" answered a receptionist's pleasant voice.

"Oh, good, you're open," I said, breathing a sigh of relief. "I need a good criminal attorney."

"We have four attorneys in our office who practice criminal defense," said the woman in a smooth professional tone. "Which one would you like?"

I wanted to say *the best one*, but more pertinent was, "Who do you have in the office right now that I can speak to?"

"Mr. McManus is here. The others will be in later at nine."

McManus. One of the partners. Highly driven or at least highly disciplined, if he came in earlier than everyone else. "Is he good? I need someone very aggressive and experienced."

"Mr. McManus is our most experienced criminal defense attorney in the firm. I should also tell you that he charges the highest rate."

That reassured me more than anything else. "Can I speak to him, please?"

"May I ask what this is regarding?"

"It's about the man they're calling 'an angel' on the news, the one who flew out of a burning building. I'm hoping Mr. McManus will agree to represent him."

A momentary pause that went on just a tad too long before she recovered and said, "Hold on, please."

A few seconds later, a rich, deep voice came on the line. "George McManus here. What can I do for you?"

"My name is Mona Lisa," I began automatically.

"Like the painting?" Derision seeped into the deep baritone voice. "Look, lady, isn't it a bit early to be starting prank calls?"

Well, crap, this wasn't beginning well. "Forgive me," I said stiffly. "My full legal name is Lisa Hamilton, and I'm looking to obtain legal representation for the man calling himself Jarvis Condorizi."

"The winged wonder? And why would you do that, Ms. Hamilton? Are you a relative of his?"

In a very distant way, I could say, but I had a feeling any more of what McManus perceived as nonsense, and he would just hang up the phone. I chose my next words carefully. "No, I'm an interested party that wishes to see his rights protected, and I am willing to pay you for any service you might render in that regard."

As I'd imagined, talk of money grounded the conversation more firmly. "Has he broken any law?" McManus asked, getting down to business. "Done any criminal acts?"

"All he's broken, as far as I know, is the window of his apartment building."

"Then why do you need my services?"

"Because I'm on my way right now to get him out of the hospital, and I need someone with legal clout to help me ease him gently out of the hands of the police officers, FBI, and whoever else might happen to be there with him. Is that something you see as within your abilities?"

"Police, yes. FBI, maybe not if they're paranoid and view him as a threat to national security, or as an alien from outer space." Which he actually happened to be, I thought, wincing, though many generations down the line.

His words ran a chill through me, but I was glad to see McManus taking my proposal more seriously. "Then all I ask is that you do your best to get me in to see him, and I will take it from there."

"Are you a friend of his?"

"Yes." That I could answer truthfully—though my interpretation of *friend* was not what Mr. McManus had really intended.

"I charge a lot of money, Ms. Hamilton. Four hundred dollars an hour, and I require an upfront retainer of one thousand dollars."

"No problem. I can pay you the retainer in cash."

"There's no guarantee, you understand?"

"I know," I said, feeling better about him. Tough and no nonsense—a fighter, by the way he was willing to lash into me, but he seemed to be honest. "Just do your best to keep him from being taken into custody."

"That I can promise you to do."

"Good. I'll meet you in front of Washington Hospital in half an hour."

"Wait a second. I'm not stepping out of my office without a paid retainer first. This could all be a waste of my time, a big hoax."

"Come on," I snorted. "Don't tell me the idea of being Jarvis Condorizi's lawyer isn't enough to get your ass out of that office, however remote the chance might be. What, you're too shy to speak to all the reporters waiting outside and get your face plastered on all the news channels? Give me a break. That type of exposure will be worth more to you and your law firm than what I'm going to pay you, which I'm quite sure in and of itself will be quite substantial. But hey, if you aren't willing to take a small risk, so be it. I'll just move on to the next lawyer on my list."

McManus gave a short barking laugh, the least polished I'd heard that carefully cultivated voice become. "It seems you've got some balls on you, Ms. Hamilton. All right, I'll meet you in the hospital lobby, but this had better be for real."

"Oh, no worries on that," I assured him. Sorting through

the papers, I pulled out the other list Thaddeus had given me. "By the way, I'm also looking for a good law firm specializing in public law and policy." And read aloud to him the names of the three law firms on the list. "Which one do you recommend?"

"You're talking about a lot of money here, to hire any one of those firms you just mentioned."

"Fortunately, I happen to have a lot of money at the moment."

His silence expressed skepticism, but he did give me a name. Thanking him I hung up and a short while later we were pulling off the road into the hotel parking lot. We parked around the side of the building in the shade. Hannah went inside to register us, loaded with a bunch of fifty- and one-hundred-dollar bills, while the rest of us waited in the van.

I took the opportunity to call the firm McManus had said was the best. The phone call, this time, started out better as I introduced myself as Lisa Hamilton. But it came to a notable hiccup when the receptionist, an older woman by the sound of her voice, asked what I needed, refusing to let me speak to someone until she knew what the matter was about.

"Do you know the winged man they're talking about on the news?"

"Yes," she replied.

"It's about him. Getting rights for him and other people like him," I said, hoping that would be enough to pass me along to someone else.

"What . . . angels?" she said in a distinctly dry tone of voice.

"No, he's actually a bird-shifter," I corrected, then could have kicked myself because now the woman's voice became clearly sarcastic.

"And are you a bird-shifter also?" she asked, saccharine sweet.

"No," I gritted, "but I do have his best interest in mind, and I would like to speak to someone experienced in public law and policy who might be able to help him and others like him."

"Oh," she said, drawing out the word mockingly, obviously humoring me by playing along in this silly game of pretend. "So you're saying there *are* others like him."

Her words and tone of voice had me gnashing my teeth. I took in a careful breath and said, "All I ask is that you keep watching the news and take down my phone number so you have somewhere to call if you do eventually decide someone in your office might want to speak to me." I repeated my name and telephone number twice, then hung up.

"This is not going to be easy," I said, exhaling a long, frustrated breath. "I'm getting a feeling people aren't going to believe us when we tell them who we are, even after what they saw Jarvis do."

"Not until you show them that we're not human," Quentin said, his face as grim as everyone else in the van who had heard the conversation.

"Speak for yourself!" I said. "Just kidding. No, I know what you mean."

Hannah returned with some key cards in hand. "I booked two suites right next to each other. Each with two bedrooms and a living room area with a queen sofa pullout bed. I thought that would be better than single rooms."

"It is, good thinking." She gave the change and receipt to me and I shoved the bundle at Dontaine. "Dontaine, can you take care of this? Keep track of all our expenses?"

"Of course," he answered.

"Good," Quentin said, peering sideways at me. "I thought

you were going to shove that responsibility on me, as well as driving the van, handling the GPS, and handling every other aspect involved with modern living."

"Complaining already, Quentin?" I opened the door and got out. "I thought you wanted to be seen as more than a pretty face or body. Or are you missing Mona Maretta already?"

"Ouch! Low blow," Quentin said. But his light teasing did what the smart boy had intended, easing me out of the somber mood I had fallen into.

Quentin, Nolan, and Hannah took the first suite. My three lovers and I took the next suite. Our rooms were nicely situated in the back, not visible from the road.

I dumped my three cases on the floor. "Okay, let's go."

"Not so fast," said Dontaine, taking my suitcases into a bedroom. Opening the bag that contained my dressier clothes, he hung them neatly in the closet. "Which one do you wish to wear?" he asked.

"You want me to change?" I glanced down at the jeans, T-shirt, and sneakers that I had on, and didn't see anything wrong with what I was wearing. No holes or stains or anything; they weren't even frayed.

Amber and Dante remained in the living room, their faces carefully blank. I got the feeling, however, they were both secretly amused.

"When you declare our existence to the world today, you will be representing us all," Dontaine said, smoothing the wrinkles out of one of the full-length black dresses I had brought—what Monère Queens usually wore. "It would be nice if you were dressed more presentably."

"Nuh-uh," I said, shaking my head. "No way am I going to wear a long, black formal gown."

I wanted to say, *You can't make me*, but better inspiration came to me. "If the other Queens are going to remain in hiding, we don't want to make it easy for humans to find them, right? So a black gown is definitely out. Plus, wearing all black is pretty severe. I don't want to go out looking like Morticia or anything."

"Morticia?" asked Amber.

"From *The Addams Family*. An old TV show," Dante explained.

My poor Warrior Lord didn't look any further enlightened.

"Hmm, you have a point. Perhaps something more colorful would be better," Dontaine said, his eye moving to a bright scarlet dress.

In defense, I grabbed an outfit Dontaine's friend in New Orleans, a professional dresser, had put together for me—gold slacks paired with a light green oriental shirt, and ivory ballet slippers. It was elegant and sophisticated, and much less gaudy than the scarlet dress he had been considering.

"No dress or high heels," I asserted firmly, stepping into the bathroom to change. "I might need to run if we have to make a quick getaway."

When I stepped out of the bathroom, I was met with the appreciative stares of three pairs of masculine eyes. The gleam in Dontaine's eyes was just a touch too satisfied, telling me I'd just been had. I walked over and hit him in the arm.

"What was that for?" Dontaine asked. Had he been human, he might have said *Ow!* and rubbed his arm. But tough Monère warriors apparently didn't do that.

"You played me," I accused.

"I don't know what you're talking about," Dontaine replied innocently, but a pleased smirk leaked out despite his best efforts to suppress it. Amber and Dante didn't even try to hide their grins from me.

Unable to help myself, I smiled. "Okay, Slick. You got me to change into a nice outfit. Let's go now."

"Three more minutes," Dontaine said, dangling my makeup bag in front of me with a pleading, coaxing look that clearly said, *Please, milady, you're going to be representing us all.*

Giving in, I sat down at the end of the bed. "No more than three minutes," I grumped, looking at my watch. "I'll be counting."

Using a deft, steady hand and full Monère speed, he had my hair and makeup done with ten seconds to spare: a quick application of smoky eye shadow, contouring blush, and red lipstick; my hair was a simple brush out, a squirt of gel onto his hands, and artful scrunching. Simple things that somehow gave me a salon-styled look.

A complete transformation, I noted, looking in the mirror. "I don't know how you do that, Dontaine."

"It's all in the hands," Dontaine said with a wink, "and a good haircut. Now we are ready to go."

And we were, I saw, running my appreciative gaze over the three gorgeous men behind me who had also taken the time to change into neater attire, making them even more mouthwateringly scrumptious.

I smiled in sudden anticipation. "Watch out, world. Ready or not, here we come."

TWENTY-FIVE

"THERE'S QUITE A crowd of reporters," Hannah said worriedly as we came in sight of the hospital. We had parked the van three blocks down and walked the remaining distance, in case we needed to make a quick, anonymous getaway.

"I'm picking up three Monère guards posted around the hospital," I said. The local territory Queen's men.

"Me, too," Amber confirmed. His golden eyes scanned the area, lingering with unease on the crowd of reporters and cameramen restlessly gathered thirty feet away from the front entrance in an area that had been sectioned off with yellow tape by the police, who were also quite visibly present. I saw two squad cars, counted three police officers outside, and glimpsed a dark uniform inside the glass entrance doors.

"Amber, can you stay out here and stand guard, in case our arrival spooks Jarvis into flying out another window?" I asked, looking up at our most conspicuous member. "I know the Queen Mother informed the local Queen not to touch

Jarvis, but your presence out here might keep her men from overreacting if he tries to bust out unexpectedly."

Amber agreed with obvious relief. He glanced up at the hospital, looking puzzled. "That's odd. I'm not sensing Jarvis at all."

"Neither am I," I said, "but it's a stone building. If the walls inside the hospital are built with cinder blocks like the hospital I used to work in, it'll mask most, if not all, of his presence."

Mr. McManus was seated in the waiting area and was easy to pick out. He looked exactly like what he was: a high-priced attorney, wearing a three-piece suit and spit-polish black shoes. Beneath the bushiest eyebrows I'd ever seen, sharp intelligence gleamed out from a pair of deep-set eyes. Wavy russet hair, sprinkled with distinguished gray, framed a craggy, strong-boned face. An expensive-looking briefcase sat by his feet, and the fingers of his right hand drummed impatiently as he scanned the faces of everyone entering. His gaze touched on us briefly, then moved on.

His sharp eyes swung back, refocusing on me as I made my way over to him.

"Mr. McManus, I presume?" I said, extending my hand. "I'm Lisa Hamilton. Thank you for meeting me here."

"You're much younger than I expected," he said, frowning as he shook my hand.

"And you sound even better in person than you do over the phone," I returned. I had been expecting his voice to be less vibrant somehow, but it was even richer and more resonant in person, almost professional quality like what you heard announcing commercials.

"How old are you?" McManus demanded, his bushy brows scrunching together like caterpillars wriggling toward each other.

"Twenty-one. Don't worry, I'm legal." In that one sense of the word, at least. "Let me introduce my friends to you."

Everyone exchanged courteous nods.

"Here—before I forget," I said, handing him the thousand-dollar retainer fee. The cash was wrapped in a sheet of hotel stationery with the top letterhead ripped off, leaving just a blank sheet. An envelope would have been nicer, but all of them had been imprinted with the hotel's name and address.

McManus counted the money and slipped it inside his suit pocket. He glanced at me, waiting expectantly. When nothing more was forthcoming, he said, "One pointer, Ms. Hamilton. Always ask for a receipt in any cash transactions."

A good point, though it made me feel as young as he said I looked. Business transactions were not my forte. "Can I have a receipt?" I asked.

McManus took out a business card and printed out the amount he had received on the back. Dating and signing it, he handed it to me, completing our transaction.

I pocketed the business card/receipt. "So are we your clients now?"

His thick brows twitched. "I thought you were engaging my services to represent Jarvis Condorizi solely."

"For the most part. But if I and my friends get into trouble upstairs, I trust you'll come to our aid as well."

"Of course. But that will increase my time, and your expense."

"Understood." We walked to the bank of elevators, bypassing the visitor's desk.

"You know where he is?" McManus asked when I pushed the "up" elevator button.

"The burn center, most likely." The elevator doors opened, and I entered, holding the door while the rest trooped inside.

"Don't you need a visitor's pass?" McManus asked.

"I thought it would be better just to go straight up. Your presence should be enough to get us in."

Clearly, McManus didn't like this, but he didn't comment. Scanning the directory posted on the wall, I pushed the button for the fourth floor.

"Not all of you will be able to see him," McManus said as the doors closed and we started going up.

"Most of them will wait outside the burn unit. It'll just be Hannah and me, and you, of course, going in to see Jarvis."

Dontaine, Nolan, and Dante turned to gaze at me. Only Quentin seemed unconcerned.

"He is a wounded male," said Dontaine too quietly for McManus to hear.

"Which is why it would be best if only Hannah and I went in," I answered. "The presence of other males will only agitate him."

"And a Queen's presence will not?" Dante asked with acerbic bite.

"Consider me both bait and protection for Hannah," I murmured. "Don't worry, Nolan. I'll make sure he doesn't hurt Hannah."

"It is both of your safety I am concerned about," Nolan said.

"Mona Lisa is right," Hannah said quietly. "This way will be the least threatening to Jarvis, and therefore the safest for us."

"Excuse me, did you say something?" McManus asked, glancing at me. He had obviously seen my lips moving.

"No, just talking to myself," I answered blithely.

That didn't appear to lend him any more confidence in me, but at this point I didn't care as the lift came to a gentle halt and the doors opened to the fourth floor.

We left the men waiting unhappily in the sitting area and

made our way to the Trauma and Burn Center. Visiting hours were posted on the glass doors, from nine a.m. to nine p.m. It was a few minutes past nine. Perfect timing, though our number of visitors was not as ideal. Most hospitals allowed only two visitors in at a time, not three, and only relatives were permitted into the intensive care units.

Then we were in the burn unit and the smell of it hit my sensitive nose—burnt flesh beneath the astringent, industrial smell all hospitals had. I caught the feel of Monère presence, but that, too, was faint, much fainter than it should have been, but I would have known, even had I not felt him, where Jarvis was. There were two policemen posted outside the room directly across from the nurses' station, with a crowd of other bodies inside and outside of the room: nurses in their flowered-top scrubs and young-looking doctors in white coats and dark blue scrubs. Hospital interns and residents, I realized with a start. Must be a teaching hospital. Two FBI types stood outside the room next to two seated police officers. There was almost an equal number of people inside his room gathered around the bed, all of them gloved and gowned, blocking my view of the occupant.

McManus stopped in front of the nurses' station, waiting patiently for one of the busy nurses. But what I felt made me too uneasy to wait.

"I can't discern his heartbeat," I said to Hannah. Everything was beating human fast, and that should not be; Jarvis's heart should have been half the normal rate, but everything I heard was going at least sixty to eighty beats a minute. The only reason for a Monère's heart to beat that fast was extreme stress or severe injury. And it wasn't because he had sensed us: none of the heartbeats had sped up. That, coupled with the weak presence I felt emanating from him, had me severely worried.

"He shouldn't be this weak," I said softly to Hannah.

"No, milady, he shouldn't," Hannah agreed.

"We can't wait. Follow me."

I dashed past the guards, moving at full, blurring Monère speed, and entered the room, dodging around bodies until I saw him. And then I stopped, frozen solid with shock and dismay.

"Oh no," I whispered.

My words, the feel of my presence, drew Jarvis's eyes directly to me, past all the people gathered around his bed.

There was a sudden exclamation as people caught sight of me and Hannah. *Hey, who are you? You can't come in here without a gown! How did you people get inside the room?* But I had eyes and ears for only one person—Jarvis.

Ash-blond hair curled in loose waves around the lower strands singed. He had the face of an angel, an archangel, with strong, noble features and vivid blue eyes. No wonder people were calling him an angel.

Those blue eyes grew huge and wide, the only part of him that moved. The rest of him was still.

He lay on his stomach, facing the far end of the room where Hannah and I stood. His face was the only visible part of him that was not burned. A tented-sheet canopy had been erected over him and I caught a glimpse of his neck and upper arms from where I stood: they were completely scorched, ugly charred burns mixed with raw, blistered flesh, everything smeared liberally with a gooey paste.

An older doctor sitting near the bed turned around to look at me, unblocking some of my view so I could see the unblemished back of Jarvis's lower thighs and calves emerging from the other end of the tented canopy. As I watched, the IV catheter the doctor had just inserted into the back of Jarvis's knee was slowly pushed back out, the white anchoring tape no match for the strong rejection of Jarvis's body to the inserted foreign object.

The doctor muttered a foul curse and glared at Hannah and me, as if we were to blame for what must have been the one-hundredth failed attempt to put an intravenous line into him.

"Please," Jarvis said, looking at me with clear panic in his eyes. He had been so utterly still, not even breathing, so that it was like watching a rock suddenly come alive as he levered himself up off the bed, disrupting the canopy above him.

Amidst the sudden uproar of voices, Jarvis slid down to kneel in front of me, his horribly burned arms spread out wide, out to his side. "Please, milady, she's innocent. She doesn't know anything."

Only then did I realize the protective nature of his gesture.

The *she* he referred to was the girl Jarvis had leaped out of bed, stark naked, to shield: the young teenager sitting on the other side of the bed, Kelly Rawlings, the runaway. Both of her hands were swathed in white bandages up to the forearm. Had Jarvis been at full strength, I would not have felt her much weaker presence—a Mixed Blood, as I had suspected. But with his energy signature almost as weak as hers, it was easy to discern.

Jarvis thought I was here to kill him and the girl.

"I'm here to help you," I told him, "not to harm either of you."

He stayed kneeling, clearly not trusting my words, begging me with his eyes to spare the girl's life. For his own life, not one word or plea.

"Jarvis, what are you doing?" the girl exclaimed. "Get back in bed. You'll infect your wounds!"

"Stretch out your senses, Jarvis, and see for yourself that I am like her," I told him.

He did and his eyes widened even more in confusion. "But . . . you are a Queen."

"And also a Mixed Blood. I give my word, I am here only to help."

"What is the meaning of this and who are you two?" demanded one of the suit-wearing men. There were two of them inside the room. Well, actually four of them now; the two others posted outside had come into the room as well.

"They are Jarvis Condorizi's friends," McManus said, pushing his way in past the interns, still tying up his gown. "And I am his attorney. Who are you?"

"FBI," the man snapped, flipping out his badge. "Special agent in charge, Richard Stanton. I wasn't aware he had asked for a lawyer."

"His friend here, Lisa Hamilton," he gestured to me, "obtained my services on his behalf."

I waved at Special Agent Stanton.

Stanton's brows, less bushier than McManus's, lowered in glowering disapproval. "And who the hell, Ms. Hamilton, are you?"

"I am a Monère Queen. A representative for our people." My cool and calm statement drew a shocked breath from Jarvis.

"Are you hurt?" Kelly asked, coming over to Jarvis.

"No, I'm fine, Kelly." He kept his arms spread, blocking her attempt to come around in front of him. "Sit down and stay behind me."

At his urging, she settled back into her seat, her brown eyes fixed intently on me, her gaze none too friendly.

"What's a Monère Queen?" Stanton demanded.

"Um—perhaps a sheet for his modesty," I said, waving a hand at Jarvis.

Kelly pulled a sheet off the bed and draped it over Jarvis's lap from behind.

"A Queen is what they call a lady of light," I explained. "Someone who is able to draw down the rays of the moon and share its energy with her people."

"And who the hell are your people?" asked Stanton.

"My friend, Hannah, here. And people like Jarvis," I answered. "Kelly, too, if she wishes."

Jarvis trembled almost violently at my words. I wasn't sure if it was dismay from what I was revealing to the humans here or from the agonizing pain from the burns and the position he still maintained, kneeling on the floor.

"That doesn't answer my question," Stanton growled. "Who are the Monère? I've never heard of them."

"We are the children of the moon," I answered. "Its descendents."

Jarvis made a horrible, panicked sound deep in his chest. "Please, milady. They may be able to hear you outside. You will bring them all down upon us."

"There's nothing to fear, Jarvis. I'm here at the request and approval of the High Court. I've been appointed an ambassador, of sorts, to represent our people. We're taking advantage of the opportunity you provided to go public."

The shock of my declaration, on top of his pain, proved too much for Jarvis. He swayed, looking faint, and I moved quickly, lightly grasping his face to keep him from falling.

With that contact, the moles in the palms of my hands flared to life and power was pulled from deep within me, drawn by Jarvis's pain. It flowed out of me and spread into him. Carefully, I stepped back and released him.

"You took away my pain," Jarvis said, looking at me with awe, trembling but no longer swaying unsteadily.

"Just the pain," I told him, "and only for a little while. Will you allow Hannah to lay hands on you? She is a healer."

My claim set off the disgruntled physician who had been

working on Jarvis when we had come in. "A healer? What can she do that we can't? I can't even get a blasted IV to stay inside him."

"His body will naturally expel any foreign object," Hannah explained, her gentleness and compassion obvious to everyone in the room. Turning back to Jarvis, she asked, "Will you allow me to help you?"

Jarvis nodded his silent assent.

Hannah came to stand in front of him and I moved back. Jarvis remained kneeling on the floor.

Everyone cried out in protest as, without ceremony, Hannah laid her ungloved hands gently on Jarvis's burnt shoulders and pushed down through the gel until her hands came in contact with his skin.

"Quiet!" I commanded, glaring at them. "None of you can help him, only she can. Let her work!"

"She'll infect his burn wounds!" sputtered the older doctor, obviously the senior physician in the room.

"We do not get infections," I said as I felt the gentle flare of Hannah's power. "Our body naturally heals our injury. He should have been half healed by now."

Agent Stanton snorted. "Then why hasn't he?"

"I don't know," I said, watching Hannah.

Agent Stanton and the doctor, whose name tag read *Dr. T. Hubert*, came around the bed to stand next to me, and saw most clearly what was happening as Hannah swept her hands down Jarvis's arms. Wherever her hands touched, the wounds healed into perfect unblemished skin, but only for a second. As soon as her hands moved on, the healed skin quickly melted back into angry, raw wounds.

"Dear lord!" gasped Dr. Hubert. At his words and expression, the rest of the onlookers crowded closer for a better view.

"Everyone stay where you are," Agent Stanton ordered sharply. "Agents Dutton and Maloney—over here."

The two agents made their way over to Stanton, McManus following behind them.

"I'm his attorney," McManus said, returning Stanton's glare. His jaw dropped, however, when he caught sight of what Hannah was doing to Jarvis's hands—the all too brief, temporary healing.

Hannah lifted her hands to Jarvis's unburned chest, hovered a moment over his heart, then moved her fingers down his abdomen.

"Is it the gel smeared over his skin, Hannah?" I asked. "Is it interfering with the healing?"

Pain and sadness darkened her compassionate eyes as she drew her hands away. "No, milady," Hannah said. "He's too injured for me to heal . . . too weak."

"Weak? How can he be too weak?" I asked. "He was powerful enough to be a threat to his Queen. Powerful enough to do a partial shift of just his arms."

"What energy he had, he used in their escape from the fire. He does not have any reserves left to heal himself. Mona Lisa . . . he's dying."

Kelly made a choked sound.

"I didn't know we could die from burn wounds," I said, astonished. Other than sun poisoning, I thought we could be killed only by having our heads severed or our hearts removed. Jarvis's head and heart were obviously intact.

"Neither did I. His heart is severely damaged—much like Amber's was when you first met him, almost dying from the punishment his Queen inflicted on him."

Hannah was talking about sunlight. Amber's former Queen had roasted Amber in bright sunlight. Was heat the common element? Had the burning heat of fire done to Jarvis what several hours of direct sunlight had done to Amber?

"There's nothing you can do?" I asked.

"No, I'm sorry, milady. It's beyond my ability—his heart and other organs are starting to shut down. He will start to fade soon. It's been too many years since he has Basked and it has weakened him."

"You and your family didn't appear weak, and you were rogues for twenty years. He's only been without a Queen's light for three years."

"We did weaken, but none of us were ever injured as severely as Jarvis. If we were, we might not have recovered, even with my healing talent."

"Who the hell are you people?" Agent Stanton said in a blustery demand.

"Quiet, please," I said. "I need to think."

The FBI agent bristled like a rooster. "I demand an explanation."

"I'll be happy to give you one," I said sharply, "but I'd like to see first if there's a way to save this man—if that's all right with you? Or do you not care if he lives or dies?"

"Your healer just said she can't save him," Dr. Hubert said, subdued, all his anger gone, eyeing us with curiosity and wariness now.

"Please, milady Queen," said Jarvis. "I don't mind dying. But Kelly—she's innocent. I've told her nothing of us. Please, I beg you to keep her safe from our people." Placing his injured hands on the floor with a squishy sound, he abased himself before me.

Kelly cried out and reached for him, but there was no safe place to put her hand. His back and shoulders were as raw and damaged as his poor arms and hands, and his head was too far away, bowed down at my feet.

I hadn't been flustered before—excited and nervous, yes, but not flustered like I was now.

People gasped. I felt my face flushing. "Um, Jarvis?"

"Yes, milady Queen."

"You have my word. Kelly will not be harmed. Now, please get up off the floor."

Jarvis slowly lifted up and rose to his feet. The relief I had started to feel evaporated as the sheet across his lap fell to the floor, leaving him naked in front of me.

He was a couple of inches taller than me, I noted, and fairly big. Maybe I should have been wary or frightened of him, a Monère warrior who was wounded, and therefore at his most dangerous. My men would certainly have had a conniption fit. But looking into those oddly defenseless, guileless blue eyes, it wasn't fear I felt, just more embarrassment—on his behalf and mine.

Carefully keeping my eyes fixed on Jarvis's face and chest, I bent and retrieved the fallen sheet, draping it low around him like a towel, keeping it below the burns ending just above his buttocks.

Kelly grasped the sheet behind him, and I left it to the girl to preserve her companion's modesty, more for our sakes than his—like most Monère he didn't seem to mind being naked. "Jarvis, can you lie back down on the bed, or would you prefer to sit in a chair?"

"A chair, please," said Jarvis.

Kelly brought her chair forward, and Jarvis eased himself down onto it.

Laying my hand on his chest, I drew away the additional pain the movement had caused, and he sighed a breath of relief. "Thank you, milady Queen."

"You can call me Mona Lisa, or just milady."

He nodded, ducking his head in a shy gesture that I

thought hugely ironic. Flashing a roomful of people didn't
faze him the slightest, but being allowed to address me by
name made him shy. It made me want to crush the neck of
the idiot Queen who had turned him rogue. He was a gallant
blend of meekness, courage, and odd innocence. He would
never be a threat to her or any other woman. His friend Kelly,
on the other hand, was an entirely different matter for all
that he sought to protect her. Though she was young, she
had a toughness in her eyes that he lacked. I wondered if that
was their relationship: he protected her physically, but she
watched over him in all other ways.

I closed my eyes a moment to shut out all the distraction.
I had a choice here. I could let Jarvis die. His death would
not hurt our cause; it might even help it, cementing his hero-
ism in the public eye. Or I could try to save him, and in
doing so, show more than I had intended this first round
and risk alienating people, frightening humans, and outrag-
ing Monère.

But I had no choice, really. I could not stand by and let
this valiant rogue die when I had the means and ability to
save him. I could only try to do it in the least shocking way
possible. Grabbing him and running was out of the question;
the bright rays of the morning sun outside would finish Jarvis
off. It would have to be here, in front of witnesses.

I turned to Agent Stanton. He was the real authority I
had to deal with here. "I can save him and heal him," I told
Stanton, "and everyone can stay and watch, but I will need
the help of one of my men. He'll be unarmed and won't make
any trouble as long as your men don't make any threatening
moves like drawing their guns."

"Our guns will stay in their holsters," Stanton said, "as
long as your guy doesn't make any aggressive moves in turn."

"He won't. I would appreciate it if you can inform the policemen stationed outside."

Stanton nodded to the agent next to him, and the man began winding his way through the crowd.

"Dr. Hubert," Stanton said, clearly irritated. "Can you clear out some of your people? It's too crowded in here."

The doctor kicked out two nurses and three young interns. That still left almost a dozen people in the room.

"Dontaine," I said in a normal tone of voice. "I need you."

A scarce moment later, I felt Dontaine's presence outside, heard him say politely, "Excuse me, please."

Dontaine entered the room in full, stunning glory. Everyone looked dazzled, no doubt expecting some big bruiser to enter, not someone who looked like a living, breathing Adonis. Dontaine didn't need a sword; he simply smote them all with a blinding smile. A few in the room embarrassingly came close to swooning, and not just the women, I noted.

"Tone it down a little, Dontaine, will you?" I said with a dry smile.

The wattage dimmed. "Yes, milady."

He walked straight to me, people parting before him like the waters of the Red Sea. The rogue, however, knew him for the threat he was.

"Easy, Jarvis," I said. "My word that Dontaine will not harm you or the girl. I need him to help me bring out my light to share with you."

By the sudden hot, sensual change in Dontaine's expression, I knew he had mistaken what I intended. *No*, I tried to convey in the severe look I shot him, *we're not having sex!*

"What are you talking about?" Agent Stanton asked. "Bring out what light?"

"Jarvis has not bathed in a Queen's light for six years;

that's why his energy is nearly depleted. I need Dontaine's help to ignite my light so I can share it with Jarvis, similar to what we do when we Bask, pulling down the moon's light."

"And how will this guy help you do that?" Agent Stanton asked, eyes narrowing.

"By kissing me. Nothing else," I said to Dontaine, making things clear. "Just kissing."

Dontaine's emerald bright eyes sparkled with a delight that was out of proportion to what I proposed, until I realized why he seemed so pleased. Because I had called him instead of Dante.

"And how will kissing you help bring out this light you're talking about?" Agent Stanton asked.

"We glow only in pleasure," I said, lifting my face to Dontaine. As Dontaine lowered his head to me, all my awareness of the watching audience, the nervous rogue, the skeptical FBI agent . . . all of it suddenly dimmed as Dontaine's mouth lowered until he was just a few inches away from my lips.

"Just a kiss?" Dontaine murmured. "Quite a challenge."

"I have full faith in you." I watched Dontaine's emerald eyes darken to forest green, watched his eyes dilate, the expanding black iris chasing the green color out to the very rim.

Those firm, lovely lips lowered to airbrush their way across my check, over my jaw, not touching, just the light, stimulating buzz of his presence against mine, and then those lips landed light as a butterfly on my neck, grazing the exact spot where Halcyon had sunk his teeth into me. It had long healed. No trace remained of my skin ever having been pierced there. But it was still incredibly sensitive.

I shivered, bit back a moan as I felt Dontaine's tongue with sudden, electrifying sensation. His teeth grazed skillfully, precisely, there against that invisible bite wound for an eye-rolling, heart-pounding moment before moving down the bend of my neck, torturous nibbles of pleasure mixed with that gentle buzz of sensation that was something I felt only with Dontaine whenever my skin contacted him. With delicate finesse, Dontaine slowly released more of his power into the contact until there was a significant bite, tiny electric shocks dancing along my skin, mixing the biting pain of it with the pleasure of his tongue, teeth, and lips, running it over and over where Halcyon had left his invisible mark.

I gasped, quivered.

"My lady," Dontaine said, his husky voice vibrating my ear. "You are alight."

My skin was glowing, soft and pearlescent, the inner moonlight we carried inside us brought to the fore. Jarvis gazed at me with wonder and hungry yearning in his eyes. The expression in Kelly's eyes, however, was not just wonder but fear. I felt the same reaction from others in the room, but had to shut it out and ignore it for now.

"Keep touching me, Dontaine," I murmured as I knelt by Jarvis's chair.

Dontaine's finger lightly stroked over my sensitive neck as I placed my hand on Jarvis's uninjured thigh. His body, the one part he could not voluntarily control, stirred, tenting the sheet covering his lap. I felt hunger in him, not just the normal physical desire of warrior for a Queen, but an even more visceral one of all the drained and depleted cells in his body thirsting for the illuminated light in my hand resting against his skin. So close and yet unable to pass across the barrier of his own unlit skin. It was partly from his weakened state and partly because, as I had explained, we glowed only in pleasure. Just resting my hand on his leg was apparently not eliciting enough pleasure.

I lifted my other hand to Jarvis's face. Felt him shiver beneath my touch as I leaned forward and kissed him with warm sensuality. He liked it, but not enough to glow. There was too much learned fear and intimidation of who and what I was—Queen—to relax into the desire. More drastic measures, like a hand job, were looking more and more eminent. But I really wanted to avoid that if I could. Not the greatest first impression to make here.

My glance shifted to Kelly, standing beside us. A stormy expression was in her young, street-hardened eyes. She hadn't liked me kissing Jarvis, not at all. Made me wonder if the nature of their relationship was less platonic, on her part, at least, than what I had presumed.

I drew back but still kept my hand on his thigh. "Kelly, maybe you should try. Kiss him. Try to bring out Jarvis's light."

Jarvis jerked beneath my hand. "No, milady, please. It's not like that between us. She's my friend—a child."

"Hush, Jarvis," I admonished, squeezing his thigh. "Kelly's hands are bandaged. She can't touch you any other way. I will not force her, if she does not wish to, but if she is willing, you must let her try."

"The *child*," said eighteen-year-old Kelly, "is willing."

"Kelly—"

"Shut up, Jarvis," she said, moving in front of him. "Close your eyes and think of England or something."

He made a rough sound of laughter that stopped abruptly when Kelly leaned forward and touched her mouth to his. It began as a chaste and gentle kiss, then slowly deepened, became more heated. His eyes closed, but I was pretty sure he wasn't thinking of England.

Light gathered slowly on Jarvis's skin like creeping dawn, just the faintest spark, but that was all I needed. The barrier between us dropped and my light rushed into him. And not just my light but my power. I thrust it into him. Thrust it the same way I had learned to push power out of my hand in a concentrated blast of energy. Healing power was different, more natural, but Jarvis's body was nearly depleted; it hungered for what I had to give him.

A wash of power, of energy, of shared light blasted out from me to him. A moment of dazzling brightness that drew cries, and then the light dimmed and was gone from my skin, but lingered still on his in a soft afterglow that slowly faded into his perfect, unmarred, unblemished skin.

His wounds were completely healed, the full thickness of his epithelium fully restored.

I stood so that I could see his back, and found it as perfect as the rest of him.

A shocked roomful of faces stared back at me; more than one mouth was agape.

"He's healed," Kelly whispered. And then a pandemonium of sound and voices—exclamations, questions, demands— broke out.

TWENTY-SIX

I T TOOK A few moments for the initial hysteria to die down. None of the shouted questions had been answered because as things had started to quiet down, Kelly said, "My hands no longer hurt. Take off my dressings."

Since I was closest, I ended up unwrapping the gauze from her hands, wincing when I saw the tender, wet redness of her skin from fingertips up to forearm.

"That looks tender," I observed.

Her reply was, "You should have seen what they looked like before."

That surprised me. "You mean they're better?"

"Much better," said Dr. Hubert, coming over to examine her. "She had second-degree burns. Now they're only first-degree. But that's nothing compared to this patient's improvement." Fascinated, the doctor ran his hands carefully down Jarvis's arm. "Does this hurt?" he asked.

"No, sir," Jarvis answered.

"Unbelievable," the doctor muttered, lightly pinching up

a fold of skin. "Full epithelium—dermis, subcutaneous tissue, and fatty latter. Everything's been restored."

He marveled over Jarvis's healing while I puzzled at Kelly's hands. "You were touching Jarvis"—kissing him actually—"when I healed him. Some of the healing must have spilled over to you a little."

"This isn't a little," Kelly said. "My hands were blistered, the skin broken, weeping out clear fluid."

"They still are," I noted.

"That's the ointment they smeared on me," Kelly said. "Yuck, I have to wash my hands."

I caught a nurse's eye. "Can you bring some clothes for Jarvis and something to wash the goop off his skin with?" It took her a little bit of time to make her way out of the room. Unfortunately, it had gotten even more crowded in here. All the nurses and interns who had been banished had rushed back inside during the light show we had just put on.

"Watch them," Agent Stanton muttered tersely to the agent beside him and went to examine Jarvis, giving me, Dontaine, and Hannah as wide a berth as he possibly could.

Great, I thought. I heal someone—two someones, actually—and now Agent Stanton was afraid of me.

"I didn't know I could heal a Mixed Blood," I said to Hannah. Even if it was just a partial healing.

"It is more than I would have been able to do," the healer said.

It suddenly hit me then. I had healed without sex, without orgasm. With only just some neck nuzzling.

The nurse pushed her way back into the room with some blue scrubs identical to ones the doctor and interns were wearing, with a washcloth, towel, and basin of water in her hands.

"I can wash him," Kelly offered.

"Let the nurse do it, Kelly," I told her. "That way she can see for herself that he's really healed. And you should probably take it easy with your hands; they still look pretty tender."

"They don't hurt."

"That's likely just a temporary effect. You'll probably start to feel pain again in another hour."

Agent Stanton finished his inspection of Jarvis and made his way back beside the other two agents.

"May I examine him also?" McManus asked.

"Ask him." I turned to Jarvis, who was being carefully washed by the wide-eyed nurse. "Jarvis, this is Mr. McManus, the attorney I hired to represent you. Do you mind if he examines you also?"

"No, milady."

I made a help-yourself gesture to McManus.

"Okay," Stanton said. "What the hell did you just do?"

"Monère Queens have the ability to draw down moonlight," I said, trying to explain, "which acts as a revitalizing energy source for us. We are able to share this light with other Monère."

"It's daylight. There's no moon outside," Stanton said flatly. None of the feds were going for their guns, but their attitude of let's-play-along-with-the-poor-deluded-girl was gone now. They were treating us, treating me, like a definite threat now.

"The light we draw down is stored within us, inside our body. With Dontaine's help, I was able to pull it out and share it with Jarvis."

"You also healed him. Or did he heal himself?"

"No, I healed him. But my healing ability is a little different from Hannah's, harder to access and more erratic."

"And more powerful," Hannah asserted.

"I'd trade that for better control," I said.

"You are getting that," she said with a smile. "Very well done, milady."

"You called Kelly a Mixed Blood," Stanton said. "What do you mean by that?"

"It means that she's half human and half Monère." I could tell by Kelly's startled glance she hadn't known that before. "That's probably why I was able to partially heal her."

"Can you heal other people like that?" Dr. Hubert asked. "Other patients here?"

"No, I'm sorry. Our kind of healing only works for those with Monère blood. Hannah can tell you more; she's worked with humans before."

"Humans?" Agent Stanton said in a sharp tone. "So you admit that you're not human."

That drew McManus's attention away from Jarvis.

"The Monère are a race of people who once lived on the moon over four million years ago before our planet became uninhabitable," I said.

That drew a lot of startled looks, but no one jeered at my claim, not after what they'd just witnessed.

The nurse was done washing Jarvis and had helped him put on the blue top. Without a shred of self-consciousness, he stood, letting the sheet drop, and pulled on the pants.

I didn't like the way Agent Stanton was staring at us. Definitely time to go.

"Kelly, perhaps you'd like to change out of your hospital gown as well," I suggested.

"I'd rather she stay with me, milady, if you please," Jarvis said.

I asked the nurse to bring Kelly's clothes. She readily agreed and scurried away.

"How soon can you discharge Jarvis and Kelly?" I asked Dr. Hubert.

"I'd like to keep them for another day for observation," he answered.

"That's not usual practice. There's no reason now for them to remain in the hospital."

"*Nothing* about this is usual," he replied.

"Then they'll sign themselves out against medical advice," I told him as the nurse returned with Kelly's clothes. Obviously feeling the tension, the smart girl stepped into the bathroom to change.

"Jarvis, do you have any shoes?" I asked.

He retrieved a battered pair of sneakers from a small closet and slipped them on.

"You're just going to leave?" Dr. Hubert said, scowling deeply.

"Yes. Sorry, Dr. Hubert. Thank you for everything you and your staff have done. If you can bring the AMA forms, Jarvis and Kelly can sign them and we can be on our way."

The doctor stalked out of the room, and Kelly came out of the bathroom, fully dressed.

"Anything else you two need to get?" I asked.

Kelly and Jarvis shook their heads.

"Okay, then. We'll sign the AMA forms on our way out." Or not. When I tried to walk out of the room, two FBI agents blocked our way.

"Excuse me, please," I said politely.

"Sorry, ma'am, can't do that," said the shorter of the two.

"Why not?"

"Because we have to take you into custody," Agent Stanton answered behind us. They had boxed us neatly between them.

I glanced at McManus and he quickly stepped up to the

plate. "For what reason are you taking my clients into custody? They haven't broken any laws."

"Doesn't matter. They're not human," Stanton said. "They're coming with us."

Ah, so that was how it was going to be.

I laid a hand on McManus's arm, halting his protest. "That's okay, Mr. McManus. We'll see you downstairs in front of the hospital. Jarvis, please bring Kelly along. Stay close to me." I could have used compulsion to make the two agents step away but wanted to introduce that in a more delicate manner, so for now I simply sprang over the two agents and dived over the policemen standing guard outside. I hit the ground in a neat roll and sprang back to my feet, the others behind me, moving at supernatural speed.

"What the hell!" a guard exclaimed. "Where did they go?"

By the time he finished speaking, we were a hundred feet away, down by the elevators where Nolan, Dante, and Quentin sat waiting for us.

I told Jarvis, "They're with us. Everyone down the stairwell."

"Just close your eyes and keep your feet and head tucked close to my body," Jarvis said to Kelly, whom he was carrying in his arms. Her lips were white. All this seemed to be new to her. I was surprised she hadn't squeaked in alarm. Tough gal.

It took us less than ten seconds to climb down four flights of stairs, gaining a couple minutes of lead time.

I pushed open the ground-level door, walking out into sunlight.

"Where to?" Jarvis asked, more nervous about my own men than by whoever else might be out here.

"There are reporters waiting in front of the hospital. I'm going to speak to them now, tell them who we are. Do you wish to come with us?"

"You told me to stay close to you, milady," he said uncertainly.

"It would be safest for you that way, but we're about to go public. If you would rather not be a part of that, we can part ways here and now. Or you can join us, be part of our group."

"Join you, milady?" he said, looking confused. "I'm a rogue."

"So were Hannah and Nolan, and their two sons, Quentin and Dante," I said, gesturing to the Morells. "I don't have a problem with former rogues."

"Former? I don't understand, milady. Are you asking me to serve as . . . as one of your men?"

"Yes, Jarvis. I'm offering to be your Queen."

Stunned disbelief ran across his face. He began to drop to his knees, still holding Kelly.

"Please don't kneel again," I said, stopping him with a quick hand under the arm. "A simple yes or no will do."

"And Kelly?" he asked hoarsely.

"She's welcome to join us also."

He set her on her feet, asking her silently what her decision was.

"I'm staying with you," Kelly said, "wherever you decide."

Jarvis swallowed and said, "Then, yes, milady. Please . . . I would like to serve you, if you will have me."

I smiled. "Then consider yourself sworn into my service. Welcome to the family."

I sensed a familiar presence coming quickly around the distant corner. "Easy," I said to Jarvis, when his head jerked up, "it's just Amber. He's with us."

Amber came into sight and Jarvis's eyes widened in astonishment. I wasn't sure if it was from Amber's huge size or the gold medallion chain he wore.

Jarvis turned dazed-looking eyes to me. "And the other three males I sense nearby?"

"Are the local territory Queen's men, I believe. I'd advise you to avoid them until we can make your changed status more clear."

Jarvis nodded.

"Okay, everyone's here. Let's go do this."

We walked around to the front of the hospital, toward the thick throng of reporters. Several of them glanced our way. A few eyes zeroed in on Jarvis, then dismissed him as they took in his obviously uninjured appearance. But one attractive blonde reporter continued to gaze sharply at Jarvis and Kelly, especially Kelly. Her school photo had been running on the news.

"That's them! Come on, Jack," she cried, grabbing the arm of her cameraman. The other reporters turned back to stare at us then rushed toward us in a mad scramble.

The blonde reporter reached us first. "Are you Jarvis Condorizi and Kelly Rawlings?" she asked, sticking her mike in front of Jarvis.

He flinched back a little and looked at me. I nodded.

"Yes," Jarvis answered.

Questions came pelting at him fast and furiously. Jarvis glanced desperately at me, clearly overwhelmed. I motioned for him to wait. Stepping around the excited reporters that thronged around him and Kelly, I made my way with the others to the standing mike set up near the taped-off area for the reporters. Gently tapping the microphone, I happily noted that it was turned on just as Stanton, his three agents, and the two policemen burst out the front door with guns in hand. Catching sight of us, the nearby reporters, and running cameras, they halted abruptly. Before they could decide what to do next, either point their weapons at us or drop them less conspicuously down by their side, I spoke into the microphone.

"As he just confirmed, that is Jarvis Condorizi and Kelly Rawlings." My voice echoed nice and loudly out from the set of speakers, capturing everyone's attention. "FBI agent in charge Richard Stanton and his men, standing right over there——" I waved my hand at them, and several cameras zoomed in on them. "——wanted to take us into custody. We politely declined and made our departure out one of the side exits."

Half the reporters dashed back over to us. "Who are you?" the blonde female reporter who had first spotted us asked, first one there, once again.

"My name is Lisa Hamilton. I'm a Monère Queen serving as ambassador for the Monère people residing here in America. The Monère, as I explained and demonstrated to the doctors and nurses upstairs in the burn unit, and the FBI agents here, are descended from a race of people who once lived on the moon over four million years ago, before our home planet became uninhabitable. We were here long before Christopher Columbus ever sailed the ocean blue, and have lived in secret among you, until now. Our people have many gifts; one of them is shape-shifting. Jarvis, for example, is a bird-shifter. Jarvis, are you well enough to show them your wings?"

"Yes, milady." He made his way over to me. No one spoke as Jarvis took off his top.

With a simple pulse of power, he lifted his arms and shifted them into beautiful, magnificent wings. Where his hands used to be were long gray-and-black-striped feathers; the color transitioned into startling, pure white along the top. The ease with which he performed the partial shift was quite impressive.

"What is your name?" I asked the quick-footed female reporter. She was not only pretty but young, only in her late twenties, and obviously highly intelligent, debunking the stereotype of all blondes being bimbos.

"I'm Meredith Tanner with Fox News."

"Jarvis, would you mind if Meredith touched your wings?"

"No, milady."

With mike in hand, Ms. Tanner stepped forward and touched a wing with her fingers. "Oh my God," she breathed into her mike. "They're real feathers."

"Ms. Tanner, if you don't mind stepping back please. Thank you, Jarvis, you can shift back now, if you wish."

Another pulse of power, and the feathers melted away, replaced by fingers, hands, and skin once more. A moment of stunned silence, and then a tall, athletic-looking male reporter near the front thrust his mike at me. "What other gifts do the Monère people have?" he asked.

I loved these reporters—not one single mocking glance or scoff of disbelief.

"We are faster and stronger, and our senses much keener. What is your name?" I asked.

"Charles Kramer with NBC News."

"Charles, to help me demonstrate, would you mind racing me?"

The reporter blinked then smiled eagerly. "Sure. Where to?"

"How about if I race you to the curb and back, here to my left? That way you won't need to shift the cameras around. I'd recommend you keep your shots angled out wide instead of zooming, so you don't miss anything."

Charles nodded and said into his microphone, "Okay, I'm ready when you are," and handed his mike to the reporter next to him.

"On the count of three," I said. "One, two, three . . . Go!"

Charles sprinted forward. Before he had taken two steps, I was waiting for him by the curb, fifty feet away. To everyone watching, all they would have seen was a blurred streak of movement.

I heard gasps and comments like "Did you see that?" and "Holy shit," which the home stations would hopefully bleep out. The expression on Charles's face as he ran up to where I waited for him was one of awe and amazement, mixed with excitement.

"Do you have a watch or handkerchief or something to give me as proof that I was actually here at the curb, here with you, and not just a fancy hologram? I'll return it to you, of course."

He removed his watch and passed it to me. "My God, are you really that fast?"

"Yup. See you back where we started." I streaked back to my original spot in front of the cameras to a lot of startled gasps and white faces. No one fainted, luckily. Holding up Charles's watch, I said, "Here you go, folks. Proof that I was actually there at the curb and that it wasn't some cleverly manufactured illusion. You'll also be able to see that it's real when you play the footage back in slow motion."

Charles returned, puffing hard.

"Thanks for the watch, Charles."

A reporter near the back yelled out the next question. "Are the others with you also Monère?"

Gotta love these guys, they recovered quick; not even a second of silence had passed.

"Yes," I answered, "let me introduce them to you. From my left here is Nolan Morell, his wife Hannah, and their sons, Quentin and Dante. Behind me is Dontaine. The big guy over here is Lord Amber. And you all already know Jarvis and Kelly."

"Is Kelly a Monère also?" asked another reporter.

I hesitated. "Do you want to answer that question, Kelly?"

"No, you can tell them," Kelly said, her face carefully set without any readable expression.

"Kelly is what we call a Mixed Blood, half human and half Monère. Something I believe she was not aware of herself until today."

More questions were thrown at me. The crowd outside the hospital had gotten much larger now, I noticed, including more policemen. A lot of people from the burn unit had also come outside.

I held up my hand and the shouting subsided. "I and my friends are here as representatives for the Monère people residing in the United States. We would like to live openly among you in peaceful harmony, and that is the reason why we have come forward. Unfortunately, people like FBI Special Agent Richard Stanton over there"—I waved to him again— "feel that since we are not fully human, that we don't have any rights, and he wishes to take us into custody even though we have not harmed anyone or broken any laws." My pleasant smile disappeared. "Let me make this very clear. This is a one-shot deal. We are here now, ready and willing to talk about a peaceful and legal coexistence between our people—that is my greatest wish. However, if you persist in your efforts of trying to grab us and hold us against our will, brandishing your guns, and threatening us with violence, I can promise you this: we will simply disappear and go back to living secretly among you, something we have been doing for millions of years."

I let that sink in for a second before continuing. "Let me introduce you to George McManus, our attorney from the law firm of Adams, McManus, and Kent—and also Dr. Hubert, who is Jarvis's and Kelly's physician, and some others from the burn unit. They can tell you more about what they saw and heard upstairs." I waved them to come over. Stepping back away from the microphone, I said softly, "Jarvis, if you can grab Kelly and follow us, we'll leave now. Our van is parked several blocks away."

With cameras still filming us, we ran, blurring out of sight, nothing more than smeared streaks of speed; one moment there, the next moment gone.

Twenty-seven

I T WAS SORT of anticlimactic to pull into the back parking lot of our hotel and exit the van without anyone gaping or pointing at us. For now, our anonymity was still intact, though I didn't trust it to last for long.

"Jarvis."

He turned to look at me.

"Dontaine, Amber, Dante, and I will be here," I said, pointing to our door. "You and Kelly will be staying in the suite next door with the Morell family. Is that all right?"

"Yes, milady."

"You both did well. Let's get some rest while we still can, then we'll grab something to eat. After that, we'll get some clothes and supplies for you and Kelly. How does that sound?"

Jarvis seemed both bemused and discomfited on my seeking his opinion. "Of course, milady."

"Don't forget to put the *Do Not Disturb* sign on your door," I told Nolan, and made sure to hang our own sign outside on the door handle.

"So what do you think?" I said as soon as we were inside. "Do you think it went badly? Did I totally blow it?"

"I thought it went well," Dante offered. "You made our purpose and our good intent very clear. The next step is up to them."

We talked for another half hour. The general consensus was that we had handled things pretty well—as best as the situation allowed, anyway.

"You guys must be feeling tired," I said, noting the time. It was ten thirty in the morning, long past our normal bed-time. "So who gets what room?"

"Where would you like us to stay?" Dontaine asked, his face carefully bland.

"Oh, no you don't," I said, walking to the bedroom where Dontaine had unpacked all my stuff. "You guys work out the bedding arrangement. One person can stay with me, but no sex, just sleeping."

I was already in bed when Amber came into the room with a suitcase.

"The other side," Amber said, claiming the side closest to the window.

I obediently moved over and watched Amber undress. He was a beautiful beast, I thought, watching him strip down and walk into the bathroom with that lack of self-consciousness all Monère males seemed to possess. From the flashes I remembered of my first life, I hadn't been shy about baring my body either, and yet now I was. How did that work? Was modesty natural or something learned?

Any further thoughts scattered when Amber returned and slid into bed with me.

One good thing about this hotel was that they didn't skimp on the curtains. The ones in our room were heavy and thick, blocking out the morning sunlight almost completely; just a thin sliver of light on either side of the drawn curtains penetrated into the room.

"Who got the bedroom and who's taking the pullout sofa?" I asked.

"Dante is taking first watch. Dontaine is sleeping in the bedroom."

I turned on my side, and he pulled me in tight, spooning his big body around me. "They'll switch in a couple of hours."

"I'll take the third shift," I offered.

"That's mine. You can stand watch after me."

"Which probably means there won't be any watch to take after you," I grumbled. "I'm not a delicate flower that will wilt at the least little bit of work, you know."

"Hush, we know that," Amber murmured, his voice a pleasant rumble behind me. "Close your eyes."

My lids obediently shut. I thought it would take a while to settle down, but I drifted easily into sleep moments later with Amber wrapped snugly around me.

When I blinked my eyes open, hours later, the slices of light coming into the bedroom were much dimmer, and I was alone. For a big man, Amber could move with surprising stealth. He had left the bed without waking me.

I got up and used the bathroom. The television was playing when I stepped out into the living room area where not just the people in our suite, but also everyone from next door, were gathered. They had turned on the volume when they heard me get up, so I had already heard part of the news reporting. But seeing it was an entirely different experience.

Every news channel was playing the announcement I had made in front of the hospital. I'd never been on TV before and had never seen myself this way. It was not the same as looking at your image reflected in a mirror or seeing it captured in a photo. It was more objective. Truly how others perceived you.

With my hair so fashionably styled, and the clothing and makeup bringing out the exotic lift of my dark eyes, I could honestly say that the woman on TV was attractive. Not gorgeous like the people behind me, but there was a grace and elegance and command that was indeed riveting, especially set against my obvious youth.

I had changed. And it wasn't just the new highlights in my hair or the better haircut, although that did indeed help. It was my attitude, my confidence—my awareness of who and what I was.

The ugly duckling had transformed into a graceful swan Queen.

I had a moment to absorb this altered perception of myself before Quentin said to me, "We're the biggest story out there. They've been playing this all day."

He flipped to a channel showing Dr. Hubert in front of the hospital describing what he had seen in the burn unit. Another channel showed Jarvis pulling off his blue top, his bare arms morphing into gloriously feathered wings. Yet another station was playing the blurred streak of me running to the curb at full Monère speed, leaving the tall reporter looking as if he had been caught flat-footed at the starting point. They followed with an immediate replay at slow speed. Watching this, I was struck by a stunning realization. "Oh my God," I said unsteadily.

"What is it?" Amber asked in a harsh rumble. All the men tensed and looked alertly around for a threat.

"We did it!" I laughed. "We really did it!" I felt shocked, amazed, and exhilarated as it sank in. "The whole world knows about us now."

"Don't mind her," Quentin said in a loud aside to Kelly and Jarvis. "Our Queen's a little slow when she first wakes up."

"And how would you know, little bro?" Dante asked, swatting his brother up the backside of his impudent head.

"Hey, you're just older than me by six lousy minutes, and I know by how she just reacted." Quentin flashed me a grin. "Milady darling, the whole world has known for over eight hours now."

"That's *milady darling Queen* to you," Dante growled.

"Boys, stop teasing," Hannah chided her sons with off-handed casualness.

I laughed again. "That's okay, I deserve it. It's just that it really didn't hit me until I saw us on TV. Has it really been eight hours?"

"It's just past six in the evening," Nolan said.

Jarvis's stomach growled. His face reddened when everyone glanced at him.

Another laugh bubbled out from me. "Let's go get something to eat."

I ended up sandwiched between Amber and Dontaine in the middle row because my face was too recognizable now. Nolan, Hannah, Jarvis, and Kelly sat in the back row, with Quentin driving and Dante riding shotgun.

Doing a search on the GPS, Quentin drove us to the closest fast-food restaurant, a McDonald's. We went through the drive-through and parked a short distance away to eat.

"The meat's overcooked," Dante grumbled, biting into his Big Mac, which he had ordered without cheese.

"Shut up and eat," Quentin said cheerfully, biting into his Double Quarter Pounder, minus cheese also. "Not like all of us can march into a steak house and sit down and eat without being recognized."

"Maybe we can order takeout at a restaurant next time," I said. "A steak restaurant, if you want, though I don't understand the preference you guys have for rare meat. This Filet-O-Fish is delicious."

Dontaine shuddered beside me. "Mona Lisa, I love you with all my heart but your taste in food is atrocious."

"Fish," Amber mumbled, his grimace as heartfelt as Dontaine's shudder.

"Monère men," I said, turning to wink at Kelly, who had opted out of the beef everyone else was eating for a chicken sandwich. "Something's got to be wrong with their taste buds, not ours."

Sitting next to her, Jarvis wolfed down his second burger. I had doubled his order of two hamburgers. A good call, it seemed, as I watched him unwrap his third burger.

"Do you need any more food, Jarvis?" I asked.

"No, milady," he said around the big bite he had just taken.

"You were injured. If you're still hungry, let me know."

"Yes, milady."

"Were you able to get some sleep?" I asked Kelly.

"Some—about five hours," she said, eyeing me warily. "All the men address you as *my lady*. Am I supposed to do the same?"

"Not if it makes you uncomfortable. You can call me Lisa or Mona Lisa, if you prefer."

"What's with that?" Kelly asked. "Mona Lisa?"

"*Mona* is a title for Monère Queens. Since my name is Lisa, I'm addressed as Mona Lisa. If I had been named Kelly like you, I would be addressed as Mona Kelly."

"Huh. Mona Kelly. Doesn't have quite the same ring to it as Mona Lisa does," Kelly said with the first smile I had seen her give.

I chuckled. "No, I guess it doesn't. But still, I wish I'd been named something else."

"Where to next?" Quentin asked when everyone was done eating.

"Can the GPS tell us where the nearest mall is?" I asked.

"That it can." His fingers flew quickly over the touch screen.

We were at the mall five minutes later. I turned on my cell phone as we pulled into the parking lot and found ten messages waiting for me. The first was from a Mr. Harry Wagner from the law firm specializing in public law and policy where I had been so nastily rebuffed by the receptionist. I put it on speakerphone so everyone could hear.

"I apologize for not returning your call sooner but I was not aware you had called until now. I would very much like to speak to you," the voice said, giving a phone number.

"Does anyone have a pen and paper?" I asked.

"No need," Quentin said, flipping open his cell phone. "I can jot his name and number on the notepad application." The guy was an obviously experienced texter. "See? What would you people do without me?"

"Get along just fine without you," Dante said, messing up his brother's hair.

The next several messages were all from McManus, our attorney. The first one started out calm. "This is George McManus. Give me a call. My cell phone number is . . ."

The next one that followed: "I'm still here talking to reporters, police, and FBI on your behalf. Call me."

The third call: "My office is getting flooded with phone calls. *New York Times*, *Washington Post*, *USA Today*, and a bunch of local reporters want to interview you. Call me back soon. I'm still on the clock. You're racking up a huge bill, lady. Call me!"

McManus's voice was even more agitated in the next message, informing us that he and his office staff were getting hammered with requests from the media. "For God's sake, Barbara Walters called, along with every other news channel in this country. Even some from England, Australia, China, and India. I don't know what to tell these people. Call me, dammit!"

The ninth message was from Harry Wagner again.

"Mona Lisa . . . Miss Hamilton. I want to apologize on behalf of my receptionist again and assure you that our law firm is the best in the country for your needs. We have the clout, reputation, and political connections to help you gain rights for your people. No other law firm can match our expertise, or the breadth of services we offer our clients. In addition to influential lobbyists, we have media relations specialists and any other outside experts you might need. Please call me so we can discuss this further. Our office has already closed for the day, but you can reach me anytime at my private number." He rattled off a different phone number from what he had given previously, repeating it twice.

"Did you get that, Quentin?" I asked.

"Yup," he said, his fingers busy typing on the keys. "Boy, does he seem eager for our business. Sounds like the receptionist got her lazy and sarcastic ass kicked."

The final message was from McManus, called in less than half an hour ago.

"It's six o'clock, Ms. Hamilton, and I've gotten over two hundred emails. Your bill is four thousand dollars now. Call me!"

Flipping the phone closed, I looked at everyone in silence. "Wow. I guess a lot of people want to talk to us."

"Four thousand dollars!" Hannah said, harrumphing

loudly. "I hope that's not in addition to the retainer we gave him."

"Nope, it's not," Dontaine said, doing a quick calculation. "Four hundred dollars an hour and ten hours of his time so far. Minus the one-thousand-dollar retainer, we owe him another three thousand dollars and counting, until you call him and tell him otherwise."

"Call Wagner first," Dante suggested. "If you like him, we can transfer everything to their media relations specialist to handle. Their services might be even more expensive," he warned, "but it sounds like McManus is out of his depth."

Wagner answered on the first ring.

We talked.

I liked what he had to say, up to the point when I asked him how much it would cost, and found out he couldn't give me a figure until we sat down with him and a few other members of his firm, and discussed in exact detail what our goals were. That, he said, would take an hour, at the very minimum.

When I asked if he could meet in half an hour, Wagner politely said that was unfortunately not possible as it was very late in the evening, and offered to meet with us nine a.m., first thing in the morning. That resulted in an explanation from me that we usually slept during the day and awoke around six at night, the time when their office closed. There was some more discussion on whether we could meet earlier in the morning or in the early evening, with Wagner's law firm extending their business hours to accommodate us. We both agreed the earlier the better, and we settled on seven a.m. the next morning.

My next call was to McManus. He picked up on the third ring. "McManus here," he growled.

"It's Lisa Hamilton, returning your call."

"About time!" he roared. "Why the hell didn't you call me back sooner?"

"We were sleeping and my phone was turned off. I just turned it back on and got your messages. Thanks for fielding all the calls for us."

"Expensive damn answering service, at four hundred dollars an hour."

"I agree. We'll be happy to take over from here. How about we settle things tonight?" I offered, since there was no guarantee of a tomorrow if things went sour, and gave him the name of the mall we were at. We agreed to meet in half an hour—how long it would take him to drive here—at the outdoor restaurant I had glimpsed next to the mall entrance.

"Including the time it'll take me to drive there, that will be a total of eleven billable hours," McManus said.

"We'll have three thousand four hundred dollars in cash waiting for you," I assured him.

"Good. I'll have a receipt ready and can hand you all of your messages. Who do I tell people to call when they contact my office looking for you?"

"It'll most likely be one of the three law firms I mentioned to you. I should have a name and number for you early tomorrow morning."

"Good luck," he said. "They're even more expensive than I am."

I said good-bye and hung up. "Ouch," I said, wincing. "Even more expensive . . . that's hard to believe."

"What do we do now?" Kelly asked. "Sit here for half an hour waiting for the lawyer?"

"Yeah. Sorry," I said. "If we go in to buy stuff now, chances are some of us will be recognized and we have to make a quick exit. Best to wait until McManus is here."

"Why?" asked Dante.

"Why what?"

"Why do we have to run?" Dante asked in a reasonable tone. "If our goal is publicity, here will do just as well as any other place. We don't have to wait until tomorrow to call any of the reporters back. If we stay here, they'll come to us, and the outdoor restaurant of the mall will be as good a spot as any other to talk to the media. We're lucky the police haven't tracked us down yet. They know our names now and my mother used her driver's license to rent this vehicle."

"This van is one of their most basic models. I doubt it has a tracking system installed," Quentin noted. "But if they know the make, model, and license plate of our rental, Dante's right. Cops will probably be on the lookout for it now."

So it was only a matter of time before they found us. That put things in better perspective. Cops, bad. Media and publicity, good.

We took another few minutes to iron out our plans and yet more discussion to divide ourselves up into three groups. Amber, Quentin, and I were assigned to get a laptop— Quentin had insisted having a computer was essential. Dante would go with Jarvis and Kelly to buy stuff for them and to grab some hats and sunglasses. Dontaine, Hannah, and Nolan would hit Staples for basic office supplies, like pens, envelopes, and notebooks.

Kelly's mouth dropped open when Dontaine opened the briefcase full of cash.

"That's a lot of money," she said, her eyes as round as saucers.

"I thought so, too, at first. But it's going real fast," I said mournfully watching as Dontaine counted out McManus's fee, eliminating two of our stacks.

Dontaine reminded everyone to get receipts and started doling out money to the three groups.

"Just a sec," Quentin said. "I used the guest computer in the lobby while you guys were sleeping. Per the U.S. Treasury web site, the Treasury stopped printing all the larger denomination bills after World War II. So all the five-hundred-, one-thousand-, five-thousand-, and ten-thousand-dollar bills are collector items." That eliminated the entire bottom row of money. He rifled through the remaining stacks, removing some of the older dated fifties and one-hundreds. "Keep these separate, as well," he said, handing them to Dontaine. "They also might be collectible."

That left only a few pitiful stacks of money for our immediate use, I noted with a sigh. "Hannah, if you can hang on to the briefcase, that will free up Nolan's and Dontaine's hands."

Hannah nodded.

"Okay, don't forget," I reminded everyone. "When everyone's done shopping, each group will get a separate table outside at the restaurant. Amber will guard our table while Quentin and I talk to reporters. Likewise, Dante will keep an eye out, freeing Kelly and Jarvis to answer questions, and Nolan will stand guard while Hannah and Dontaine talk to the media."

"Milady, you wish us to talk to reporters?" Jarvis asked with discomfort.

"Yes, six of us answering questions will be better than just me talking."

"What are we allowed to say?" he asked.

"Easier to tell you what to avoid. Don't mention Prince Halcyon, the Queen Mother, the specific names of any Monère Queens or the territories they rule, or any details about what hurts or weakens us. Talking about Hell or NetherHell or my brother is also a big no-no. Do you and Kelly know about me and Dante? Our past history together?"

"No, milady," Jarvis said.

"Good, so you won't have any problem there, but that's something you shouldn't talk about either. And no mentioning curses or reincarnation or anything like that." The list of things-not-to-mention was longer than I had thought.

"But everything else is fair game," I told him. "Don't worry about it too much, Jarvis. Just answer whatever you feel comfortable answering. If they ask you a question you don't want to answer, you just say something like, 'I'm sorry, I'd rather not answer that,' and refer them to me. Okay?"

He nodded glumly.

"Same goes for everyone else. Any questions you don't want to answer, feel free to refer my way, or change the subject to something you don't mind talking about. Oh, and no mention of New Orleans for now—that was where we came from," I explained to Kelly and Jarvis. "They may eventually find out but we'll wait for them to dig it out."

There was some more haggling about where we should park the van.

"Not here in the mall parking lot," Dante said. "It's too easy to block the mall exits."

We ended up deciding to park on a small road across from the back entrance of the mall. We drove back to the mall, dropped everyone off near one of the smaller entrances, then Quentin, Amber, and I parked the van. When traffic thinned, we zipped our way quickly back, going into Best Buy.

"Go on in ahead of us," I told Quentin. "It'll probably be better if Amber and I stay a little apart from you."

Good-looking boy that he was, Quentin would draw eyes, but not like Amber would through his sheer size.

Sure enough, as soon as we walked in, the young employee standing by the door immediately looked at Amber, and then of course me, standing next to him. Recognition dawned and his mouth dropped open.

I gave him a smile as we walked by then steered us toward the back part of the store. We ended up in an aisle across from the big-screen TV section, keeping a distant eye on Quentin who had gotten a very eager employee to help him choose a laptop. The few people we passed stopped to look at us but no one had approached us yet. A small crowd, however, was starting to gather, taking pictures and video with their cell phones. Good thing we'd separated from Quentin; no one seemed to recognize him. All the attention, so far, was focused just on us.

Someone changed all the televisions to a news channel, so that suddenly all the screens were featuring a close-up shot of yours truly. They were rerunning my announcement in front of the hospital. The angle widened to show the rest of my group standing behind me, including the very large and distinctive-looking Amber.

"Hey, that's you two, isn't it?" asked a brave, pimply faced employee who looked like he was still in high school.

I nodded confirmation.

"Cool," he said, coming over to talk to us, and that broke the ice. More people converged around us, ringing us in a loose semicircle that had Amber tensing next to me.

"We're fine, Amber," I said, squeezing his arm. "They're just curious."

I answered questions and even signed autographs. The crowd was very well behaved, probably out of respect for Amber and his intimidating size, but that could just be the cynical part of me talking. A few brave people even asked Amber for an autograph, which he gravely gave, after I explained that they just wanted him to sign his name for them. Pretty soon, almost everyone in the store had drifted over to us, except for a few shoppers and salespeople who craned their necks curiously our way but still went about their business.

It wasn't long before the manager of the store, an older man with thinning hair and glasses, pushed his way through the thick crowd, saying, "Everyone, please continue your shopping. You cannot gather here. Everyone, please continue your shopping . . ."

Two mall security personnel followed behind him, a thin man and a short woman.

"Ms. Hamilton," the manager said with a strained smile. "How can we help you in our store?"

"My friend is buying something. We're almost done." I was happy to see Quentin at the register paying for his purchase. He made his way over to us, and the crowd parted for him as if sliced open by his beaming smile and outrageously good looks.

"I thought you were just buying a laptop," I said, eyeing the two large boxes and blue shopping bag he was loaded down with.

"There was a very nice combo sale on a laptop, printer, and carry bag. I also got a ream of paper, ink cartridges, and a memory key. You gotta admit that was a pretty quick purchase." To buy all that in under ten minutes, it really was. It just hadn't felt that way. It had felt like forever.

"Any change left?" I asked.

"Fifty-five dollars and change."

I sighed. Another thousand dollars spent.

I took the shopping bag and passed one of the boxes to Amber to free up a hand for Quentin to sign autographs with, which he did with an easy, charming smile that accelerated quite a few hearts. Our boy was definitely not shy.

"Sorry about that," I said to the hovering manager. "All

done now. Do you want us to leave the fast way or would you rather we walked out at normal speed?"

He blinked nervously. "Uh . . . we will walk you out, at normal speed," he said.

"The parking lot exit then," I said, nodding toward where we had entered. Much better than going through the mall with this crowd.

The security guards made a path for us through the crowd. Cell phones went up on either side of us, with numerous clicks and flashes as we passed by. One last photo opportunity when the young employee near the exit checked our purchased items against the receipt, and then we were out the store. People spilled out the doors, following us.

"Amber, Quentin. Ready to run? Last one there is a rotten egg," I said, taking off.

We left the crowd behind in a burst of speed, running until we came around to the main entrance.

"Last one there is a rotten egg?" Quentin repeated as we entered the restaurant. "I cannot believe you said that. It's probably being posted on the Internet right now."

"What does that mean?" Amber asked.

"It's just a childish taunt," I explained, smiling. "A way of saying *let's race* and *I'm going to beat your ass.*"

People began noticing us almost immediately. A college-aged girl with her hair pulled back in a long brown ponytail watched with a shocked expression as we approached her hostess stand. Her mouth wasn't exactly hanging open, but it was close as she gazed from Quentin up to Amber. Me, she barely glanced at.

"I'd like three tables outside," I told her. "The ones closest to the velvet ropes, please."

"Um . . . ah . . . how many people?" she asked, clearly flustered.

"Three at each table. Six others will be joining us soon, so if you could seat us and reserve two other tables next to the velvet ropes, I'd appreciate it."

Something about sitting down to eat kept people away who would otherwise have approached anywhere else. An equally flustered waitress came over, stumbled through the specials, and asked if we wanted anything to drink.

"We're ready to order now," I said. I ordered a virgin piña colada, one of my favorite drinks, and a fruit and cheese platter appetizer dish. Quentin ordered two bottles of Coke, unopened, for both himself and Amber.

"I do not wish to drink anything," Amber said after the waitress left.

"It's just polite custom," I explained. "If you're going to take a table at a restaurant, you have to order something, even if it's just a drink, to pay for taking a seat another paying customer could have occupied instead."

Nolan, Hannah, and Dontaine arrived at the same time our drinks were brought out. The rest came ten minutes later, loaded down with shopping bags.

"What took you guys so long?" I asked, having eaten all the fruit and half of the cheese on my platter.

"Sorry," Dante said. "We were recognized."

"We weren't." Dontaine grinned.

"Yeah, but none of you guys were wearing surgical scrubs," Dante countered.

Kelly and Jarvis were wearing newly purchased shirts and pants, I was pleased to see.

Soon after, McManus made his way through the gathering crowd, which had quickly thickened into a substantial size as shoppers entering and exiting the mall all stopped to stare at us.

"Congratulations," I said to McManus, handing him the

bundle of cash Dontaine had counted out, "you made it before any reporters did."

The bristly-browed attorney counted the money and passed me a large yellow envelope. "Your receipt is in there, along with all your messages and emails. You're expecting reporters?"

"We've been sitting here for fifteen minutes. What do you think?"

"You planning on talking to them?" McManus asked.

"You betcha."

"Do you want me to stick around?" he asked.

"At four hundred dollars an hour? No thanks, although you're more than welcome to stay on your own time. I have your cell phone number. If we need your services again, we'll call you, but likely as not, we won't. If the police try and take us into custody, we'll just go."

His brows slanted down. "You mean do that speed-away thing?"

"Yeah, and you won't ever hear from us again."

"Just me or the whole world?" he asked.

"Both."

"Moment of truth, huh?"

My heart gave a little thump. I hadn't realized it until he put it so clearly, but yeah, that's what this would be. "My terms were pretty clear. The government's had a whole day to decide what they're going to do."

"Cops are going to be coming here soon."

"I know."

"Then I hope, for everyone's sake, no one overreacts."

"Me, too."

The first reporters sped into the parking lot, with more news vans following right behind them. Mall security had flocked out, and local police screeched in with the FBI right on their heels—one big 'ole party. All new faces, I noted. Last but not least, a couple of carloads of men and women wearing Homeland Security Windbreakers poured out and quickly organized the milling law enforcement personnel to have them push the crowd back farther away from us. So far none of the officers or agents had made a move on us or drawn their weapons. McManus, I saw, had decided to stay and was talking to a couple of reporters himself.

Quentin and I sat across from each other, close to the velvet ropes, which so far none of the reporters interviewing us had attempted to cross. More media flocked in front of the other two tables. Most were from local stations, but there were several national networks represented: CNN and MSNBC, even BBC World News, broadcasting live, it seemed.

"Mona Lisa!" a male reporter called out. The use of my Monère name caught my attention, had me turning to him. "Why do your people call you Mona Lisa?"

I explained, as I had done earlier to Kelly, that Mona was a title added before the first name of a Queen. "The word *Mona* means *of moonlight*. Why Monère sometimes refer to Queens as Ladies of Light."

"What other gifts do your people have besides shape-shifting?" asked another reporter.

"We're much stronger than the average person."

"How much stronger? Able to lift a car?" someone asked.

"I've never tried it," I said, "but probably yes."

"Can you demonstrate your strength for us?" the same voice asked.

"I'll be happy to, if you have something you don't mind being destroyed, like a rock."

Someone quickly ran off to search for a rock. Another

resourceful cameraman handed me a small metal flashlight, the size of my palm. "How about this?" he asked.

"Do you mind if I crush it?"

"Sure, go ahead, if you can."

I took him at his word, closing my fingers around the handle. When I released it, the metal under my hand had been mangled and squeezed down, showing the crushed batteries inside. The cameraman took back his flashlight with an astonished expression. My demonstration grabbed the attention of not just the reporters around my table but also garnered the intense interest of some of the watching law enforcement standing several yards away.

Someone ran back with a big rock about twice the size of my palm. "Is this okay?" the man asked, obviously one of the news crew.

"Sure," I said. "You can help me demonstrate, if you don't mind."

He nodded eagerly.

"Go ahead and squeeze the rock. Try to break it with both hands."

He clutched and strained, squeezing the rock. It didn't break. He passed it to me under the bright lights of the filming cameras. Taking it in my left hand, I closed my fingers and squeezed with gentle pressure. Dust and small bits of rock crumbled out from where I held it. "I could have crushed it completely, but I wanted to leave something behind, so that you could see that the rock is real and as hard as it looks." I gave the rock back, with the impression of my fingers nicely grooved a good inch down into the stone.

"Are you a lefty or a righty?" a reporter asked.

"I'm right-handed." And I had used my left hand.

"What other gifts or abilities do you have?" asked a female reporter.

Another moment of truth. "I am also able to compel people with my gaze."

"Compel? What do you mean by that?"

I was suddenly very conscious of all the filming cameras. All the people possibly watching right now around the world, and how frightening this next thing might seem to them. How easily it could all blow up in our faces. But it had to be disclosed now, before we met with any policy makers.

Course decided, I took a breath. "Compelling someone means that I am able to control someone's actions for several minutes, take over their will."

A second of profound silence. Then the female reporter asked, "Can you show us?"

"If you have any volunteers, I can demonstrate. We can also test at what range and limit of distance my ability works."

"I'm willing to be your guinea pig," she offered, "as long as I hear first what you're going to make me do." Brave lady. Because after this, she was certain to be grilled and examined by the FBI and Homeland Security, and who knows what other agencies.

"How about if I tell you to squawk like a chicken, flap your arms, and hop on your left leg?"

"Okay," she said, laughing nervously. "I don't mind doing that."

"Let's start at a distance of about three feet away," I suggested.

Handing her mike to another reporter, she backed up about a yard. "What do I need to do?"

"Just look at me and try not to do what I tell you to do."

I captured her gaze with a small thrum of power that drew the attention of the other Monère around me. Their eyes all turned to me, as did all the reporters talking to them.

"What is your name?" I asked.

"Maria Camille Ortega, from NBC4 Washington."

"Maria," I said, raising my voice so everyone could hear me clearly. "I want you to squawk like a chicken, flap your arms, and hop up and down on your left leg."

She started squawking, flapping her arms, and hopping.

"Stop," I told her.

Maria froze, hands under her armpits, standing on one foot like a flamingo.

I released her from the compulsion. Watched her come back into awareness.

"Did she just make me squawk like a chicken?" she asked her cameraman.

He nodded.

"Oh my God, I really did?" She didn't look like she believed him.

"Did my eyes change?" I asked loudly.

"Yes," said one of the reporters who had had an up-close viewing of everything. "They lightened in color and grew kind of sparkly."

A policeman stepped forward, a black middle-aged man with a tough, no-nonsense face. "I want you to try that on me."

"Have you ever yodeled, Officer?" I asked.

"Never."

"Good, then we will see if I can make you yodel. But first I ask that you hand your gun to one of your fellow officers, so they won't get too nervous."

"Why?" he asked. "You think you could make me shoot someone?"

"If I wished to, yes. But that is not my wish. I don't want anyone to feel threatened enough to draw a gun on us, because the moment they do, my mission here is over. All of us here will disappear, and I don't want that. I want everyone to be aware of both our powers and their limitations, so no one can claim later that I tricked or bespelled anyone."

Another policeman walked over, probably his senior officer, and held out his hand. The first policeman reluctantly handed over his piece and walked over to me, stopping a few feet back from where the female reporter had stood. All the cameras shifted around so they had a good shot of us both.

"Is this far enough away?" he asked.

"How far would you estimate the distance between us?" I asked.

"I'd say about five feet."

"Are you ready?"

He nodded.

I brought forth my power. "Yodel for me."

The cop snorted. "Ain't working."

"Please step one foot closer to about four feet away."

He did so and I repeated my command. This time I felt my eyes capture him. He yodeled, loudly and clearly, almost professionally.

"Son of a bitch," the other cop muttered, the one holding his gun.

I released my compulsion. Watched the blankness ease away from the other man's expression. "See," he said smugly. "It doesn't work." He turned to look back at his fellow officers. Their expressions made his shoulders tighten. "It didn't work, right, guys?"

"You yodeled, man," another policeman said.

"Come on back here, Jackson," ordered the man holding his gun.

I waited for him to trot back to his other members before announcing to the reporters, "My range limitation for compulsion seems to be about four feet."

"Can any of the others here do that?" called out a reporter near one of the other tables.

"As far as I know, just Dante and me," I answered. "Anyone else here able to use compulsion?"

The others shook their heads.

"Which one of the men is Dante?" shouted another reporter.

"Dante is the man standing at the middle table. Quentin, do you mind switching places with your brother?"

"No problem," Quentin grinned, going over to the other table to take Dante's place. Dante took his brother's vacated seat next to me.

"Dante, how far is your range?" someone asked.

"I do not know," Dante said.

"Speak up louder," another person shouted.

Dante repeated his words with more volume.

"Any volunteers to help him find the answer to that?" I asked the watching crowd.

A surprisingly large number of hands went up, including some from the restaurant staff. I chose a male waiter and beckoned him over to come stand in front of Dante.

"Why don't we start at a distance of five feet," I suggested.

"You think my range is greater than yours?" Dante said, smiling faintly.

"I'm pretty sure it is," I said, smiling back, and suggested he have him sing "Happy Birthday."

"Try to resist him," I told the volunteer.

"Believe me, ma'am," the waiter said, "I will. I don't have any singing talent, at all."

There were a lot of audible gasps as Dante's pale eyes turned solid silver and began to glow. He gave his command.

The waiter started singing, loudly and robustly and as awfully as he had claimed.

He stopped when Dante told him to, and was released from the compulsion.

Following instructions, the waiter took one more step back. Standing six feet back, this time he was able to resist Dante's efforts. "Jesus Christ," he yelped when Dante's eyes changed color. "Look at his eyes!"

"It seems like six feet for you, Dante, as your maximum range." I thanked the waiter and quietly asked him to bring me the check for the three tables.

"Are we leaving?" Dante asked.

"No. They seemed to take that well, but I thought it best to pay before I forgot. Or in case we have to leave in a sudden hurry."

I told the reporters we were done with the demonstration, but added that we would be happy to speak more with them on an individual basis, whereupon they flocked back around each table. We chatted with reporters for another thirty minutes, but unfortunately none of the watching crowd left. They stayed and more people joined them until a thick mass stood beyond the perimeter the police had established around us.

An FBI agent approached our table, stopping a carefully measured seven feet away. "Ma'am, you should probably end this now. We would be happy to let you continue if there weren't so many people around, but the crowd is getting too large."

"I was just noticing that myself," I told him. Then asked, "Are you going to just let us leave?"

"Yes. We'll even escort you out of here, if you allow us." Cameras were rolling, recording our interaction, microphones held out to pick up our conversation.

"No orders to take us into custody?"

"Very specific orders not to unless you act aggressively and give us reason to."

"We won't. We're here as peaceful envoys."

"Then it might be best, for your own safety, if you can avoid any more of these, uh, open, public gatherings. Large crowds can all too easily get out of hand."

"So what do you suggest?" I asked. "Private interviews with the media?"

The man nodded and said to my surprise, "Yes. Our department's media liaison would be happy to make the arrangements for you."

"Thank you but there's no need," I said, politely declining the offer. No way was I going to let the FBI arrange meetings for us in places where they could easily trap us. "I'll try and do as you suggested, though. What is your name?"

"Jim Carmichael. I'm the FBI agent in charge."

He was older than the other agents, fit and lean with dark, serious eyes. Responsibility seemed to rest easily on his shoulders. "I like you much better than Agent Stanton," I told him.

"That's good to hear, ma'am."

His words caused a painful wince. "Please don't *ma'am* me. I have to be at least ten years younger than you."

"How old are you?" he asked in a direct and yet still polite manner.

"I'm twenty-one." They had to have all my data by now.

"How would you like me to address you then?"

"Mona Lisa will do."

"Mona Lisa, then. I'd appreciate it if you could wrap things up."

"No problem." Dante had taken care of the bill.

"Would you want us to escort you through the crowd?" Agent Carmichael asked.

"No, thanks," I said, standing. "We'll take the quick and easy way out of here."

I called for everyone's attention, thanked them for their time and interest, announced that we were leaving, and suggested that they do so as well. In a lower voice, I said, "Okay, everyone, grab your stuff. Jarvis, if you could get Kelly."

The reporters fell back as we all stood and gathered our things. Two yards away from the loose perimeter, I gathered myself and leaped, sailing over everyone's head, twenty feet, thirty feet . . . landing behind the watching crowd a short distance away in the parking lot. Amber thudded lightly down beside me, the others following closely behind.

With a last jaunty wave to the crowd, we sped away.

EPILOGUE

THAT NIGHT, WE started returning the messages that various members of the media had left with McManus. Most weren't available so late in the evening, but a surprising number were and took our phone calls. Quentin played secretary, using a newly purchased notebook to begin scheduling interviews.

The next morning, we sat and talked with Harry and five other attorneys from his law firm. We spent the first half hour of the meeting discussing exactly what the Monère were, which was, technically, a nonhuman alien species, even though Monère had lived here on this continent before the word *America* was even coined. But aside from the messy legal issues of proof backing up our earlier settlement on this land, which we did not have as far as I knew, and the even trickier question of biology, our legal experts decided that the best approach was to seek American citizenship. Even a monkey would be granted basic human rights once it became a citizen, they said.

And McManus was right. These guys were far more expensive than he was, to the collective tune of two hundred thousand dollars for their services, which would include finding a senator or congressman who would be willing to sponsor and initiate a bill in Congress, on behalf of the Monère.

If and when the bill was passed in Congress, it would then go to the Senate floor. If and when *that* bill was passed in the Senate, the President would then have to sign off on it before it became official law. Lots of *ifs* and *whens* and other tricky steps involved, not the least of which was a congressional hearing that I and the others would likely have to testify at. Wagner and his politically savvy team of lawyers and experts would shepherd us through this entire complicated process. Oh, and the price he quoted was only an estimate; it might go as high as three hundred thousand dollars, depending on how much money they needed to grease the wheels to win the support of key people.

Politics, I discovered, was a very high-priced business.

I called the two other law firms on my list, with a much clearer understanding of what services I needed, and browbeat them into giving me a rough quote over the telephone. They gave close to the same figure. We signed with Wagner's law firm. They were supposed to be the best, something I comforted myself with as I forked over a hundred thousand dollars to them, the first chunk of their payment. I remembered to get a receipt.

Barbara Walters wanted us to fly out to New York for an interview on her show, *The View*. So did Diane Sawyer for *Good Morning America*, Matt Lauer for the *Today Show*, and Regis and Kelly. On the west coast, Jay Leno and Ellen DeGeneres were also eager to get us on their shows. I told Quentin that we were staying put, and asked to have them come to us instead. The west coast shows ended up

interviewing us via satellite out of a local DC studio, as did
Regis and Kelly. Barbara Walters, Matt Lauer, and Diane
Sawyer, however, flew out to DC to interview us in person.
But, hey, if it only takes an hour flight from New York to
DC, why not, right?

There was more chatter about us being angels, what
with Jarvis's winged appearance and the doctors' and nurses'
description of me glowing when I healed Jarvis's burns. But
that died down when Barbara Walters asked me during her
interview who my sweetie was. Was it Dontaine or someone
else?

My answer was that it was several someone elses. That
I was in committed relationships with Amber, Dante, and
Dontaine.

As the big studio cameras zoomed in on each of my men
as I pointed them out, I could almost feel the collective pulse
of watching America skitter in appalled and scandalized
titillation.

That pretty much cut down the talk about us being angels.

The interviews that followed focused almost entirely on
the sexual relationship of Monère Queens and their warriors.
I might have answered the questions with maybe a little too
much frankness. Our interviewers couldn't seem to get away
from the sex part of it and the fact that three lovers was considered uncommonly chaste for a Monère Queen.

All in all, the people who flew out to meet us and interview us in person considered it well worth their effort, with
record ratings for their shows.

The location of our hotel was discovered on the third day.
Frankly, I was surprised it had taken that long.

I saw FBI Agent Jim Carmichael again when he and his
men showed up with some local police to keep the crowd of
reporters and gawkers under control. Agent Carmichael and I

agreed that staying at the hotel would no longer be possible. Just as well, it was getting pricey at seven hundred bucks a day for two suites.

Money was leaving our briefcase at a very steady and alarming rate.

We bought a used van with sixty-one thousand miles for a little over half the price a new one would have cost. After all, why pay for something brand new when there was still no guarantee we'd be sticking around?

So far, so good. The U.S. government and I had an unspoken understanding. We would play nice as long as they did. Why rock the boat? They were getting tons of information about the Monère from us, freely and willingly given. But I didn't know how long I could trust that to last.

Quentin found a furnished six-bedroom home for us to rent an hour away from DC. It ended up being a third less than what staying at the hotel would have cost us. That it was in a gated community was even better. Still, even with the added distance, reporters kept climbing up the side of the hills where it wasn't fenced, and hiking in. We had to hire a private security company recommended by our law firm to not only patrol around outside the house and escort trespassing reporters back out the front gates, but also to sweep the house on a daily basis for bugs. We'd found quite a few of them.

We had taken the first step. People knew about us now.

Those same people were still clueless that the same supernatural race that had generated their tales of angels and werewolves were the same ones spawning their mythology about demons and Hell. And I wanted to keep it that way for as long as I could. Preferably until the Monère gained legal rights.

Was it reasonable to expect humans to live alongside

people who could crush their skulls with a simple flexing of their fingers? That was an argument already being aired.

My rebuttal back was: Wouldn't you want to know who and what we really were instead of living next to us in ignorance, as many were doing even now? To have us not only protected by the same rights but also restricted by those very same rules?

There was also talk about how our talents and abilities could benefit everyone. A huge untapped resource, people were saying.

It was a start. A good start even.

Now we had to see if we could finish it without screwing it up.